WHE

L✹VE
Calls

CELESTE O. NORFLEET

WHEN LOVE

Calls

ARABESQUE®

WHEN LOVE CALLS

An Arabesque novel

ISBN-13: 978-0-373-83111-1
ISBN-10:   0-373-83111-0

www.kimanipress.com

Printed in U.S.A.

To Fate & Fortune

To Charles, my friend, my love, my support, my security, my heart, my hero, my husband, you're the man of my dreams always and forever. Here's to another twenty years!

Chapter 1

"I'm going to jail."

"No you're not."

"Oh, yeah, I'm going to jail," Alyssa Wingate muttered as she readjusted her crooked name tag again. "I guess I can always plead temporary insanity. Yeah, that's it. I'm sure the courts will be lenient with me. After all, this is my first real offense, if you don't count that bat incident a few years back."

"Shh…"

"I've always played by the rules, never broken any laws… well, except for that mattress-tag thing, but that wasn't my fault. I was only trying to see the price. And besides, I bought it anyway, even though I didn't really want a fourteen-hundred-dollar king-size mattress. Oh, who am I kidding? I'm getting tossed out of here and then I'm going to jail."

"Shh… You're not going to jail," Nina Hall whispered, as she stood beside Alyssa.

"Yep, I'm going to jail," Alyssa repeated with certainty as she glanced around, ready to be handcuffed and taken away.

"Would you please stop saying that? There's no reason we shouldn't be here. This is a major event and we were invited."

"Correction, our boss was invited and couldn't make it. We swiped the tickets, then snuck into the VIP reception."

"That doesn't matter as long as we're cool."

"Maybe I'll get lucky and just get probation and have to do, like, a million hours of community service. I could do that," Alyssa said, nodding to herself.

"And stop rambling on like that, people are beginning to stare," Nina hissed, smiling and greeting a passerby. "Good evening, how are you? What a wonderful turnout."

"I'm not rambling. I'm just practicing what I'm going to say, so that when I get arrested for stalking a U.S. senator, the judge will see that I'm truly sorry as I throw myself on his mercy."

"Oh, God, you're insane and overly dramatic. If I didn't know any better, I'd say you were pretending, but your goody-two-shoes act is far too perfect."

There was a buzz of excitement across the room. Heads turned, but Alyssa looked the other way, straightening her name tag one last time. "I'm going to jail."

"Shh, and stop fidgeting."

"I'm not fidgeting."

"Then what are you doing?"

"It's not me. It's my name tag. It keeps drooping, slipping, flopping…"

"Whatever, enough with the seven dwarfs already."

Alyssa finally straightened her name tag, took a deep breath and looked up, smiling. Her pecan skin shone, her smile radiated and her almond-shaped, dark eyes sparkled with crystal clarity. She was the spitting image of her grandmother. "Okay, I'm ready."

"Good, you look fantastic. You need to smile more often."

"Thanks," Alyssa said, appreciating the compliment. It was something she had to teach herself to do. Compliments were rare growing up.

"You'll be great." Nina nodded her assurance.

"Yes, I'm calm, I'm cool, I'm collected and I'm relaxed. I know everything there is to know about the honorable senator from California. He's single, served two terms as a congressman, then was elected to the Senate at twenty-nine years old. He took office a year ago on his thirtieth birthday, making him one of the youngest senators in U.S. history. He sits on several congressional committees and subcommittees, inherited a vineyard in Napa Valley from his grandfather and, by all accounts, is drop-dead handsome."

Nina stared at her while shaking her head in growing disbelief. "Wow, girl, you are obsessed."

"I prefer the term *well informed,*" Alyssa corrected.

"Still, of all the politicians to pick, you chose the one who is firmly against lobbyists."

"It was a no-brainer. He may be staunchly against political lobbyism, but he's also pro universal health care and Social Security reform. And if I can pull him in, Pete will have no choice but to offer me a position as a lobbyist. And to clarify his position, he's not against political lobbying, he's against 'excessive lobbying and the perks that follow, which make politicians useless to the people they're supposed to represent.' That's a direct quote from his Web site, by the way."

"I have no doubt. But be that as it may, he's still a tough nut to crack. I heard that as soon as he hears the word *lobbyist* he calls security and has the person thrown out."

"I doubt that," Alyssa said.

"Well, you know him better than I do. Hell, you know him better than anyone does, probably even his assistant."

"You make me sound like some kind of stalker."

"If finding out everything there is to know about a person is stalking, then the shoe fits, dear."

"I did it to help others."

"Uh-huh, right."

"What's that supposed to mean?" Alyssa asked.

"You know what it means. You like him, you're attracted to him."

"Of course I like him. He's a good politician."

"Nah, not like that, you like him as a man and, if I didn't know any better, I'd say you more than liked him," Nina said as she stared at her friend suspiciously.

"Well, now, it's a good thing that you know better," Alyssa said sternly, hoping to end this conversation. She looked around, feeling Nina's eyes still on her. She was right, of course; her little investigation had turned into more than professional interest. She did feel something for him. She wasn't sure what it was, but she definitely felt something. "Okay, I'm ready, let's do this. Where is he?" She smiled through clenched teeth.

"Umm—" Nina looked around the crowded reception area quickly "—it doesn't look like he's here yet."

"But he's got to be here. I'm ready now." She raised her voice slightly, drawing glances from those around her.

The *he* whom she referred to was Senator Randolph Kingsley, one of the most discriminating senators on the hill and one who personally vowed to limit the influence of special-interest lobbyists. He and another senator were co-sponsoring a bill that would curtail influence by capping the amount of gifts, services and political donations lobbyists could make. It was an uphill battle, but it was successful so far.

Most lobbyists stayed far away from Senator Kingsley. Approaching him at a public function was risky, but one that Alyssa was willing to make for her cause.

"Alyssa Wingate, would you please stop that and calm down? You're a nervous wreck. You'll do fine. Just relax. You know all the material. You practiced a million times on the way over here, so chill," Nina said, then jumped when a passing waiter startled her by offering her an hors d'oeuvre from his tray. He stared at her strangely. "Thanks," she said breathlessly, then grabbed a miniature crab cake off the tray and dropped it into her mouth before the waiter could even offer her a napkin. "Now, look. You've got me all jumpy and nervous."

Alyssa adjusted her bogus name tag again and continued to look around, knowing that she didn't belong there. These were the powerful political elite, senators, congressmen, business executives and corporate heads, community leaders. And then there was her, no status, no family name, no money and no nerve. "I need to leave. People are staring at me," she muttered to Nina.

Nina smiled warmly and turned away. "That's because you're acting as if you don't belong here."

"I don't belong here. We don't belong here."

"Shh... Just relax and smile as if this is the most natural thing in the world, a simple after-work reception on Capitol Hill. We do it all the time." She smiled and greeted another person. "Hello, how are you this evening? Wonderful turnout, isn't it?"

"Maybe he's not coming tonight." Alyssa looked around.

"He's coming, just relax. I spent all afternoon on the phone finding out his itinerary for this evening. He's got three events scheduled tonight—a Senate meeting, a photo shoot for a magazine, this reception and one other reception later on. So if we don't get a chance to talk to him here, we can catch him at the next one."

"Brilliant," Alyssa said.

"I like to think so."

"What if he skips both?"

"He won't."

"Hey, that's not three things, that's four things."

"Whatever, he's coming, so stop stressing, and if everything I hear about him is only half true, he's probably half-a-second ahead of schedule."

Alyssa squinted and continued to look around.

"Stop that. Just put your glasses back on. I swear, you're gonna get frown lines squinting like that."

"No, I won't, and I can see fine far away. It's up close that things get a bit blurry."

"Honestly, if you don't want to wear your glasses, then why didn't you just wear your contact lenses like everybody else?"

"I was too nervous to put them in."

"You should have done it."

"And intentionally poke my finger in my eye, are you kidding? Why would I want to do that?"

"How about so that you could actually see and not squint, maybe?"

"No, I mean, do you know all the things that could go wrong?"

"Only for you, Alyssa. Knowing you, you'd probably try to put the lens in and cause a blizzard in the Brazilian rain forest."

"Ha-ha, not funny."

"Actually I was going for reality and not so much humor." Nina looked around again, smiling warmly. "You know, what we need is a drink in our hands. Everybody has a drink. We'll blend in with a drink. Wait here, I'll go get us a—"

"What, are you crazy? I'm not waiting here by myself, looking like a nut. No drinks. I don't drink anyway. Well, maybe a glass of champagne to celebrate the new year and maybe a small glass on my birthday. Oh, and I did have a glass when my grandmother celebrated her birthday and—"

"You're rambling again."

"Okay, you're right. No rambling, got it."

"Relax, I'll be right back."

"Nina, no, wait…" Alyssa said as her friend walked away, and several guests turned and glanced at her. "Hi, how are you? Good evening. Miserable weather outside, isn't it?" She plastered a fake smile on and nodded until they turned away. "I'm going to jail," she muttered again.

"Excuse me?"

Alyssa froze in place, hoping that if she didn't move and didn't breathe, the person tapping her shoulder wouldn't notice her anymore. She was obviously wrong.

"Excuse me, aren't you—"

"No, sorry, not me. You have the wrong person," she said, turning away slightly and looking desperately for her friend.

"Funny, I could have sworn that you were Alyssa Wingate." *Oh, Lord, busted.*

Alyssa sighed, then turned around, ready to accept her punishment. "Oliver Watts?"

"Hey, it is you," he said.

"Oliver Watts," she repeated.

"Yep, it's me, in the flesh," he answered with his usual boyish charm.

"Not now, go away, Oliver," she said quietly as she pivoted slightly. He stepped back into her line of vision.

Oliver Watts, a pesky neighbor several years younger, stood chuckling. "So, what are you doing here?" he asked, obviously ignoring her request.

"Shut up," she hissed. "Do you want to blow my cover?"

"You have a cover?" he asked, still chuckling, then tilted his head to glance at her crooked name tag. "Sundari Adia

Nomalanga. Where did you get that goofy name tag? And who is Sundari Adia Nomalanga?"

"Shh," she hissed, then readjusted the tag again. "Keep your voice down. I'm not supposed to be here." She glanced around, smiling and nodding. "Sundari Adia Nomalanga is my alias. As I said, I'm not supposed to be here."

"No kidding. You stick out like a flower in Death Valley. What are you doing here?"

"I'm undercover," she whispered.

He burst out laughing. Several people around them turned and smiled at the couple. Alyssa was horrified as she tried to walk away from him.

"No, wait, I'm sorry, you just caught me off guard. But really, what are you doing here?"

"I need to speak with Senator Kingsley."

"He's not here yet."

"Duh, yeah, I know that. I'm waiting for him."

"Okay," he said, still half chuckling.

"What are you doing here? I thought your mother said that you were in Nepal or Mongolia somewhere."

"I was, now I'm back. I'm supposed to be hanging out at a gallery opening across the street, but I noticed this shindig going on over here, so I decided to stop by."

"That's it, you just walked in, no cover story?"

"No, first I told the sentry at the door that I was a secret agent on assignment and that my contact was inside with my forged papers," he said, and chuckled at his ridiculous story, then looked at her face. She was grimacing and he laughed out loud again. She turned away. "No, seriously, I just walked in, no big deal. Don't tell me you had an elaborate story…"

She glared harder and he laughed more.

"You know what, you're right. I do stick out. I don't belong here. I'm gonna leave."

"Alyssa, what are you doing?" Nina said, handing her a martini. "Here, take this. It'll relax you."

"I don't belong here. I can't do this, I gotta go."

"Alyssa," both Oliver and Nina began. They stopped and looked at each other, then turned back to see their friend cutting through the crowd toward the main exit.

"Excuse me. Excuse me," Alyssa said, parting through the thickest part of the crowd. Still holding the glass, she got bumped from behind, turned, then turned again only to bump into a solid chest, spilling her drink down the front of his tie.

"Oh, rats, I'm sorry." She shook her head, then quickly produced a lace handkerchief from her purse and began dabbing her suit and the man's tie in front of her. "Ever have one of those days when everything seems to go wrong?" she moaned out loud.

"Repeatedly," the man said as she continued dabbing them both with her handkerchief.

"Yeah, okay, that's not coming out. Here, take my business card and send me the cleaning bill. Believe me, I'm good for it. I'll send you a check."

"Thanks, but don't worry about it."

"No, really, I insist. I'm good for it," she said, continuing to dab at his tie.

"All right, if you insist," he said, taking her card.

"Uh, why don't I take care of that, sir?" another man said, suddenly standing at her side.

"Actually, I'm kind of enjoying it, Kent."

Alyssa stopped dabbing with the handkerchief, looked up into gorgeous dark eyes and glared. "Playtime's over, jerk."

"Too bad." He smiled and shrugged.

She smirked, pushed around him with her elbow slightly poking him in his side, then continued through the crowd, meeting Nina and Oliver as she got to the other side of the room.

"How did you beat me here?" she asked.

"Oh, it was easy," Nina said. "We didn't stop to fondle Senator Randolph Kingsley on the way over."

"That was— No, he didn't even look like— I can't believe this— I just spilled— I just called him— Oh, crap." She turned around, seeing him standing slightly above the crowd, looking in her direction. He smiled and nodded amiably. She closed her eyes and grimaced as someone walked up to him and blocked her view. "Crap," she repeated.

"All right, you have your in. Just go back over there," Nina declared.

"Are you crazy?" Alyssa said, pulling Nina over to the side. "He already thinks I'm some kind of nutcase. Oh, and that's beside the fact that I just called him a jerk to his face."

"You called him a what?" Oliver said, chuckling. "That's great. Only you would call one of the most popular senators in the country a jerk to his face."

"Tell me you didn't," Nina butted in, after glaring at Oliver. Alyssa nodded ruefully.

"Uh, ladies—" Oliver began.

"Not now, Oliver," Alyssa said, obviously still upset.

"I'm just saying…" he proclaimed, glancing up and noticing Senator Kingsley scanning the room, obviously looking for someone.

"What am I going to do, Nina? The whole idea of coming here tonight was to make a good impression on the man."

Oliver continued to watch the senator look around. "You know, I kind of think you might have made that good impression, 'cause if I'm not mistaken—"

"Oliver, please," Alyssa said. "Okay, what do we do? How do we salvage this?"

"Okay, let me think," Nina said as the two of them moved away again, then put their heads together.

Oliver followed them, noticing that the senator's eye followed them, as well. He smiled, enjoying the cat-and-mouse game being played, even though the two mice had no idea that the cat was watching them. "You know, maybe you don't need to do anything. Maybe—"

"Shh." Nina silenced him once again, then turned back to Alyssa.

"Alyssa—" Oliver began.

"Oliver, please, this isn't a good time."

"You're right, maybe now isn't exactly a good time. I'm sorry," he said, chuckling and looking beyond them, seeing Senator Kingsley moving through the crowd and making his way in their direction with his eyes on a single target. "But you might want to—"

"Oliver, please, this is serious," Alyssa said.

"I'm sure it is, but still, you might—"

"Come on, give her a break, can't you see she's upset?" Nina said, turning to Oliver and handing him the empty glass.

"Alyssa, I'm sure that whatever happened with the good senator was nothing," he said, smiling openly.

"What are you still doing here? Go away," Nina said.

"Nina, the man must think I'm crazy. I pour a drink on him and call him a jerk, then elbow him in the ribs as I walk away."

"Alyssa, please tell me you're joking. You assaulted him, too?"

She frowned. "Not joking, but in my defense, he was a total jerk at the time."

"You're absolutely right. I was, and I do apologize." The seductive voice behind her sent an instant wave of warmth through her.

"Is that— Is he…" Alyssa asked, whispering to her friend and pointing over her shoulder.

Nina nodded slowly while smiling and looking up. "Good evening, Senator Kingsley. How are you, sir?"

"Fine, thank you, Nina Hall," he said, glancing at her name tag.

"Oliver Watts, sir, good to meet you. I'm a huge fan."

"Good to meet you, Oliver." They shook hands, and then the senator redirected his attention. "Excuse me, we didn't actually meet back there. I'm Senator Randolph Kingsley, and you are…"

Alyssa turned slowly, regretting the next few minutes. Their eyes met.

He smiled. "You're slouching," he said, tilting his head to the side while looking at her chest area.

"Oh, sorry, I…" Alyssa said, straightening up instantly, taking a deep breath and thrusting her breasts forward.

He smiled, and tried hard not to chuckle, then pointed to her lapel. "Uh, no, I meant that your name tag is kind of slouching." He tilted his head again to try and read the small badge attached to her lapel. "Sundari Adia Nomalanga, that's a unique name. I don't believe I've ever heard it before. Is it African or Indian?"

"Actually it's both."

"Does it have a meaning?" he asked.

Oliver and Nina looked at each other and rolled their eyes, knowing that this would definitely get them all kicked out of the reception.

"Yes, it does. Sundari is Hindu and it means *beautiful one.* Adia is Swahili and it means *gift from God.* And Nomalanga is Zulu and it means *sunny.*"

"How appropriate," he said as his eyes lit up.

Oliver and Nina glanced at each other again, exchanging a sly smile.

"Sir, a clean tie, and they're ready for you over here." A

man stepped up to the senator quietly, handing him a duplicate of the slightly stained tie he wore.

He nodded. "Thanks. Kent Larson, meet Ms. Sundari Adia Nomalanga, Ms. Nina Hall and Mr. Oliver Watts."

Kent looked at each in turn, shaking hands and nodding after each introduction. "Nice to meet you all," he said, then refocused his attention on Randolph. "They're waiting over here."

"It was a pleasure meeting you, Ms. Hall, Mr. Watts, Ms. Sundari Adia Nomalanga. Excuse me."

"Uh, one thing, Senator. I'd like to meet with you possibly to discuss Social Security reform with respect to—"

"Senator, this way, please," Kent said.

Alyssa frowned when he turned away. "—to discuss…"

He turned back to her while reaching into his pocket to get a card. "Call me at the office. We'll talk."

"This way, sir," Kent said, guiding him through the crowd toward the center.

"Now, that's an impressive man," Nina said breathlessly, smiling.

"Absolutely. I must have been insane to think that I could just walk up and talk to him," Alyssa said. "I thought I was prepared, but I don't think there's enough preparation for him. Talk about charismatic."

"He's smooth and just too cool," Nina added.

"Hey, what am I, chopped liver?" Oliver chimed in.

"Who are you?" Nina finally asked. "Alyssa, who is this person? Do you actually know him?"

"Sorry, Nina Hall, friend and coworker, meet Oliver Watts, next-door neighbor when we were growing up."

"And close personal friend," Oliver added. "Hellooo, Nina." His smile was broad and genuine.

Nina sized him up instantly, then, knowing Alyssa's age

and seeing that Oliver was a few years younger, came to two likely conclusions. "Babysat or tutored?"

"Both," Alyssa said, still looking through the crowd to hopefully spot the senator again.

"Excuse me, I take exception to the term *babysat.* Alyssa and I hung out together."

"Come on, that's all we can do here tonight," Alyssa said, slightly disheartened.

"What, we're not staying?" Oliver said as a waiter walked by with a tray of hors d'oeuvres. He quickly grabbed three crab cakes and a napkin.

"We're going. You can stay," Nina tossed over her shoulder as she followed Alyssa.

Oliver popped the first crab cake into his mouth and followed them outside. "Where are you parked?" he asked.

"Across the street over there, next to that art gallery, why?" Nina asked suspiciously.

"Great." He popped the second crab cake into his mouth. "I'm going that way, too. You may escort me."

"Is he kidding? Who are you exactly and why are you tagging along uninvited?"

They started walking down the front steps, then paused to walk around a huge black sedan parked out front. "Now, that's a car. If you have to travel, that's the way to do it," Oliver said, nodding his head approvingly.

"It's probably the senator's," Nina said.

They walked around it, then paused again for traffic before crossing the street. They headed for the parking lot, and then both Nina and Alyssa stopped short when they came to the art gallery's front display. There in the window was a poster-size photo of Oliver, smiling, charmingly boyish.

"Oliver?" Alyssa said, surprised.

"Oh, that's right, I knew there was someplace else I was

supposed to be tonight. Must have gotten my directions crossed. Come on, let's check it out, it might be fun," he said, then stepped between them, grasped both women's arms and escorted them inside.

"Oliver, Oliver," a taut prissy woman shrieked, near hysterics, as soon as they entered. "Where have you been? I was worried sick that you might have taken off again like last time. Oh, never mind, you're here now. Come, come, come. There are dozens of patrons here who are dying to meet you. Come on, I've already sold six paintings, so a grand appearance from you wouldn't go unnoticed."

"You can thank these two lovely ladies for getting me here safely," Oliver declared.

Then, almost as an afterthought, she noticed Alyssa and Nina. "I'm sorry, ladies. This is a private reception for guests and patrons only. The gallery will be open to the general public tomorrow morning at ten o'clock."

"Jacks, Ms. Wingate and Ms. Hall are my personal guests this evening."

"Oh, well, in that case, please enjoy," she said in a snobbish tone, obviously annoyed to have them there.

"Here you go, Jacks, I brought this for you," Oliver said, handing her the last crushed-up crab cake in the napkin.

"Oh, really? How nice," she said, peeling the napkin open and looking down at the squished mess in her hand. "Thanks." She smiled up at him, seeing his very serious, very pleased expression. "Shall we? This way, please."

Jacks led the way through a maze of guests standing before large paintings. The gallery was just as crowded as the reception they had just left. "Oh, by the way, this is Jacks, my agent and personal promoter. She's a true gem," Oliver said.

She turned quickly. "Nataliya Parker-Price Duosette.

Charmed, I'm sure." She turned back, waved across the room, then quickly made her way through more guests.

"Oh. So, where did the name Jacks come from?" Alyssa asked.

Nataliya turned again and looked at Oliver, apparently not very amused.

He smiled happily in all sincerity. "Actually that was my idea. I think she looks more like a Jacks, don't you?"

"Indubitably," Nina said seriously, using the same snobbish tone and following his lead.

Jacks began clapping her hands. "Excuse me, excuse me, people. People, please, might I have your attention?" The room began to settle down with only a few hushed voices still chatting, Oliver's being one of them. "Ladies, gentlemen, honored guests, patrons of the arts, I have the distinct pleasure of introducing our guest of honor…" she began, then unfolded a small piece of paper and started reading the list of accolades.

"Thought I was just some knucklehead off the street, didn't you?" Oliver whispered proudly to Alyssa and Nina, still standing between them.

"You're still some knucklehead off the street," they returned in unison, as if on cue. Alyssa and Nina chuckled silently at the coincidence.

"…the brilliant artistry of our honored guest, a man far beyond his years and time. Please join me in welcoming artist, Renaissance man, genius…"

"No wonder you have a big head. Look what she fills it up with," Nina whispered in a low voice.

"…Oliver Watts."

Oliver laughed at her remark, then raised his hand as the guests began applauding wildly and he stepped up to take center stage. Nina laughed and shook her head. "Who exactly is that guy?" she asked, joining in the applause around her.

Alyssa smiled and applauded gingerly. In reality, her thoughts were still half a block away, looking into Senator Randolph Kingsley's eyes. "Good question," she uttered quietly. "Who exactly is that guy?"

Oliver began talking. As usual, his engaging personality and boyish charm captivated everyone in the room. Nina and the other assembled guests listened intently, but Alyssa had tuned out. She stepped back and excused herself, walked toward the perimeter of the room, then inched her way away from the main gallery.

Standing by the window, she watched pedestrians hurry by on their way to wherever they were going as cars sped toward their destinations. Then, for some reason, her thoughts veered to him, Senator Randolph Kingsley. Where he was going next, what he did to relax, what he watched on television, what he liked to eat, what his childhood was like, if he was seeing anyone.

"Whoa, where did that come from?" she said to herself.

Getting caught up in the excitement of the evening was one thing, but daydreaming about one of the most prominent senators in the country was another. He was an African-American, single, straight male, and she was certain that half the female population—black, white, brown and purple—had designs on him.

She was a nobody, from nowhere and had nothing. So her chances of attracting someone like him were nil at best. Although there was always a chance, it happened, but only in Cinderella fairy tales where the prince would sweep his love off her feet and they'd live happily ever after. Sure, she'd have a slightly good chance only if she was the last female on earth and, even then, she'd be skeptical. Low self-esteem was her best friend, but so was being realistic.

Chapter 2

Across the street Senator Randolph Kingsley smiled dutifully, shook hands and joked with the invited guests. His public persona was set on automatic. He did what every U.S. senator did in these settings. He morphed from a political wonk into a personable, energetic, public servant. There was no handbook, just the commonsense notion that one must always respect the office.

Although he might have had a momentary lapse in judgment earlier that evening, no one witnessed it except her, her being Sundari Adia Nomalanga. The name was curious and the flopping name tag was ridiculously humorous. He chuckled to himself and, appropriately enough, timed it perfectly with a local community leader's joke.

Those around him laughed, as well, giving the local politician exactly what he wanted, center stage. Randolph smiled as a photo was taken and continued basking in the political limelight.

Randolph, to his surprise, had no idea what the flow of conversation was around him because he pretty much stopped paying attention when Sundari left, and that wasn't like him. He was distracted. Adia, he thought to himself, was indeed a gift from God. She was lovely in an unpretentious way that was natural and unassuming.

Like so many others before, women came in and out of his life constantly, most with aspirations of owning a vineyard in California, a home in the Capitol Hill area and maybe taking permanent residence at the White House, but he was always very selective. Political groupies were like kryptonite. And he avoided them like the plague.

Seeing what obsessively fanatical women had done to political careers in the past had definitely made him cautious. Scented, perfumed, adorned and sexy, they came in an unending procession, all with one goal.

The prize, ever elusive, was the senator at their side. It didn't matter what had to be done, to whom or how often, the end justified the means and these women meant business.

Of course, he wasn't a saint; he'd done his share of dating—models, actresses, executives, lawyers, schoolteachers, even a doctor or two. They were all sweet and loving women with plenty to offer, but he just never really clicked with any of them. His heart was never in any real danger, because he knew exactly what each woman wanted.

They were users and he accepted that fact.

His last date was a surgeon who was more into her position at the hospital than him. In a complete turnaround, he was her arm candy, a trophy to be taken out and displayed at opportune times. His prominence in politics and his vineyard in California only added to her prestige. And the fact that he personally knew Matthew Gates, a fixture in business and on several hospital boards, including hers, added to his appeal.

Ambitious to a fault, she had a reputation for single-minded focus. She wanted status and that meant a seat on the hospital board. Once he suggested her name to Matthew for consideration, she all but dumped him. He wasn't surprised or brokenhearted, and he was easily consoled, since his heart wasn't attached. Granted, he'd been used and betrayed before.

Once, in college, the captain of the cheerleaders used him to help her pass trigonometry, and then she dumped him after she'd gotten a passing grade. Back then, he decided to lie low as far as romance was concerned. It worked for him then as he focused instead on his studies and future career.

All's fair in love was his motto now. Pity, the doctor never did win a seat on the board, but she did try to come back into his life, though they both knew it wasn't going to happen.

Then, like now, he took a brief hiatus from romance. But being who and what he was, rumors floated around the Hill constantly. Who is he sleeping with, who is he dating, who can we match him up with? Everyone wanted in on his life and women called him constantly. They wanted a piece of him, "a just-in-case piece of him," his half sister, Juliet Bridges, would always say.

Now he prided himself on his discretion. And up until a year ago, he used Juliet, a retired ballet dancer, as his companion for social events. But now that she was married, he went to receptions alone and left alone, with only his assistant at his side. Not exactly how he wanted it, but he accepted that's how it was, at least, for the time being.

He knew his life lacked something, and only now was he beginning to understand what that something was. Success and achievements were fine, but being alone without someone to share them with was no longer enough.

Lost in his thoughts, he looked around the room. Wealthy, smiling faces greeted him in every direction. Men wanted to give him their business cards. Women wanted to give him their phone numbers. He made it a rule never to accept either, but instead directed them to Kent, who readily filed them—where, he had no idea. This was obviously just another political reception where some lobbyist wanted desperately to hand him an obscene amount of cash for his campaign fund, no strings attached. Yeah, right.

But even with all the nonsense that came along with his position, this was still the best job in the world. True to his dreams from his freshman years, he stayed focused on what he wanted to accomplish. And even though special interests were parked at his door, he made it clear that his vote wasn't for sale at any price.

Just then, a woman standing across the room caught his attention. He could only see the back of her, but the possibility instantly stirred his imagination. Was it possible? Was it her again? The suit looked similar, but the hair was slightly different. Either way, he couldn't tell for sure, and she was too far away to get a good look.

Earlier, with a simple touch, she'd gotten his attention like no other woman had. Even now, he smiled thinking of her. Curiosity forced him to walk across the room. He focused on the back of her head and started in that direction. Apparently he'd found what he was searching for. What he needed now was a matchmaker.

"Good evening, Senator."

A quick chill instantly shot through him. He'd been blind-sided. He knew that voice—strong, steady and firm. It was as if he conjured her up. He turned and looked down slightly. She smiled back up at him. He chuckled and shook his head. "I was just thinking about you. Is it my turn?"

Louise Gates smiled. "Whatever are you talking about, Senator Kingsley?"

"Hello, Mamma Lou. You look lovely and enchanting as ever," he said, then reached down, kissed her cheek and swallowed her up in his arms. She was a most welcome sight.

"Oh, stop, making an old woman blush. Shame on you. But you, look at you, all over the place, on television, in newspapers and magazines. You're almost impossible to keep up with. I'm so proud of you," she said, wiping the lipstick from his cheek.

"Thank you, Mamma Lou, where's…" he began, then paused and waited a second before he held out his hand. "Ah, here he is. Colonel Wheeler, sir, how are you? Good to see you again."

"Fine, fine, my boy. I would ask how you're doing but I already know. Very impressive, very impressive."

"Thank you, Colonel. I try. When did you get into town?"

"Last night. We're staying with Tony and Madison and the babies," Colonel Wheeler said.

"How are they?" he asked Louise.

"Oh, everyone's just fine, busy, they send their love and the twins are adorable, of course," Louise added.

"I have to get over there, but I've been so busy, I haven't had the time."

"There's always time for family," Louise said.

"You're absolutely right, Mamma Lou. Are you staying around the capital long?"

"Madison and Tony are taking care of the annual auction at the antique store, so we're just pitching in to lend a hand."

"I might just get you two to pitch in and lend a hand on the Hill." They laughed heartily, knowing that he was doing an excellent job as the newly elected senator from California. "I was just asking Mamma Loù if it was my turn now."

"And I was just telling the senator that I had no idea what he was talking about," Mamma Lou said.

Colonel Wheeler chuckled. Randolph looked at him for sympathy. "No, no, I'm sorry, son, nothing I can do. Over the years I've been offered bribes, pleaded to, cajoled, sweet-talked and even wheedled, but trust me, nothing works. I am unequivocally and most definitely, out of it. Like so many others before you, you're on your own."

"Excuse me, I'd take offense to this conversation if I weren't such a good sport," Louise said.

"And we love you for it," Colonel Wheeler said happily.

"Hear, hear, that surely deserves a toast," Randolph said, nodding to his assistant, who quickly guided a waiter in their direction. A tray of champagne appeared. Each took a glass. "To Mamma Lou, forever wonderful, and to you, Colonel Otis Wheeler, forever the statesman by her side," Randolph said.

"And to Senator Randolph Kingsley. Congratulations, son, a fine career, we are all very proud of your success," Colonel Wheeler added.

"And to love," Louise said quickly as the men were poised to sip. Colonel Wheeler just cleared his throat and chuckled, always half expecting something from his special love. But Randolph nearly choked, sputtering as he took a small sip.

Randolph laughed heartily and Colonel Wheeler joined in. "So, Mamma Lou, have you chosen her yet?"

"Who, dear?"

"My future wife."

"No, have you?" she asked. A spark lit in his eyes and gave her his answer. "You have, haven't you?"

"I didn't say that," Randolph said.

"Of course you didn't." She smiled. "You didn't have to, dear. It's all over your face."

"How does she do it?" Randolph asked Colonel Wheeler.

Colonel Wheeler shook his head. "I'm just an innocent by-stander, not even here."

"Sir, we have one more reception after this," his assistant said quietly.

"Yes, right." Randolph turned to Louise and Otis. "As al-ways, it's been a pleasure. Please stop by the office if you're gonna be in town for a while. I'd love to take some time and show you around."

"We'd love to. Thank you," Louise said, holding her face over as he kissed her cheek again.

"Take care, son. Don't let 'em rattle you too much," Col-onel Wheeler added.

"I'll try not to," Randolph said, shaking hands. He nodded and started toward the exit as his assistant led the way. Mo-ments later, through a crowd of fond farewells, he was on his way out the door.

"That's a man who is going to go far in this town," Otis said assuredly. "He's got a good head on his shoulders."

"Indeed, and as we all know, two heads are always better than one," Louise added.

Colonel Wheeler chuckled, then laughed. There was no stop-ping her, and not having received an out-and-out refusal from Randolph, his special love was already busy planning.

"The car's out front. This way, sir," Kent said.

Randolph followed.

The rain had stopped, but the air was still muggy and the sky was sluggish to let go of its drizzle. Randolph looked up at the sky and took a deep breath. It wasn't the sweet scent of his vineyard home outside San Francisco, but the air was fresh and clean and it felt good to be out, at least for a bit.

Thankfully work waited for him, filling the empty hours before he'd finally fall asleep alone every night. Quietly, that's how he rolled, keeping a low profile and trying to remain out of the headlines as much as possible. In D.C., it was the best thing to do.

Walking down the steps, he looked up, and saw the art gallery across the street. He remembered thinking earlier about stopping in if time permitted. Of course, it never did. He watched as a small group of passersby hurried inside. That's when he spotted her, Adia, standing at the window staring across the street.

She was looking at him and his body reacted with an intensity he'd never before experienced. From the instant he saw her, she affected him like no one else ever did.

Caution might have told him that he'd picked up yet another ardent admirer, but his instincts said otherwise. He smiled and again considered a quick run across the street. Then just as the thought began to rest comfortably...

"Sir, I checked with traffic. There's an accident en route, we'll lose seven minutes with the detour. Unfortunately you'll be three minutes behind schedule, but it's unavoidable. We need to leave now."

"That's fine," he said, still looking at Adia. "Kent, do me a favor, jot down the name of that gallery across the street."

"Of course," he responded without question.

Randolph smiled. He was truly blessed and his life was charmed. But it was also empty, devoid of something, and he was starting to realize what that might be.

The door ajar, he got into the backseat and looked across the street. She was still standing there. Through the dark smoked windows he could observe her without notice. There was something about his Adia that made him smile even now.

Dressed in a navy suit and modest heels, she wasn't as glamorous as some of the woman he dated. Nicely rounded, she wasn't model thin. But there was something about her. He wasn't sure just what. He smiled, remembering the name tag tilted on her lapel.

Chapter 3

Senator Randolph Kingsley. Alyssa'd seen him on television, read articles about him in newspapers and magazines, but still, she wasn't prepared to meet the man in person. Wow.

Seemingly larger than life in other venues, he was really just a guy. Maybe more attractive, more interesting, definitely more charming, but still, just a guy. She looked up through the window of the art gallery just as he came down the front steps of the reception across the street. She wasn't sure, and of course, it was absurd to even think, but she could have sworn that he saw her standing there and smiled her way.

She watched him get in and the car drive away. She had his card, but this was no flirting opportunity. She needed to talk to him about serious business. He had something she wanted and she intended to get it.

"Your friend is completely insane," Nina said behind her. "I love it."

"Oliver, yeah, he always was, even as a kid. His parents were overprotective and spoiled him rotten, giving him everything he thought he wanted and then some."

"Oh, then his family's got money, huh? Nice."

"No, they're just a very loving, giving family."

"Figures, I'm always attracted to men without money. Must be some kind of pheromone I send out. That's all I need, to hook up with a starving artist…then again, he is adorable…unless of course, you're interested," she said with a very obvious hopeful lilt in her voice.

"Interested? Me? In Oliver?" Alyssa asked. Nina shook her head. "Nina, you hit it on the nose earlier. I did babysit Oliver for two years. He drove me crazy, he was irritating and he tortured me at every opportunity. He was like Dennis the Menace on espresso. No, I'm certainly not interested, he's still like a little brother to me."

"Just checking because…"

"Why because?" Alyssa asked.

"Well, he seemed kind of attracted to you."

"Residual affection, I assure you. He had a schoolboy crush on me once, but that was years ago."

"Okay, you're sure, then, 'cause he is kinda cute."

"Yeah, he was always a cutie and the girls used to go nuts for him, but if I remember correctly he stayed to himself a lot, artistic temperament, I guess."

"Don't tell me he's gay."

"No," Alyssa answered quickly, "definitely not. He was always a ladies' man. He had them lined up outside his front door."

"A ladies' man," Nina said with added interest.

They turned to see him gesture toward a huge painting, detailing some elaborate brushstroke and design. "Nina," Alyssa began. Nina smiled, but didn't answer. She just kept staring at him as if to size him up. "Nina," she repeated.

"I might as well," Nina said offhandedly as if to herself.

"Might as well what?" Alyssa asked. Nina smiled, but again didn't answer. "Nina…" she said, shaking her head, "don't break his heart."

"Me, never, no, of course not," she said, glancing back across the room, seeing Oliver show another painting with exaggerated, animated grandeur as only he could do. "So, I thought I'd hang around a bit longer. What about you?"

"Umm, actually I think I'm gonna head back over to the office. I want to get a jump on something I was working on earlier," Alyssa said.

"Work, this late? It's after eight o'clock. Even I don't want to be hanging around that office after dark. We've had three break-ins already, you do know that."

"Yes, and I'll be fine and I'm not staying too late."

"Okay, well, take care, see you tomorrow."

"Yeah, oh, and please tell Oliver I said goodbye."

"Sure thing."

Alyssa walked out and hurried to her car. Not fancy, not stylish and not new, but it served her well, getting her from point A to point B. She got in and drove through the wet streets of D.C. Even at this late hour, traffic was miserable. By the time she pulled up to the corner next to the building, she was anxious to get to work. She locked her car, then pulled up the security gate and unlocked the front door. She went directly to her desk, turned on the computer and started working.

The reception, predictably, was stiff-necked and boring. Every wannabe–political groupie was there. Press coverage had a tendency to bring them out in droves. Political sound bite chatter, hysterical laughter, less-than-genuine smiles and self-righteousness posturing abounded.

Randolph played along, yet was always careful to avoid politically compromising situations. He listened and smiled and commented when asked. He heard the same lame joke four or five times, told slightly differently, but he laughed each time. He answered and deflected the same questions over and over again.

"No, I have no intention of running for higher office at this time. Yes, I'm enjoying myself in D.C. Yes, it's very different from my home in California. Yes, I actually live on a vineyard. No, I'm no wine connoisseur. Yes, I do hope to wed and have a family someday. No, I don't have a timetable for my personal life. No, I don't go on blind dates. Yes, I'm sure your daughter, sister, cousin, niece is very nice, but I make no exceptions."

Randolph smiled politely each time he answered, but made sure he got his message across. For some reason, he had assumed that questions from the press would be difficult, but they were nothing compared to questions from those interested in his personal life.

Scanning the crowd, he finally spotted a friendly face and gradually made his way across the room. "Hey, buddy, took you long enough to get here. Remind me never to extend an invitation without having a car pick you up." Trey Evans smiled as the two men shook hands.

Longtime friends and business associates, they recently had found themselves related to each other when Trey's cousin, J. T. Evans, married Randolph's sister, Juliet. They also found themselves at the top of Louise Gates's infamous matchmaking list. "How've you been?"

"Busy," Trey said.

"How's my portfolio?" Randolph asked.

"Making money," Trey answered easily.

"That's what I like to hear. Come on, let's get a drink. I could use one."

The two men talked and joked then walked through the crowd toward the bar, occasionally stopping to chat with other guests. Moments later, they sipped club soda as several guests repeatedly came up and held lengthy conversations. Kent, ever vigilant, interrupted Randolph.

"Thanks, Kent," Randolph said as the other guests took the hint and moved on.

"He's pretty good. I could use a man like him on my staff."

"No way, my office would probably collapse without Kent around to hold it together."

"That bad, huh? Looks like you need to give him a raise. You look pretty tired."

"Just busy. These twenty-hour workdays are murder."

"Tell me about it," Trey agreed. "My client list is insane. Then a few months back, I took as a client one of those million-dollar lottery winners. Big mistake, the man insists on making the most insane investments. He's killing me. Every two minutes, he's calling me with another bright idea. Twice, I had to actually stop him from being scammed by con artists. He even sent money to one of those bogus Nigerian fraud scams."

"What?"

"I kid you not. I have no idea what is wrong with these people."

"Your guess is as good as mine."

"I finally got him to sign a waiver with a capped allowance. And still, he calls me every day wanting to opt out," Trey said.

"It's almost impossible to stop a train wreck. What are you going to do?"

"I finally had to lock him into a high-penalty note."

"Is it working?"

Trey looked at him and both men shook their heads. "I'll tell you, Randy, I haven't taken the time to really enjoy myself in months, and as for a little bit of romance, man, it's nonexistent."

"My heart bleeds," Randolph joked. "Speaking of romance, Mamma Lou is…" he began.

Trey instantly whipped around in full panic mode. "Here? Is she here, where?" he said.

Randolph started laughing. "No, at least I don't think so, but hey, you never know…she might be."

"Not funny. That little old woman is a menace. I'd rather take my chances with a thief in the night than do a one-on-one battle with her." Randolph laughed again. "It's not funny," Trey repeated, still glancing around.

"She's not that bad."

"Oh, you can say that because you have the whole United States government protecting you from her. Who do I have? Nobody."

"Come on, lighten up."

"Yeah, I don't think so. Anyway, so what about her?"

"She and Colonel Wheeler were at a reception I attended earlier."

Trey smiled, then laughed out loud. "It's you, man. It's your turn." He held his hand out to shake. "I'm sorry, Randy, but what can I say? Better you than me. It's been nice knowing you, brotha."

"You act like she has me marked or something."

"She does. Obviously you've never sat down and talked to Tony, Raymond, Dennis, J.T. or Juwan, not to mention her two sons, Ray and Matthew. And heaven knows how many others we don't know about. All happily single men until she targeted them. Bull's-eye, each and every one."

"But happy, each and every one, right?" Randolph said.

"Oh, yeah, they're happy. Deliriously, mind-blowingly,

ecstatically happy. I've never seen my cousin J.T. so happy in my life."

"So, what's the problem if she plays matchmaker? She's obviously pretty good at it."

Trey looked at him suspiciously. "Wait a minute, is this some kind of matchmaker intervention? Is Mamma Lou gonna pop up around here or something?"

"No, of course not."

"Just checking 'cause, man, you're starting to sound like you want to be matched up."

Randolph tilted his head and looked across the room. A woman walked by with the same style of suit and build as Adia. "Excuse me a minute," he said, and hurried to catch up with her. Unfortunately it wasn't her. But the idea that he would seek out a woman who looked like Adia was telling. He walked back over to Trey.

"Well?" he asked.

"Well, what?"

"Did you get her name and phone number?"

"No."

"Late-night date, wake-up call, anything?"

"No, it was the wrong woman."

Trey shook his head. "I see. Mamma Lou has you spooked, doesn't she? You're actually running after women now." He shook his head and sucked his teeth.

"Spooked? Me? Whoa, look who's talking. The mere mention of her name has you getting double whiplash. You nearly broke your neck doing a one-eighty. The last time I saw action like that, there was a possessed kid floating four feet above the bed."

"Nah, nah, I was just joking, I was just messing with you. You see, Randy, when it comes to Mamma Lou and her matchmaking, I have a theory…" Trey began.

"Oh, no, here we go again," Randolph said, rolling his eyes toward the ceiling, having heard his fill of Trey Evans's many theories.

"No, no, no, it's very simple…" he began.

Randolph listened, first nodding, then shaking his head, then just plain cracking up laughing. They finally shook hands and agreed to disagree.

"So, what are you doing next weekend?" Trey asked.

"Working, what else?" Randolph said, just as he had every weekend since his first election. "Why, you have a double date set up for us?"

"Nah, but why don't you sit in on our game?"

"What game?"

"Poker night, once a month or whenever we can get together. It's usually at Tony's place in Alexandria, since he's more centrally located, but next week, I believe, it'll be at J.T.'s new place in McLean. That is, if it's finished being remodeled. If not, then it's at my place."

"Sounds like a bet. Count me in," Randolph said.

They shook hands, then pounded fists. "All right, you go back to doing your senatorial thing and I'll be over here doing mine," Trey said, seeing an attractive woman pass by and smile at him. "Later."

Randolph smiled and shook his head. Trey was funny and smart and the best money manager in the business, but when it came to woman, he was a total scoundrel and completely clueless. Then he chuckled to himself as the reality of the statement settled in. When it came to women, every man was completely clueless.

Alyssa yawned. She squinted at the clock on her desk, then glanced up at the clock on the wall. It was almost ten o'clock. She'd been at it far longer than she intended, but she was impressed by the result. All she had to do now was print it out.

The office and storefront on a small street in a questionable neighborhood was quiet late at night. Businesses and mostly everything was closed at this time, and she kind of liked it that way. No distractions except those rolling around in her mind.

Ten minutes later, after changing the empty ink cartridge and adding more paper to the bin, she stood at the office printer and pressed the green button. Old, clumsy and loud, the printer begrudgingly spat out her precious document's twenty-seven papers. Then, since the printer didn't have the capacity, she collated her revised proposal by hand.

That's when she first heard the sound. The front door opened and closed and a disembodied voice called out. Her mind dashed in several directions. She looked toward the only other exit on the first floor, but it was way across the open space and she would never get to it without being seen.

She ducked low beside a desk, crouched over and spotted her purse containing her vile of pepper spray, her stun gun and cell phone. It was also too far away. Hearing footfalls coming in toward the rear where she was hiding, she reached up, grabbed the phone on the desk, pulled it down and dialed emergency.

"Hello, anybody here?" the voice said.

"Send help," she whispered into the receiver, then gave the address.

"The phone line is lit. I know somebody's here, so please just come out. I'm not going to hurt you, trust me please."

Alyssa frowned. How many burglars, murderers, rapists or thieves said please? "I have a gun, don't move," she shouted.

"Okay, I won't," he said calmly.

"I'm gonna give you one chance. Get out of here now. I already called for help and I don't want to shoot you."

"Well, that's good because I really don't want to get shot," he said.

Alyssa frowned again. Either the dregs of society were getting friendlier or she was talking to… She stood up quickly, hoping to startle him. She didn't. He stood in the doorway still in the shadows. "Who are you and what do you want?"

"Adia?"

"Your name is Adia?" she asked.

"No, not me, you. Adia, Sundari Adia, is that you?"

"Senator Kingsley?"

"Yes, may I?" he asked, then took a step farther into the back area.

"What are you doing here?"

"I believe you mentioned something about wanting to meet with me. Well, here I am," he said, smiling and oozing charm. "Actually I just happened to be passing by and saw the gate up and the lights on in the back, and since the front door was unlocked and open…"

"Crap, I forgot to lock the door again?"

"Again. Not exactly smart this late at night."

"Yeah, tell me about it. But I thought you had another reception to attend this evening."

He smiled. "Why, Ms. Nomalanga, it seems you know my itinerary better than I do."

"Not me, really. Actually it was my friend, coworker, really. We work together. We kind of snuck in before, but we were doing it with the best of intentions. I can't really explain, but—I know this sounds strange. Oh, never mind. I give up. Whatever I say is gonna come out sounding like I'm a stalker."

"Are you?" he asked.

"Am I what?"

"A stalker," he said.

"No, no, no, of course not. It's just that I work here at the

Foundation for Senior-Citizen Reform and I needed to talk to you, since you're on the Senate Special Committee for the Aging. We, the foundation, don't have the major funding that some of the larger lobbying firms have, but we have persistence and drive and a very serious cause."

"You're a lobbyist?" he asked more seriously.

"Me, no, not exactly, I'm in-house support."

"Even so, I presume you know my stance on lobbyists and special interest."

"Yes, I do, but this is different."

"It's never different, Ms. Nomalanga," he said, taking a step back to walk away.

"No, please wait, don't go." She hurried over, reached out and grabbed his arm, then instantly released him as he turned back to her.

"So everything this evening was so that you could talk to me about senior-citizen reform?" he asked.

"Basically, yes," she said, taking a decidedly professional stance. "I borrowed the invitation and crashed the private reception."

"That's a very gusty move just to talk with me."

"It's for a good cause. And as for the other part, I didn't intend to spill a drink on your tie and call you a jerk and poke you in the ribs, but yes, I went to the reception to talk to you."

"That's too bad," he said.

"Why is that?"

"I thought maybe…" He paused, almost blushed, then looked away. "Never mind, my mistake. I'll tell you what. If you have a proposal, I'll be happy to have a member of my staff look it over."

"Your staff."

"Yes, is that a problem?"

"No," she said, then, "Well, yes."

"Which is it, no or yes?"

"I may be relatively new at this person-to-person lobbying thing, but I do know politicians and they very seldom seriously entertain what their staff rejects and I can't take that chance."

"Oh, really?"

"Yes, really, this is important and one of these days, you're gonna be old and you're gonna want somebody to fight for you, and if you don't care now, then by then it'll be too late." He smiled through the entire time she ranted. "Fine, smile, laugh, enjoy my zeal." She turned to walk away.

"No, no," he said, taking her arm before she moved away. He pulled her closer. "I'm not laughing at you, I'm admiring your passion. Do you get this passionate about everything in your life?"

She smiled, slightly embarrassed. "Well, maybe not pizza with anchovies but pretty much everything else."

"I'll have to remember that, pizza, no anchovies."

They stood there a moment, just smiling. "We should really get out of here. It's late and…" She turned to walk away again, but this time, he pulled her into his arms and kissed her.

Afterward, breathless, she laid her head on his chest, stunned by his kiss, by her reaction to his kiss. "Wow, this was definitely not how I expected the evening to go."

"Nor I," he said, backing away. "I'm sorry, that was unprofessional and wrong. I don't know…"

"Well, I guess I should apologize, too, then."

"For what?" he asked cautiously.

"For this." She flung herself at him, locking her mouth to his, wrapping her arms around him. The kiss was full of passion as he opened to her and she opened to him. The tangle of tongues wrestling made their passion soar.

His hands, one holding her tight, the other caressing her breast, felt like heaven on her body as she pressed even closer beneath his suit jacket, resting her hands on the firmness of his buttocks. Pressing, pushing together even more seemed impossible, yet they attempted the feat anyway.

He caressed her face with his hands as his gentle kisses slowed the hunger but not the desire. Tasting, licking and savoring the moment, they kissed in slow, steady resolve, feeling every pleasure.

A throat cleared behind them. "Sir," his assistant called out with his back turned to them, while they were still locked in a passionate embrace.

Randolph instantly held Alyssa away as he took a step back, putting distance between them. "Yes, Kent, what is it?"

"Sir, we have a situation."

Two seconds later the sound of sirens was heard as several police cars careened down the street and surrounded the small storefront building. Blinding lights flashed through the front window and calls to surrender rang out.

"This is the police, come out now."

"Sir?" Kent turned to him, questioning.

"Just do as they say, we'll straighten it out later."

"Yes, sir." He immediately spoke into a small phone and their driver instantly stepped out and placed his hands on his head and leaned against the big black car.

"All right, inside the building, come out now."

Kent looked at the senator and nodded, then walked out. Randolph followed with Alyssa at his side.

"Yep, I'm so going to jail," she muttered to herself.

Chapter 4

"Alyssa Wingate," Nina muttered, still half asleep, "this had better be good. Do you know what time it is?"

"It's good. I'm in jail."

"You're in what?" Nina sat straight up in bed.

"Don't panic," Alyssa warned.

"Don't panic? You call me at this hour, tell me that you're in jail and then you tell me not to panic. Are you kidding me?"

"Okay, you can panic a little. Senator Kingsley is here with me. We're being detained."

"Senator who? He's what? You're what?"

"You're panicking."

"You're damn right I'm panicking. What happened? Why is the senator in jail with you? Did you follow him to the other reception? Oh, we are so fired."

"We're not fired, and actually I'm being detained. He's just hanging around to make sure I'm okay. I think."

"Excuse me, you have a United States senator hanging around a police station at twelve midnight just to make sure you're okay. Are you kidding me?"

"No, not kidding."

"Alyssa, what happened after the art gallery?"

"I'll tell you when you get here. I need you to stop by the office, get my purse from my bottom drawer and bring my ID. Unfortunately, I'm still supposedly Sundari Adia Nomalanga."

"Should I ask and do I even want to know?"

"Probably not and not really," she said.

"Okay, give me the precinct address. I'm on my way."

Half an hour later Nina showed up with Alyssa's purse. She was escorted into a small office where Alyssa stood staring out the window. "Girl, you have so much explaining to do."

"Later, I'm just tired now," Alyssa said.

"All right, ma'am," the officer said, then looked down at the driver's license in his hand. "Ms. Wingate, you're all set. The Senator vouched for you, you're free to go." He placed her purse and ID on the desk and turned to leave but then turned again. "But it might be a good idea to keep the proper ID on you and when you're working late, lock the doors behind you."

"Yeah, thanks," she said.

He walked out, leaving the door open behind him. Alyssa glanced at the door as he left. Senator Kingsley stood across the room, chatting easily with a few uniformed officers. He glanced in the open door. Seeing Alyssa, he nodded and then looked away casually.

"Come on, let's go," Nina said.

"Yeah," Alyssa said, picking up her purse and ID from the table.

Nina drove back to the office, asking dozens of questions, but Alyssa wasn't in the mood to elaborate. She told Nina the basics about forgetting to lock the door and that the senator had been driving by and, seeing the door open and the lights on, had come inside.

"Then what?" Nina asked anxiously.

"Then nothing. I heard a noise out front and called the police. They came and drove us all to the station to get more information. In the excitement I forgot to get my purse, and the only identification I had was that stupid name tag."

"That is so weirdly spooky," Nina said excitedly.

"What is so weirdly spooky?" she asked, not in the mood for Nina's mystical mystery mumbo jumbo. Nina Hall, a proud descendant of Creole grandparents, was born and raised in New Orleans and prided herself on the ways of mysticism. Deathly afraid of voodoo or anything like it, she was a firm believer in karma, kismet, destiny and the charms of the nec-romantic.

"That you were in jail tonight."

"Scary, annoying and a pain in the butt, but not something I'd call weirdly spooky."

"No, don't you remember? That's what you kept saying at the reception. You did this to yourself, you cursed yourself."

"Nina, please, it's almost one in the morning, no voodoo this late." Nina looked at her, her mouth open in shock. "Sorry, no mystical kismet this late."

"But don't you see? You did it. It was like you saw your own future and you incorporated Senator Kingsley into it. You made it happen."

"Yes, I made it happen. I spilled the drink on him, I forgot to lock the office front door, called the police and forgot to get my purse."

"See, see, you see?"

"I see that I'm tired and sleepy and that we're a block away from my car."

"We're being followed," Nina whispered, glancing up in the mirror, then quickly looking away.

Alyssa turned around and squinted. She saw darkness and a few street and traffic lights and the corner they had just turned. "I don't see anything."

"We just turned the corner, wait until they turn, too," Nina said as she pulled up right in front of the building.

They both sat, staring behind them. No car ever turned. "Nina, it's late, it's dark and you just imagined it."

"I could have sworn someone was following us all the way from the police station."

"Don't worry about it, we're safe." Alyssa looked at the office. The security gate had been pulled down and the locks already secured. "Thanks again, Nina," she said, "I really appreciate you coming out this late."

"No problem. Call me when you get home."

"I will. Drive safely. See you tomorrow."

Alyssa got into her car and drove straight home. She grabbed a quick shower and curled her hair. Tomorrow was a workday and she needed to look presentable even if she had dark circles and bags under her eyes.

She took a small glob of the face cream her mother always used and plastered her face to remove the last remnants of makeup. Using a tissue, she wiped and washed her face, then blotted it dry. Light and mirror didn't lie. She tilted her face from side to side. Even without the aid of her glasses she could see that she was the exact image of her grandmother, Allie.

Every photo, every video and every film confirmed it.

Allie had been diagnosed with Alzheimer's two years earlier but refused to accept it. Her memory was weakening daily and Alyssa felt completely helpless. All the dreams the two of them talked about and whispered about over tea and cakes were lost to her now. But it was the helplessness that was so punishing. The disease was bad enough, but the fact that the government didn't seem to regard seniors as an important constituency was deplorable.

So as a registered nurse and geriatric specialist turned lobbyist, she intended to do her best to change things for the better. That's why she chose to approach Randolph Kingsley. He was the newly appointed vice chairman of the U.S. Senate Special Committee for the Aging and he seemed sympathetic to the cause.

But now she didn't know what to think. He flirted with her and she called him a jerk. He kissed her, she kissed him and then as soon as somebody else showed up, he stepped away. What was that all about? Of course, the first thing she assumed was that he was ashamed to be seen with her. What else could it be? After all, she wasn't some gorgeous model or actress. She was just plain old Alyssa Wingate from Washington. D.C.

Alyssa yawned and trod barefoot into the bedroom of her small one-bedroom apartment in a building on a narrow street. She collapsed back onto her king-size bed, and for once, enjoyed the pleasure of completely stretching out spread-eagle on its softness.

She closed her eyes and considered the evening, far different than what she had imagined. Then she smiled, remembering the kiss. It was nice, really nice—full and passionate. His tongue had slipped inside her mouth. She licked her lips, hoping some remnant of him remained, but her mint toothpaste had washed him away.

So what was she supposed to make of the senator—a lecher lusting after whatever he wanted, a liar professing his integrity or just a man succumbing to impulse? She sighed, considering each, then decided to think about it tomorrow.

* * *

Randolph talked and joked easily with the police officers as he unconsciously toyed with the laminated name tag. After Alyssa and her friend left, he nodded to Kent, who moved to his side and suggested they retire for the evening. Randolph agreed. Then after shaking a few more hands, he said a few parting words and left. Once outside he started thinking about the last few hours. It was definitely not what he had expected.

"Interesting evening," Randolph said to himself when he got into the back of his car.

"Excuse me?" Kent said, following him inside.

Randolph looked up, realizing he'd spoken aloud. "Nothing, I just said that it was an interesting evening."

"Indeed it was. Shall we escort the ladies home?"

"Ah, just as far as the office, I think. Stalking is still a crime."

Kent smiled. "Of course." He turned and nodded to the driver, then loosened his tie and opened a small valise still on the seat beside him containing a small laptop computer.

The driver took off, following the car in front at a respectable distance. Randolph glanced out the window and smiled. It was an interesting evening. It was the first time in his life he'd been escorted to a police station. And even though he had presented his credentials as soon as he stepped outside and the police profusely apologized for inconveniencing him, he still insisted on going to the station to help with any paperwork.

It was a ruse of course. He wanted to go along to be with Adia again. He smiled, knowing now that that wasn't her name, but by now, it had already stuck and she was his Adia, his gift from God.

"I'm detailing an advanced press release. Is there anything you'd like to add about this evening's events?"

"No names," he said.

"Of course," Kent said.

"Just stick to the basics," he added.

"Of course."

Randolph nodded, realizing that it was completely unnecessary to mention that. Kent had been with him for years. Fifteen years his senior, he had come to Randolph six years ago with a troubled past, asking for a chance. He gave him that chance and they'd been loyal friends ever since. Kent, now his personal assistant, took care of the press releases, the itineraries and small inconveniences while also running his senatorial office.

"Personal memento?" Kent asked of the name tag still in Randolph's hand.

Randolph looked down, obviously unaware that he still held it. He turned it around to read the professionally scripted writing, positioned crookedly within the plastic tag holder. He tilted his head. "Sundari Adia Nomalanga, a very interesting lady."

Kent smiled, recallig the very passionate kiss he had witnessed earlier. "She is indeed, not the typical D.C. lobbyist."

"Definitely not," Randolph readily agreed. "I can't believe this evening. First the martini on the tie, then the jerk comment, the name tag, the breaking and entering and finally the police station. What was I thinking?"

"That she was an attractive, intelligent, amusing and accomplished woman."

"You know me too well."

"Basically a calamity with charm, sort of a Halle Berry meets Lucille Ball." Kent smiled, amused with himself.

"Halle Berry meets Lucille Ball?" Randolph questioned.

Kent chuckled. "Okay, it's late, bad analogy, but you get the picture. Beauty and comedy. When's the last time you hung out in a police station at one in the morning and enjoyed it? When's the last time you purposely changed your plans because of a business card and a chance meeting?"

"Good point." Randolph nodded. "Very interesting."

"Indeed." Kent turned the screen around to face him. "Alyssa Adia Wingate." He pushed a button and a beep sounded on Randolph's PDA. An e-mail and file had been transferred. "Name, phone number, cell number, address, Social-Security number—"

"What? I'm disappointed, no tax-return information," Randolph joked.

"—parents' information, grandparents' information, tax-return duplicates for the last three years—"

"Okay, thanks, I get it. You found her."

"Actually, I'd wager she found you, bogus name and all."

Randolph's easily suspicious nature was piqued. "You think this evening was planned, a setup?"

"To a certain degree, yes, of course. The reception was planned and she was obviously there to meet you. But as to the events of the past few hours, hardly. What are the chances that you'd go to her office and she'd call the police, thinking you were a burglar?" He chuckled to himself.

"Still, you said it yourself, beauty and comedy."

"The odds are a million to one, I'd wager," he said, having been down the dark gambling road before.

"Still," Randolph repeated, mulling over the possibility that the whole situation was planned for his benefit and that he had been set up or even worse that he was being manipulated. He continued considering the possibility when the car stopped a half block away and the two men watched as Alyssa got out of one car and hurried to another. Both women drove off in opposite directions.

"Shall I follow?" the driver asked, looking up in the rear-view mirror.

"No, let's call it a night. What does my day look like tomorrow?" Randolph asked.

Kent typed, bringing up the daily calendar for both of them to see. "You have an early breakfast meeting with Senator Ross at eight o'clock. Then you're back in the office until twelve. After that a meeting with Senator Bailey on the Hill, then several conference calls coming in at two o'clock. After that—"

"That's enough, Kent. Why don't you take the morning off? And, James—" the driver looked up in the mirror again "—sleep in late, I'll drive myself in tomorrow morning."

He nodded. "Sure thing, boss."

"You okay?" Kent asked, seeing Randolph's pensive expression.

"Yeah, just tired. I guess I could use a vacation. I guess we all could."

"I'll add that to my list." Kent pressed a button and darkened the screen. "One more thing about Miss Wingate, do you trust her?"

"I don't know her," Randolph said, "but I think I'd like to."

"I'll see what I can do."

James drove off slowly as soon as Alyssa got into her car and pulled away. The three men sat in silence as James drove out of town toward Virginia.

They arrived at Randolph's house a few moments later. He said good-night, got out and went inside. As soon as the lights went on in the foyer, James drove away, taking Kent home and then going home himself.

Randolph placed his briefcase on the first step, took his jacket off and loosened his tie. It was a long day and long night, but oddly enough, shorter than his last few. He went into the kitchen and grabbed a bottled water and two fried chicken legs left by his housekeeper. She always prepared a small snack for him when she knew he'd be out late.

Since he made it a point not to eat at receptions, he and Kent usually grabbed whatever they could catch on the run. Usually something James picked up for both of them between events.

He took a bite of the cold chicken leg and debated heating it up in the microwave, but it tasted so good cold he decided not to bother. A few seconds later, he tossed the bare bone in the trash, wrapped up his goodie snack in a dinner napkin, grabbed his water bottle, jacket and briefcase, then went upstairs to bed.

Chapter 5

Morning came way too soon as Alyssa crawled out of bed, stubbed her baby toe on her too-large bed in her too-small bedroom, then hopped into the bathroom to get ready for work. She brushed her teeth, washed her face, grabbed a shower and pulled out the annoying curlers. Limp and weak, her hair sagged, meaning she had to take the time to use her curling iron even though she'd suffered through the pain and torture of sleeping in curlers all night. She had a sneaky suspicion that the rest of the day was going to be just as torturous.

Dressed and out the door in record time, she'd opted against using the curling iron and instead maneuvered her long hairstyle into a French twist. She'd dressed casually in slacks, knit top and short jacket, then hurried to her car to begin her day.

As usual, traffic into the city wasn't as accommodating as

it could have been and it seemed that Fridays were always the worst, and to add to that it was her turn to pick up doughnuts and bagels for their weekly meeting. That meant a fifteen-minute detour to the bakery to stand in line to get doughnuts that would be consumed ten minutes into the meeting.

After gathering the pastries, she rushed into the storefront office to begin her day.

"Morning, all. Sorry I'm late," she announced to the small group assembled around the makeshift conference table in the side room. She dumped the three boxes of doughnuts, pastries and bagels in the center of the table, then sat down, deciding not to remove her jacket. Normally she would, but obviously Ursula Rogers was having another personal heat wave, because, even though it was warm outside for early May, she had the office air conditioner blasting full force.

"Anybody freezing in here?" Nina wrapped her arms around her body, shivering. Wearing a sleeveless low-cut top, she reached over and touched Alyssa's hand, who jumped slightly.

"Your hands are frozen," Alyssa said, moving away.

"See? Told you, I'm frozen. It's cold in here."

"You need some iron in your blood, Nina. I'm just now getting comfortable," Ursula said, fanning herself with a file folder.

Ursula's claim to fame was that in the early 1970s, she'd been a fashion model, *Playboy* cover and centerfold model, then married the governor of Maryland and become the toast of D.C. They divorced soon after, but she kept her political ties and later married a congressman who was now a political adviser. Still very attractive, she knew just about everybody there was to know and heard every speck of D.C gossip before anyone else.

Everybody looked around to their neighbor and smiled, knowing that they'd all just deal with it for the time being.

Ursula, who'd be out of the office as soon as the meeting was over, was by far the most aggressive lobbyist on the staff. She arrived early every day and pretty much controlled the office environmental system and everyone just let her have it. That was, until after she left, then all bets were off and so was the air conditioner.

"Sleep well?" Nina asked Alyssa, smirking openly.

"Yes, very. And yourself?" she said, refusing to be goaded by Nina's comment.

"Like a log, until a slight interruption."

"Oh, what a shame," Alyssa said, staring directly at her friend, daring her to mention last night. "What was the interruption?"

Nina chuckled, knowing she wasn't getting anywhere. "Crank call at midnight," Nina lied easily.

"They can be the worst," Alyssa agreed.

"Ain't that the truth?" Ursula chimed in. "My heart always jumps when the phone rings late at night. I just know it's some accident or tragedy, but then when it's some fool asking for some other fool I just want to reach through the phone line and strangle them, especially if I am sleeping soundly. And don't get me started if it wakes up my husband, Morgan."

Alyssa and Nina smiled as soon as Ursula brought up the subject. Morgan was Ursula's second husband and she took great pleasure in bringing his name up as often as possible—while, of course, singing his praises both politically and socially.

After that, the conversation around the table continued in the usual cycle. First crank calls, then phone bills, then cable bills, then what happened to the Buffalo Bills football team. After that, they discussed buffalo, pheasant and other types of meat you don't hear about anymore.

"Okay, people, we have a busy day ahead, let's get started," Pete Lambert said as he came dashing into the conference room, hurried as he usually was. He walked fast, talked fast and never took the time to slow down and enjoy anything. He always said, "Life is a game of musical chairs and you have to be fast and cagey to get the last seat." No one had any idea what that meant, but his pearls of wisdom always sounded particularly intriguing and thought provoking.

Pete wasn't your typical boss; he was a relic, a hippy flower child of the sixties who knew the lyrics to every folk and country song John Denver ever sang. He had played backup to Hendrix at Woodstock. He prided himself on being in Folsum Prison the day his one brush with another hero, Johnny Cash, sang. He was a died-in-the-wool rebel and quite often insisted on charging into every situation with guns blazing. He was Jesse James, James Dean, Frederick Douglass, and Malcolm X all rolled into one.

Admired by many, he was the bane of existence for others. When he got his teeth into a cause, look out. He was in for the long haul and not just for a few battles. And heaven help those who opposed him. His passion was unwavering and his idea of relaxation was changing the world in any way possible.

He quickly passed out a few papers, then sat at the head of the table and began the meeting. Thankfully these were always quick. "Okay, first of all, kudos to our planning committee for initiating and refining our recommendations for the current legislative session. It's been an exciting ride, but we're not home yet. Congress doesn't recess for another month, so let's see what arms we can twist in that time.

"We have three more proposals on the table. As of two days ago our Medicare and heath-care-reform request sailed through without a hitch with help from Alyssa and Nina. Thank you, ladies, for your diligent efforts."

Everyone began clapping. Nina stood and gracefully

waved as Alyssa just nodded and smiled, then blushed and laughed at her friend.

"Okay, okay, not done yet, folks. Nursing homes, age discrimination, health care are all tops on our agenda this session. Also, we're contacting several pharmaceutical companies regarding their overcharging for prescription drugs. We're investigating how to get the medication where it needs to be without it costing exorbitant amounts. How are we doing with antifraud?" he asked.

"We have a congressman and a senator whose mothers had their identities stolen a year ago, were victims of credit-card fraud, had their checking and savings accounts emptied, the whole nine yards. We're using them as our in. We've already reached out and they're both hot on the issue."

"Excellent. Okay, let's keep on top of that, shall we. We might want to make that a hot topic in September." Everyone nodded. "Also, a special side note of thanks to Alyssa, who again managed to fix the printer and save us another call to Computer Fixers on Call. It's working beautifully. Thank you again." Applause again. She blushed.

"All right, folks, any questions? Let's get started, *carpe diem,* seize the day."

With that, the day began. The staff scattered in several directions. Most left for meetings with politicians while others manned the phones and contacted volunteers.

Alyssa was an inside worker, which was just fine with her, particularly after last night. Her one and only attempt to get out ended miserably and she wasn't ready to repeat that embarrassment just yet. Luckily Nina was the only one who knew about it and she intended to keep it that way.

"I got a lead on Senator Randolph Kingsley," Nina said as she hovered over Alyssa's desk, smiling down at her.

"What is this, déjà vu all over again?"

"No, I got another lead."

"No, thanks. Been there, done that. Went to jail, remember?"

Nina chuckled. "Come on. You said you wanted to get out there and actually do something to help. Here's your chance. You said that you were tired of being in the office and not seeing any action. You said you wanted Alzheimer's disease on the list of hot topics next year. You said—"

"All right, all right. Yes, I know what I said, but that was before."

"Before what?" Nina asked.

"Duh, Nina, before last night, before actually meeting the man who sat in a police station, babysitting me at midnight."

"Oh, don't be so self-conscious and don't worry about all that stuff before," she said, waving her hand. "I can personally guarantee that you made a lasting impression, and as for him being there last night, he seemed to be enjoying himself, laughing and talking with the policemen, didn't he?"

"Yeah, well, that's what I'm worried about—the lasting impression," she said, but of course, kept to herself the passionate kiss she and the senator had shared right there in the office. A shiver flashed through her body as she remembered too vividly his lips pressed to hers and his arms wrapped around her, holding her tight.

"You got his attention, right? And isn't that what Pete always says: get a politician's attention, then get our agenda out. *Carpe diem!*"

"That's just it, I didn't get our agenda out."

"Yes, you did, I heard you."

"I got two words out, *senior citizens*. That's it. How is that a big help?" Alyssa dumped her chin on her palm and slouched on the desk. "Maybe I'm just not cut out for the one-on-one lobbying thing. Maybe I am just an inside worker after all."

"Alyssa, look, we both said that in order to make a difference, we had to get out there and do something, sometimes something drastic. Well, this is it." She leaned over and picked up the phone. "So today is that day, right?"

"Drastic?" Alyssa asked.

"Yes, drastic. Here, you have his card, call him."

"Call who?" she asked, and then realized who Nina was talking about. "Oh, no. Don't even think about it."

"Yes, call him," Nina insisted.

"No, absolutely not."

She leaned in closer and smiled knowingly. "I saw the way he was looking at you last night. If you were a sandwich, he would have gobbled you up right then and there."

"Last night was last night. The senator meets millions of people every day. I bet that he doesn't even remember me."

"Oh, please, the man stared at your mouth every time you opened it. I swear, if there was nobody else around, he would have seriously kissed you right there."

Alyssa's heart jerked at Nina's intuitive nature. "I have no idea what you're talking about. Senator Kingsley looked at everyone the same way. He has an intensity in his eyes that makes it seem that he's staring."

"Uh-uh, I don't buy it. No way, the man stared at you the whole time. Why do you think he came over after you bumped into him? I was there, too, remember. Then Oliver told me this morning that he saw him. He was actually searching and looking around the room for you. Girl, whatever you did or said must have rocked his boat 'cause you got him hooked. Hell, he even stayed at the police station, waiting with you. Don't you think that means something?"

"Yes, it means he's a nice guy."

"Yeah, he's a nice guy, all right, a nice guy who is very interested in you. You seriously need to call him."

"You're reading too much into all this."

"No, I'm not. You need to call him."

"No," Alyssa said flatly, hoping to end the conversation once and for all.

"Fine, then I will. Where's his business card?"

"Fine, then go ahead," Alyssa dared her as she pulled the card out of her purse. "Here, you want to call him. Fine, do it."

Nina picked up the business card, then checked the registry taped on every desk, dialed the main number to the Senate Building, then asked to speak with Senator Randolph Kingsley. He wasn't available, so when asked if she wanted to leave a name and number, she didn't hesitate. "Ah, yes, I'll leave my name, Sundari Adia Nomalanga, thank you."

Alyssa's mouth dropped.

Nina smiled, then walked back over to her desk.

"I can't believe you just did that," Alyssa said, watching as Nina sat back down at her desk and began typing. "What am I supposed to do if he calls me back?"

"Drastic times call for drastic measures."

"Oh, great, more drastic measures…" Alyssa stood and walked over to stand behind Nina. She leaned in closer. "What are you doing now?"

"I'm drafting an e-mail…" Nina said. Alyssa nodded, then walked away, thinking she was getting back to her job. "To Senator Randolph Kingsley." Alyssa stopped and turned just as Nina finished and sat back reading the screen, then pressed the send key.

"I'm sure that had nothing to do with me." She glared.

"Not at all," Nina said happily. "But Pete always said that we have to look beyond our fears and step up for those who can't do it themselves. Alzheimer's disease ravages thousand and thousands every year. It's time we stood up and looked at ways to change that. We need to help the caretakers to relieve the burdensome load. We need to help the research scientist find new cures. We need to help the public at large to understand that this is a silent killer that wipes away lives every day. We need to—"

"Okay, okay, jeez, what is with you today? You sound just like Pete." She paused and squinted a glare at Nina. "Wait a minute, what do you mean, Oliver told you that this morning?"

"You're changing the subject," Nina said, then placed a small piece of paper on her desk. "He's got an early meeting this morning on the Hill, and then he's back in the office after that. Maybe you could meet him on the run in between."

"Oliver is on the Hill? Why would he be—"

"No, not Oliver, Senator Kingsley is on the Hill this morning."

"Nina, I told you, I'm just not ready to press flesh and do the suck-up dance again."

"You're ready. You just need to get back on the horse and try again," she said, looking over as her desk phone began ringing. "So just do it." She pushed the small paper closer, then hurried to her phone.

The small piece of paper sat there taunting Alyssa all day. She ignored it, worked around it and did everything except set it on fire with her eyes. But still, it sat there unmoved and untouched. By the time six o'clock came, she gladly tore it up into little pieces and tossed it in the trash.

Finally, with the day well behind her, Alyssa got into her car and drove to her standing appointment. Fridays meant stopping at her grandmother's house and hanging out. She usually picked up dinner and brought it in. Chinese was the favorite. Cutting through the streets mapped out in 1790, she turned southwest following Benjamin Banneker's historic layout. From there, she curved through centuries-old streets with homes that had been around for just as long. Then she passed by newly built apartments until she arrived at her grandmother's home.

She parked in front of her house and climbed the steps to the open porch. Midway up, she turned, hearing someone call out to her.

"Hello, hello, excuse me," a petite young woman, barely out of her teens, called out as she ran down the pavement toward her. Long dark hair bounced as she approached, her light eyes sparkling with friendly anticipation.

Alyssa stepped down a few steps, expecting that the woman might need directions, since it was obvious that she was not from the neighborhood. "Do you need directions?"

"No. Hi, are you related to Mrs. Granger?"

"Yes, what can I do for you?"

"Oh, good, may I ask you a few questions?"

"About what? Who are you?" Alyssa asked, presuming that this had something to do with her grandmother's medical insurance.

"Oh, right, sorry," she said, giggling nervously. "My name is Gayle Henderson and I'd like to talk to you about your grandmother and Senator Vincent Dupree. I'm a grad student at Georgetown and I'm doing a paper on senatorial scandals and I'd like to interview you and your grandmother."

"Are you kidding me?"

"No, really, I have all this information but I need—"

"Goodbye," Alyssa said, then turned around and walked back up the steps to the porch.

"Excuse me, this isn't just for me and my paper. We can help each other. By my writing your grandmother's side of the story, all the public questions can finally be put to rest."

"Goodbye, Ms. Henderson."

"Fine, I guess I'll just have to write whatever I want to. After all, it doesn't have to be the whole truth, does it?"

"Is that supposed to be a threat?" Nina asked.

"Take it however you want. But if I were you, I'd talk now before it's too late."

"Then I guess it's a good thing that you're not me, so take your best shot. I just hope you have a good attorney to handle a slander civil suit."

"My daddy's an excellent attorney," she said in a typical spoiled-rich-girl way.

"Good," Alyssa said as she watched the young woman quickly hurry back to her red BMW and drive off.

Exasperated by the nerve of some people, Alyssa gathered the mail from the small wrought iron box attached to the front of the house and flipped through, separating the junk mail from the important mail. Afterward she glanced to see Mrs. Watts, her grandmother's next-door neighbor for over fifty years, outside sweeping her porch.

"Hi, Mrs. Watts," Alyssa said loudly, since she knew her hearing had always been a problem. And since Mrs. Watts insisted on not wearing a hearing aid, conversations with her always tended to be on the loud side. "Hi, Mrs. Watts," she repeated when the older woman turned to face her.

"Oh, hi, Alyssa," Mrs. Watts said, leaning on her broom. "How are you, baby? I saw you talking to that little mouse a few minutes ago," she yelled. "Was she bothering you, too?"

"Has she been around before?"

"Oh, heavens, yes. Allie told me that she called her at least ten times last week and now she's even started coming around. Don't know what the little pest wants, but you can bet she's trying to make a name for herself. They all do."

"What do you mean, they all?" Alyssa asked.

"Oh, this isn't the first time a hungry rodent has come sniffing around here. They crawl out of the woodwork every now and then, trying to get a piece of something to gnaw on, then go back and write about something totally false. Just a bunch of liars telling lies. Allie once tried talking to them a while back, but it turned out terrible. I warned her, you just can't talk to garbage, 'cause you get garbage in return." She paused and nodded coolly. "Are you still setting the world on fire at that place of yours?"

"I'm doing my best," Alyssa said, happy to drop the conversation as a few people walked by their side-by-side houses and looked up at them and smiled. "Oh, I ran into Oliver last night."

"Yes, yes, he told me when he called earlier, said you look just the same. 'Course, I knew that, since you stop by to visit Allie all the time. I told him that he needs to come visit me more and stop dashing around the world with his paintbrushes."

"I don't know, Mrs. Watts, I went to Oliver's show last night and his work is amazing. It's powerful and moving and the art critics love him. He's a very talented artist."

"Yes, just like my father, his grandfather. Must have skipped a generation 'cause I can't drawn a stick figure without a ruler and six erasers." She chuckled. "I attended the private opening a few nights ago. It was packed and you're right, they love him. He sold two paintings before the show opened to the public. I'm so proud of that boy of mine. I just wish he'd stop playing around and find himself a nice girl to settle down with."

"When the time is right, I'm sure he will."

"And what about you, missy, when am I gonna be invited to your wedding? I've been practicing my electric slide every week, ever since you and Oliver taught me."

"I bet you have," she said slightly louder, while laughing. "You got any other moves?"

"Oh, child, I got all kinds of moves up here," she said, pointing to her mind. "I just got to get these old feet moving in the right direction and hear some good music and I'm off. Give me some Jay-Z, some Kanye, some Chris Brown and some Nelly and I'll show you my moves."

Alyssa howled with laughter. Peggy Watts was one of the hippest, coolest older women she knew. She made it a point to stay on top of everything, and when she played her music it was just as loud as the teenagers did, but of course, mostly because she was hard of hearing.

"All right, Mrs. Watts, you keep doing those moves. I think I might have to pick up a few from you now."

"Come on over anytime. I'll show you what the kids down the block taught me last week," she said, then started gyrating her shoulder and snapping her head.

They both laughed as she went back to sweeping and Alyssa went inside. "Grandma," she called out as soon as she closed the door. "Grandma, it's me."

There was no answer, so Alyssa went into the kitchen and placed the bag of Chinese food on the counter. She saw that the breakfast and/or lunch dishes hadn't been washed, so she put the stopper in, turned on the water and added dishwashing liquid. When the sink filed with soapy water, she added the dishes and let them soak.

"Grandma," she called out again, then went upstairs and peeked into her bedroom, expecting to see her grandmother lying across the bed taking a nap. She wasn't. The television was on and the bed was still made. "Grandma," she said, continuing to walk through the other three bedrooms on that floor.

Each was neatly preserved, dresser, desk, curtains, bed perfectly made, but still no Allie.

Alyssa started to panic.

"Grandma," she yelled, now fearful that she'd fallen and hurt herself, and since Alyssa didn't call her the night before, she could possibly have been lying on the floor passed out for over twenty-four hours. "Grandma Allie."

She ran downstairs to the basement, swinging the door open, dreading the sight of her grandmother lying at the bottom of the steps with her laundry basket tumbled on top of her. "Grandma," she yelled, rushing down the steps to see that everything was in its usual perfect place.

She hurried back upstairs to the front door. The small foyer had a large antique coatrack where Allie Wingate kept her purse on a hook and her door keys on another. Both were still in place. She went back upstairs to the master bedroom's bathroom, then finally climbed the stairs to the attic.

As soon as she got to the top, she saw the door at the end of the short hall, wide-open. "Grandma, didn't you hear me calling you? I was looking all over that house for—"

She stopped dead. Her grandmother was lying on the floor, sprawled out as if she'd collapsed. She screamed, then rushed over to her side. Her nurse's training kicked in as she grabbed her grandmother's frail wrist and felt for a pulse. Finding a pulse, she placed two fingers on her neck and felt a strong, steady rhythm. She was still alive, thank God. As relief washed over her, her instincts phased to the next step, the possibility that she was hurt or injured or had fallen or passed out.

"Grandma," she said, quieter with less stress for fear of alarming her. "It's Alyssa, can you hear me?"

A slow, sleepy moan escaped as Allie took a deep breath, then opened her eyes and jumped. "Lord, child, you nearly scared the life out of me."

"Grandma, can you move, did you fall or pass out? Are you dizzy? How many fingers am I holding up? Can you tell me your name? My name?"

"Oh, stop all that silliness. I'm fine, except for seeing you here," she said, placing her hand over her heart. "You like to given me a heart attack. Look at you, you're as white as a ghost. What happened, is your father okay?"

"Grandma, you're lying on the floor, you almost gave me a heart attack. Are you okay?"

Allie started laughing. "Wouldn't that be a hoot, the two of us passed out with heart attacks 'cause we scared each other to death?"

"I seriously need to talk to you about your sense of humor," Alyssa said as she always did with her grandmother's warped sense of fun. "Grandma, what are you doing lying out like this on the attic floor?" Allie covered her mouth and yawned, then started to lean up. "No, wait, take it slowly, you might have broken a bone or something."

"I'm fine, the only thing that's broken is a dream I was having, but for the life of me, I don't remember it right now. Here, give a hand."

Alyssa braced back and helped her grandmother sit up. "Are you dizzy?"

"Child, if you don't stop all that fussing, I'm gonna toss you out that stained-glass window. It'll break my heart 'cause I love those windows, but I'll still do it."

"All right, all right I get it, I'll chill out."

"Thank you," she said, looking around at the floor covered with boxes and papers.

Alyssa sat down and looked around, for the first time actually seeing the mess around her. There were several large trunks open and an overflow of books, ribbon-tied stacks of letters, small boxes and black-and-white photos. "What is all this?"

"Here, help me up to the sofa."

Alyssa stepped behind her grandmother, placed her arms under hers and lifted her up slowly, then eased her back to the sofa behind them.

"Whew, it's hot in here. How about opening one of those windows over there to get some air moving around?"

Alyssa did as instructed, opening a few windows, letting a warm breeze in. "You need an exhaust fan in here to help blow out some of this heat."

"Always meant to get your father to put one in. Guess I just forgot to tell me to do it."

Alyssa went back over and sat on the sofa next to her grandmother. "So, what is all this?"

"Memories, picture, letters, a lifetime of treasures," she said.

"Were you looking for something in particular?"

"To tell you the truth, I have no idea. I came up here to…" She paused. "Isn't that funny? I can't remember now. Oh, well…" she said, then noticed Alyssa's concerned expression. "Now, don't you go looking at me all strange. Live long enough, it'll happen to you, God willing. There's nothing wrong with me, I'm just a bit absentminded at times, that's all."

"Okay, Grandma," Alyssa said, avoiding the obvious. She started to neatly stack the photos, letters and other things back into the trunks. She reached over and picked up a very large storage box with a bright red ribbon. "What's in here?"

"A wedding gown," Allie answered.

"A wedding gown. Whose gown, Mom's? I never saw it before," she said. "I thought she eloped. Are there photos of her in it?"

"No, there are no photos and it's not your mother's, it's mine. Henry bought it for me so long ago I almost forgot all about it. He told me that he saw it in a window one day and bought it just like that. Before he even asked me to marry him, he bought it." She smiled at the memory. "He said that he saw it and just knew that it was for me, so he had to ask me to marry him."

"Wow, that's so romantic," Alyssa said. "Do you have pictures of you in it?"

Allie smiled regretfully. "I never wore it."

"What? Why not?"

"To tell you the truth, I don't even remember. I just know that it's never been worn. I'd hoped your mother would have worn it, but she didn't. She eloped."

"May I…"

"Of course, open it up."

Alyssa opened the box and held up the most beautiful white-lace wedding gown she'd ever seen. "This is breathtaking. I can't believe Grandpa bought this for you and you never even tried it on. It's so beautiful."

"Yes, it is."

Alyssa carefully placed the gown back in the storage box and was just about to put it into the larger box when another large dress box below it caught her attention. "What's in that one, another gown?"

Allie smiled again. "Open it."

She did. Beneath several layers of white tissue she found a beautiful cream-colored silk strapless dress with beautiful embroidered flowers snaking from just below the bodice to the hip, to just below the knee where it ended in a soft flourish. There was a matching shawl with beaded fringe and a pair of silk high heels that looked as if they had never been worn. "Wow," was all she could say.

Allie smiled, admiring it happily. "Lovely, isn't it?"

"Grandma, it's magnificent. I've never seen anything like it. Where did you get it?"

"It was a gift from a very long time ago."

"From Granddad again?" she asked.

"No, not this time."

Alyssa gently fingered the perfectly hand-stitched embroidery on the side of the dress, on the shawl and on the shoes. "I've never seen anything like it."

"And you never will, I don't suppose. It was especially made just for me, shoes and all, although I never wore it."

"You never wore this, either? But why?"

"Circumstances never presented themselves."

"But this is too beautiful to just sit here in a box all wrapped up."

"I agree, that's why you should have it."

"Grandma, I couldn't. This is yours, and besides, it wouldn't even fit me, it's too small."

"Actually it would probably fit you even better. You have the added curves I never did. And I know the shoes are your size."

"Thank you, but I can't. But it's lovely, just as you said," Alyssa said, repacking it back in the box just as she found it.

"So, what are you doing here tonight? I thought you were busy."

"That was last night. It's Friday and I brought Chinese food."

"So, what are we doing sitting up here in this dusty old attic?" She stood steady and ready. "Come on, let's eat. All this talking has gotten me hungry."

"Okay, you go ahead downstairs. I'll finish with all this and close the windows, then meet you in the kitchen."

"Sounds good. I need to make a quick stop and wash up a bit but I'll be right down."

Alyssa watched as her grandmother walked easily across the large attic floor, then headed down the hall. She could hear the slight creak of the steps as Allie went downstairs to the second floor. She sighed, relieved. Seeing her grandmother lying there like that had nearly scared her to death. Alyssa didn't know what she'd do if she lost her.

Allie Granger was her maternal grandmother and the only mother figure in her life. Her own mother had died of leukemia when she was four years old and she barely remembered her, just dreamlike shadows and faint images. She was partly raised by her grandmother, and their relationship was beyond close. Alyssa was named after her and admired everything she did.

That's why she was so horrified when she witnessed the first signs of Alzheimer's disease and its ravaging effects. Her grandmother played it off and ignored it as just old-age forgetfulness, but there was more to it, and the more time went on, the easier it was to recognise and the harder it was to witness.

Alyssa finished cleaning up the attic, then closed the windows and turned the lights off. Going downstairs, she stopped and peeked into her grandmother's bedroom. Hearing the water running in the bathroom, she kept going downstairs to prepare their dinner.

A few minutes later the table was set, the food was heated, the dishes were washed and set aside to dry and still no Allie. Alyssa climbed the stairs, hearing singing. She went to her grandmother's bedroom and opened the door wide. Allie was sitting on the bed singing a song combing a doll's hair on her lap. She remarked on how beautiful Katherine looked in her new dress and nice curls and then she looked up and smiled. "Hi, don't you think Katherine looks adorable? I think she's beautiful."

Alyssa smiled and nodded as her heart filled. "Yes, Katherine looks very beautiful. But it's time that we put Katherine down so we can go downstairs to get something to eat."

"Can Katherine come, too?" she asked, as always, politely.

"Not this time. Let's let Katherine rest while you and I get something to eat, okay?" Alyssa said, heartbroken by the sight of her grandmother. "I promise, we'll eat and come right back, okay?"

Allie agreed. She set Katherine to the side and followed Alyssa downstairs. They sat and said a prayer then Alyssa fixed Allie's plate. "May I have some water, please?" Allie asked.

"Sure, of course. I'll get it," Alyssa said.

By definition Alzheimer's is a degenerative disease characterized by senility, dementia and mental deterioration affecting people sixty-five and older. With her grandmother the first signs showed themselves as classic cognitive symptoms beginning with a mild impairment when she experienced the inability to remember instances of just moments earlier. This was followed by occasional loss of memory, disorientation, confusion and restlessness.

Now she lapsed into her past. It never lasted long, but it was long enough to break Alyssa's heart.

Inhibitors and pills were wildly available, but admission was first and foremost. Allie refused to admit there was a problem. The disease always fatal, there was nothing she could do, just sit and watch as her grandmother slowly faded away.

Alyssa went to the refrigerator and poured two glasses of water, then brought them back to the table. "Here you go."

"Alyssa, why on earth did I put this much food on my plate? Look at all this food. There's enough here to feed a starving nation. I'm hungry, but not that hungry. So, how was your day, sweetheart, anything different or exciting?"

"No," Alyssa said, smiling, happy to have her grandmother back with her again. "Same old, same old."

"That's good to hear. No surprises are good."

"Yes, no surprises are good," Alyssa repeated.

"I remember when I worked at the Senate Building years ago. Back then there were only a few of us, mostly in housekeeping and such. But when I got the job as file clerk, then as secretary, I was as proud as I could be." She smiled happily. "Yes, those sure were the days."

They ate awhile in silence, then went back to talking about some of the pictures up in the attic, then Mrs. Watts next door doing the electric slide. "Grandma, tell me why you were in the attic this afternoon. It's so hot up there. If you needed to find something, I would have done it for you. You knew I was coming over today."

"Your mother, she was beautiful. You look just like her, you know that. Of course you do, I've told you that a hundred times. I had so many dreams and hopes for her but…" She shook her head sorrowfully. "But that wasn't meant to be. The moment she laid eyes on your father she was lost."

"See, about that, I don't get it. Why didn't you and Dad ever get along? It just doesn't make sense to me."

"He wasn't the one for her. He had no family, no money, no nothing. His father owned a bar, for goodness' sake. What was that to offer my child? And look at him now, he's still nothing, never was and never will be."

"Grandma, please don't talk about my dad like that. He's a good man and he did the best for me under the circumstances."

"Under the circumstances, he killed your mother."

"Mom was sick, he didn't kill her."

"I could have saved her. If I'd only known, but he didn't want me to, he wanted to control her."

"Grandma…"

"He was the wrong man for her," Allie insisted.

"He was the man she chose."

"I don't know why. The man is trash."

"Grandma, my dad is a part of me. How can you love all of me and hate him so much?"

Allie reached over and touched her granddaughter's face, seeing her daughter's eyes shining back at her. "Sweetheart, you know I love you, you're everything to me."

"Then how can you hate Dad so much if you love me?"

Allie's eyes teared up and a shadow of sadness covered her face. "I wanted so much more for her. Her future was limitless, but all they wanted was to be in love. I tried everything to stop it."

"You mean, you tried to break them up?" Alyssa asked, hearing this for the first time.

"Destiny always gets its way. But I know what being in love is like, the pain, the hurt and despair. It's never worth it."

"But you were in love once. I mean, what about Grandpa?"

Allie smiled and nodded. "He was a sweet man, but love, I don't really know…"

"What do you mean? You had to love him. You married him and had Mom with him. How could you not love him?"

"It was a different time."

"What does that mean?"

She looked off across the room with pain in her eyes. Alyssa didn't know what to make of her. She'd heard the horror stories about love so many times she could recite them in her sleep, but this new look of sadness and loss was different.

"When your mother married your father, it broke my heart, but she loved him fiercely and he loved her. Unlike so many others, their love was meant to be, but not meant to last." She continued, staring a moment, then started talking about when her mother was a teenager.

"I wish you knew her," Allie said, reaching over to hold Alyssa's hand and squeeze.

"I wish I did, too."

Alyssa smiled. Katherine was her mother, and as always, her grandmother didn't remember a thing from earlier. It was as if it never happened.

Chapter 6

With footfalls echoing in perfect harmony, two men walked through the immaculate halls of the Capitol Building. Its pristine walls of marble and slate reflected the grand achievements of the past and the ghosts that still haunted, begging their due. This was the birthplace of independence. This was Congress, the Senate Building.

Past lines of pillars and portraits, they continued into the inner chambers where lawmakers performed the enormous tasks of changing laws and governing "we, the people." It was late, but the building was still crowded.

"If I didn't know any better, I'd say we were being conned by the good senators," Randolph said quietly as they walked.

Senator Andre Hart smirked then chuckled. "Of course we're being conned, this is the federal government. Every lobbyist's dream is to have a senator in their pocket."

"Cynical?" Randolph said, smiling knowingly. His friend's

aversion to lobbyists was well known, and rightly so. His second wife, now his ex, was a lobbyist who loved, married and divorced him all to further her career. In doing so, she nearly destroyed his reputation. The experience completely blindsided him, leaving a bitter aftertaste.

"Just a little," Andre responded sarcastically.

Randolph chuckled. "I don't think the Appropriations Committee will give senators Goode and Hastings much backing for the program they're proposing. After all, they can't even rally enough support from their fellow committee members."

"They're just making noise. More than likely, what they really want to do is deflect media attention away from Senator Goode's legal troubles. The Senate Ethics Committee is still convening testimony. The two senators go way back, and I'm sure Hastings is just trying to lend a hand," Andre added.

"I can't see that making much of a difference," Randolph said. "The Justice Department is all over him. Tax fraud, obstruction of justice, interfering with a federal investigation." He shook his head. "If he's indicted and reprimanded again or caught with his hand in a lobbyist's pocket, the Ethics Committee will fry him."

Andre nodded. "Not to mention that extramarital affair and heaven knows what else he's got his fingers in. The man's way past shooting himself in the foot. He's on to political suicide."

"But that's insane. Even members of his own party are steering clear of him. Keeping a lid on this controversy is impossible. It's spinning out of control and his press aide is constantly under siege by reporters."

Andre nodded. "It's a political crisis of his own making, but nobody ever said that politicians were sane."

"True, that," Randolph agreed.

The two continued walking, talking in hushed tones discussing the ramifications of the meeting. "I think I'll give the good senator my opinion first thing tomorrow morning," Andre said.

Randolph chuckled. "What, and let him off the hook that easily? I don't think so."

"I just want to be done with it. The last thing I need is for the little twerp to be on my case for the next two days."

"But letting him sweat over the weekend would be…" Randolph began, stopping in front of Andre's office.

Andre laughed out loud and nodded. "Would be…just perfect. Yes, Senator, I like the way you think. Why should he have a good weekend? Think I'll follow your lead and let him sweat it out a bit."

"That's what I'm talking about," Randolph said. "Still, I'm wondering why they came to us. We're not exactly partial to this issue, and the fact that we're sponsoring the lobbyist reform bill should have given them pause."

"Hastings is still testing the waters and trying to put a positive spin on it. The election is in three years and his name is already on the ballot, been there since 1980. He wants to appeal to minority voters, and lassoing two African-American senators would look great for photo ops."

"Now, wouldn't that be a picture?" Randolph said. "I'll have to dig out my dad's old dashiki and Afro pick."

"Think I'll let my hair grow and get it braided."

The two men broke up laughing. They continued laughing as several aides hurried by, barely breaking stride.

"I know the word is out, but I get the feeling Hastings's heart just isn't in it," Randolph said.

"I agree, but he's backed into a corner," Andre added.

"Most definitely."

"Family expectations are the worst motivations," Andre concluded.

The two stood a moment longer, talking off topic and more about their weekend social plans.

"So, how was that event you attended last night?" Andre asked.

"Interesting, very interesting, you should have gone."

"Tickets to a Nationals game trumps a political event anyday, you know that."

"My bad," Randolph said, smiling.

"Looks like you enjoyed yourself."

"What makes you say that?" Randolph asked.

"I don't know, possibly that huge smile plastered on your face. If it got any wider, you'd have to register it in another district."

Randolph chuckled, then smiled even wider. "You know me too well. Let's just say it was an extremely memorable evening."

"How so? No, wait, let me guess. There's a woman, isn't there?" Randolph started laughing. Andre nodded. "Yep, there always is."

"She's different," Randolph defended.

"Really, what does she do?"

Randolph laughed again. "She's a lobbyist."

Andre shook his head. "Been there, done that. Suicide, man, political suicide."

"Hey, you guys hanging out in the hallways nowadays?"

Randolph and Andre turned and acknowledged another senator, Bob Wellington, coming down the hall toward them.

"Don't you know the offices are all bugged?" Andre said jokingly. Randolph chuckled, more at Bob's not-so-sure expression, knowing of course, that he'd get his aides to do a full sweep in the morning.

Randolph and Andre shook Wellington's hand, and then the three men spoke briefly.

"All right, check you later," Andre said, shaking

Randolph's hand, then adding the little extra they always did in brotherly camaraderie. Bob again stuck out his hand quickly grasping Andre's and clumsily mimicked the gesture.

"Have a good weekend," Randolph said, as always, amused.

"Nice guy," Bob said as he followed Randolph, who continued walking down the hall again.

"Indeed."

"Were you good friends before coming to the Senate?"

"We met occasionally when I was in the House," Randolph said vaguely.

"You were a congressman, too?"

Randolph nodded. "Yes, for two terms."

"Interesting. The reason I ask is that I haven't seemed to be able to gain his trust yet and I'd like to. Do you have any suggestions?"

"Maybe you should start out with gaining his respect and his friendship."

"Oh, yeah, that, too, of course, respect and friendship, sure," Bob said.

They continued walking, footfalls completely out of sync with each other.

"That was an interesting hearing," Bob said.

"Indeed," Randolph answered, never missing a step.

"So, uh, what are your thoughts about the meeting, Randolph?"

"Too soon to tell. I think I'll mull it over and see where it leads me. There are several interesting points to consider and I'd hate to jump to the wrong conclusion."

"Sure, sure. I'm gonna do the same thing. But you'd have to admit, Senator Goode made some very interesting points. The facts were right there. And anything else might be considered splitting hairs or nit-picking."

"Really," Randolph said rather than asked.

"Oh, yeah. I tell you, sometimes we are faced with challenges that make this job seem almost impossible, but every so often, we get something that is so plain and simple that it makes it all worthwhile."

"You think so, huh?" Randolph said.

"Oh, yeah, definitely," Bob said, readily agreeing.

"And influence?" Randolph asked.

"Oh, that's nothing, really. Lobbyists only go as far as you allow them. You just have to know how and when to say enough. For the most part they have little influence."

"I'd say more like significant influence."

"Ah, you're giving them way too much credit."

"Or maybe not enough," Randolph said, then smiled. The games played on Capitol Hill should be Olympic events. Javelin throwing into an opponent's back, high-jumping and pole-vaulting on morality issues, long-distance running from election to election.

"Be that as it may, we can't—"

"You're right," Randolph interrupted, "we can't resolve this tonight."

"That's just what I was about to say," Bob lied.

Randolph slowed and stopped in front of his office. The two men stood in the hall as several staffers hurried by.

"How's the family, Bob?" Randolph asked, ending the discussion. The name Wellington had been etched on the door of the Congressional Hall since the early twentieth century. The only changes were what came after it—senior, junior, the third and now the fourth. Every thirty years, the reins passed to the next generation.

The original Robert Wellington elected in 1918 was a U.S. congressman. His son, Robert Wellington Jr., followed in his father's footsteps to become a U.S. senator. His son, affectionately called J.R., opted for a seat in the Senate, then served as Secretary of Defense. And now, there was Bob. Always nervous and seemingly stressed, groomed from birth, he aimed at the top seat of power, the White House West Wing.

"Well, very well, thanks for asking. Patty and the boys are coming in this weekend. I thought I might consider driving over to Annapolis so the boys can maybe get a taste of the old navy swagger." He laughed riotously at what he assumed to be a hilarious joke. "Did I tell you I received a yacht? It's anchored there, so maybe I'll drop it in the water and see if it floats."

"A yacht. Nice toy," Randolph remarked.

"Actually Father got it for me as sort of a birthday gift."

"Nice birthday gift. Happy belated," he said.

"Oh, my birthday's not for another three months, but he knows how much I love sailing. Patty and the boys are excited to try it out. Actually I am, too."

"I'm sure they'll enjoy it."

"Definitely," he said, then glanced at his Rolex watch. "Wow, is it really this late? I'm exhausted. I think I'm gonna call it a night. Hey, how about us guys stopping at The Capital Grille to grab a quick bite to eat?"

"I'm gonna have to take a rain check on that, Bob. There are a few things I'd like to finish up before I close down shop for the night."

"Sure, sure, see you Monday. Hey, maybe we can grab a quick round of golf or a quick game of racquetball in the gym next week."

"Sure, sounds good. Give me a call and we'll schedule," Randolph said, knowing of course, that it would never happen, but as in most offices, white lies and promises swirled like cream in coffee.

"Great, I'll set it up," Bob said, then continued walking down the hall. "Have a good weekend."

"You, too."

Randolph unlocked the door to his suite, walked through the open reception area, then went into his private office. Small but suitable, the office was warm and inviting and he felt more than at home here. Decorated by a friend's mother, renowned artist Taylor Evans, the room had been enlivened with paintings and classic furnishings, blending comfort and function.

He removed his suit jacket, grabbed a bottle of water from the small refrigerator then walked over and sat down behind his desk. After a few swigs and a deep reenergizing sigh, he loosened his perfectly dimpled tie, then unlocked his computer and opened his message box.

He had been half a beat off all day long, and knowing that lack of rest would never affect him, he came to one conclusion: something or someone else had.

There were fifty-eight messages since late that afternoon that required his attention, not at all surprising. Down from the usual seventy or so, the messages had been read and scanned, then divided into categories—senate priorities, constituents, personal and nonwork-related and lastly, deferred. His secretary was extremely diligent in her duties. Deciding to skim through, he opened a few, answered a few and deleted others.

Midway through the list, he noticed that his secretary highlighted a personal message from Louise Gates. He opened and read the e-mail immediately, then responded. But his finger hovered over the send key for several seconds as he paused to reconsider.

Pressing the key could open the floodgates and irrevocably change his life. Was he ready for that and all it entailed? Louise was persistent, determined and relentless. If he pressed this key, there would be no turning back.

He walked over to the window and looked out, not really

seeing the breathtaking beauty of the city from the Capitol Building. Considering his options, he realized that enlisting her assistance was no great calamity, despite what Trey said.

He began weighing his options, considering the pros and cons of his actions, then decided quickly. He walked back over to his desk and pressed the send key. The message was sent. It was done. After a brief moment's reflection, he sat down and continued reading the rest of the messages when he came across another oddly familiar name, Sundari Adia Nomalanga. He stopped.

He smiled instantly, then opened the message. It had only five words. Coffee. Sunday. Nine. Caféhill. Adia. He smiled again, how could he possibly refuse? He typed in his reply. Delighted. Anticipating. Sunday. Randolph. He said it aloud as he typed.

"Sunday?" Kent asked as he walked in and took a seat across from the desk, then opened his PDA and began examining the small screen. "Scheduling a meeting for Sunday?"

"Yes, something like that," Randolph said. Kent Larson was his right hand, his confidant and the one person he explicitly trusted. But until he knew what was going on, he decided to keep this private meeting to himself.

"Looks like you're clear. Shall I make arrangements?"

"No, not this time, I've already taken care of it."

"Any reservations needed?"

"No."

"Good. Okay, I have the financial and GAO report you wanted," Kent said as he placed the folders on his desk. "And here are the amendments and the itinerary for the conference next week."

"Excellent, thank you," Randolph said as he took the top report, opened it and began reviewing it. "Anything else?"

Kent nodded, never taking his eyes off the small PDA

screen. "Yes, I cleared your schedule next weekend and booked you on a flight to San Francisco Friday afternoon."

"San Francisco?"

"Yes," Kent said, looking up at him. "You mentioned that you needed a quick vacation."

"Oh, yes, that's right. Oh, but we'd better make it for the following weekend. I've been invited to poker night with the guys."

"Even better. Matthew Gates is having a private fundraiser that Saturday evening. Your attendance would reflect well in the district, not to mention add weight to several upcoming local campaigns."

"Okay, tell him I'll be there."

"Will you be bringing a guest?" Kent asked.

Randolph paused for a moment. "Leave it open," he finally said, then looked at the five words again. Kent nodded and made an adjustment. "Anything else?" Randolph asked.

"Yes, Louise Gates and Otis Wheeler called, accepting your invitation to lunch Monday afternoon. She also asked to take a tour of the Capitol Building if possible."

"Will you be able to set that up?"

"Already done," Kent said.

"Good."

"This is the same Louise Gates as Mamma Lou, the matchmaker, correct?"

"Yes, Matthew Gates's mother."

"The same woman you've been hiding from for the past year and a half, correct?"

"Yes," Randolph said, seeing exactly where Kent was going with this conversation.

"And now you're inviting her to see you?"

"Yes," Randolph said, smiling at Kent's confusion.

"A matchmaker?" Kent asked.

"Mamma Lou prides herself on finding the perfect mate."

"Is she any good?"

"Apparently so. She's fixed up at least five couples that I know of—Tony and Madison, Raymond and Hope, Dennis and Faith, Kennedy and Juwan and, of course, Juliet and J.T."

"Sounds as if she's been busy."

"She has."

"It also sounds as if she's pretty good."

"She is indeed." Randolph smiled.

"So, interested in her services?"

"More like being kind to a nice lady," Randolph said.

Kent nodded as he always did when Randolph evaded a direct question. "As I said, I've already set up a Capitol tour for two on Monday afternoon. I'll have one of the assistants handle it."

"No. I'll take care of it personally," Randolph said.

Kent looked up from his PDA again. The confused frown on his face was a rarity. His job was to anticipate the senator's requests before asked. This took him completely off guard.

"You'll do it?" he asked surprised.

"Yes."

"Uh-h-h," Kent stammered. "Are you okay?"

"Yes, fine. Why?"

"You seem distracted and you once remarked that you'd rather be boiled in a vat of oil than take a Capitol tour."

"Consider this a rarity," Randolph said, tossing a folder on his desk and leaning back in the chair.

"Will do. Is that it?" Kent asked.

"Yes. Why don't you head on home? I'll lock up."

"Are you sure?"

"Yes, I want to answer a few e-mails before I leave."

"Okay, good night," Kent said, placing his PDA in his jacket pocket and securing his briefcase. "Have a good weekend."

"Thanks, you, too."

Randolph watched as Kent grabbed his suit jacket and walked out. He latched the main office door securely behind him. Randolph, now alone in the suite of offices, rested his head against the back of the chair. He closed his eyes and tried to relax.

The usual mishmash of images crisscrossed his mind—work, home, the vineyard. Then quite unexpectantly, another image appeared. Alyssa's smiling face. He opened his eyes quickly.

Chapter 7

"Hi, Dad," Alyssa mouthed through the closed glass door as the curtain pushed back into place.

Benjamin Wingate yawned wide as he unlocked and opened the door for her. "Alyssa, what are you doing here this early? Why didn't you come in through the apartment door?"

"I figured you'd be down here already, so I just thought I'd stop by and say hi to my favorite guy." She kissed his unshaved cheek and grimaced at the feel of the rough, scratchy stubble on his face.

"Favorite guy, what's that? Is there another guy in your life that I should know about?" Benjamin asked, going behind the bar and grabbing a newly washed glass from the tray.

"Oh, sure, dozens, hundreds, thousands," she said, dropping her purse on the bar counter and sitting on the bar stool beside an open newspaper and a half-empty cup of coffee.

"That many, huh?" he asked, grabbing a bottle of orange juice and filling the glass.

"Well, actually just maybe one in particular," Alyssa continued as her father placed a napkin and the glass of juice in front of her.

"Who's that?" he asked, coming back around to the front of the bar and sitting next to her. "I hope he's good enough."

"He works for the federal government."

"Everybody works for the federal government."

"Ah, but he's a U.S. senator," she said, sounding impressed.

"A senator? You could do much better."

"Now you sound like Grandma."

"Who else you got?"

"No, now, wait a minute. Let's not dismiss him so quickly."

"And why not?" Benjamin asked, still joking around. "Most politicians are just self-serving con men, looking to line their own pockets."

She took a sip of the fresh-squeezed orange juice. "He's different. I think he's got his own money. He lives in California and he's gorgeous."

"Well, I guess if I have to lose my only daughter to someone, at least he's gorgeous." They smiled and laughed at the game they played. "So, what's really up?" he asked.

"Nothing," she said, then sighed deeply. Benjamin looked at her sternly. "Well, nothing, really. I'm just a little worried about Grandma, that's all."

"What's she doing now?" Benjamin asked, then sipped his coffee and glanced at the newspaper.

"I think her Alzheimer's is getting worse. She can be lucid for long periods of time. Then all of a sudden she's back to being buried in her memories," she said. Benjamin shuffled to the next section, scanned it then turned the page. He showed no real reaction, but Alyssa knew that he'd heard her. "I went over Friday after work, and she was passed out in the attic."

He stopped looking at the newspaper and looked over at her. "What do you mean, passed out?"

"I mean, passed out, exactly that. She was passed out. At first, I was afraid that she was, you know…but she was just asleep. But it was hot up there, like over a hundred degrees or something. She was just lying there."

"Why didn't she open the windows or turn the fan on?"

"She said she kept meaning to ask you to put one in, but she forgot to. So I'm asking you, can you please put an attic fan in for her."

"I can't do that, baby."

"Daddy, I know you and Grandma have your drama, but can't you just let her—"

"It's not about our drama, Alyssa. The city code will only allow one fan in an attic that size."

"What do you mean?"

"I mean, I put a fan in that attic about two years ago. It was already over the size limit, but it was more efficient."

"You mean, there's already a fan there?"

"For two years now."

"She said she didn't have one," Alyssa said, looking at her father. "See, she doesn't even know what she has. She's getting worse. I'm glad I decided to move back in with her."

Benjamin looked at her, shaking his head, obviously opposed to the idea. "I'm still not happy about that."

"I know, Dad. But I didn't know what else to do. I'm afraid that she's gonna fall or walk off or start a fire or something worse. I have to move back in with her."

"Have you considered putting her away?"

"Putting her away?" she repeated uneasily.

"You know what I mean, in a nursing home."

"I did, but she wouldn't hear of it. She said that there's nothing wrong with her. You know how she is."

"Yeah, I definitely know how she is," Benjamin said.

"But she's right, in a way. All she needs is a little help, that's all. She's not that far gone. All she needs is to have someone look after her, keep an eye on her."

"That's what assisted-living nursing homes are for, Alyssa. Who better to take care of her than professionals?"

"I can't do that, Dad, at least not now. She's my grandmother. Besides, I'm a professional. I'm still a registered geriatric nurse."

"Are you ready to give up your life full-time? Because that's what you're saying, twenty-four hours a day, three hundred and sixty-five days a year."

"She gave up her life for me."

"You were a child, Alyssa, barely four years old. You don't owe her your life now. There are plenty of reputable nursing homes in the area."

"No, I can't do that. She gave me power of attorney and I'm responsible for her."

"That's why you need to do this."

"Is this payback, Dad, for everything in the past?"

"Don't be ridiculous, this has nothing to do with the past or with our drama. This has everything to do with you giving up the rest of your life."

"You know what, I can't do this right now. I just came by to ask you to put a fan in the attic and, since it's already done…" She slid off the stool.

"Baby," Benjamin began, holding Alyssa's hand gently, "Allie and I will probably never get along, but this has nothing to do with all that. This is about you and your life and how I don't want to stand by and see you give it up like this."

"Dad, I'm not giving up my life. I'm just moving in with

Grandma, that's all. She's got a big old house and my apartment is the size of a shoe box. I'm over there most of the time anyway, so it'll be no big deal, really."

"Baby—" Benjamin began.

"Trust me, I know what I'm doing."

He nodded, knowing that it was futile to argue with her. Ever since she was five, she knew her own mind. "When?"

"My lease is up at the end of this month anyway and my landlord is talking about turning the place into a condo. There's no way I'm paying for the same place I live in now. I really like the Mount Pleasant neighborhood, but not for those prices. Besides, it's all the way on the other side of town. I work in Anacostia and both you and Grandma live in Old City."

"Old City isn't the greatest, either," her dad said.

"That's the stigma from the 1968 riots after King was assassinated," she said.

"That was a bad time. Looting, arson, vandalism, not good memories," Benjamin added.

"But look at it now. It's really come back and every yuppie in Virginia and Maryland is dying to move back and get in on the ground floor of the upturn in the real-estate market," she said. Benjamin nodded his agreement. "See, I have it all worked out. Although I might need a little help moving…" She nudged into him to make a point.

Benjamin smiled and nodded his head. "Just let me know when. I'll be there, you know that."

"I know. Thanks, Dad."

"Okay, it's still early. How about some breakfast?" He slapped his hands together and rubbed them as if he were releasing a magic genie from a bottle. "I'll treat you to breakfast at the diner down the street. Eggs, sausage, scrapple, bacon, hash browns, toast and waffles sound good?"

Alyssa grimaced. There was no way she'd be able to eat

that much food for breakfast. "How about a rain check? I'm supposed to meet my girlfriend for coffee this morning."

"Coffee, since when do you drink coffee? I thought it was tea or nothing."

"It is. You know I don't like the taste of coffee. We'll probably meet there and just go someplace else. It's in Georgetown so there are a million places to go."

"Just be careful."

"In Georgetown, Dad, I think I'll be safe there. You know the ratio of police is three for every one civilian there."

"Yeah, but in the southeast it's one cop every fifty blocks, and he or she's usually two minutes from retiring."

"See you later, Dad," she said, shaking her head at his remark as she left. Yeah, she had to agree that police protection was more visible in affluent parts of town, leaving the bulk of lower-income D.C. to fend, oftentimes unsuccessfully and violently, for itself.

Her father's bar, Wingate Lounge, was in such a southeast neighborhood. It originally belonged to his grandfather, and like his father before him, he refused to be moved no matter what the challenges were, proudly living above the establishment in one of the small apartments. The bar had outlasted fires, hurricanes, riots and robberies, mostly unscathed but always successfully.

But that would all end soon. Her father talked about retiring, and knowing that she wasn't interested in keeping the Wingate Lounge open, his only option was to sell. She wasn't particularly heartbroken. It was the bar that had pried apart his marriage and made him give her up so long ago.

Just after her mother died, he withdrew into his work, leaving her, at four years old, to fend for herself. He was completely distraught and inconsolable. All he saw left in his life was the bar, so he clung to it, leaving no room for her.

For a long time, she hated him for leaving her. But then, with her grandmother and grandfather's help, she learned to understand his pain without losing her own. They, her father and grandmother, were unlikely allies who set aside their differences to raise her. She lived with her grandmother in her big house in a beautiful old and stately neighborhood, then hung out at her father's place on weekends. She was never allowed to go into the bar by either of them.

Alyssa got into her car and drove to meet her friend.

It was Sunday morning, five minutes before nine, and Randolph was already seated at a window seat in a small café in Georgetown. Dressed casually, he blended in perfectly with his surroundings. No one recognized him. He was just another guy sitting in a hotel café, flipping through the Sunday-morning newspaper.

A baseball cap dipped low over his eyes, he checked out those entering and leaving. A typical crowd, he assumed. They greeted each other or nodded while they busily filled their cups.

The hotel lobby was connected to the café, but most of the patrons appeared to be coming from the street entrance on the other side. There were several couples seated near him, chatting quietly, but to the side, there was a double table of six women sipping frothy beverages and eating puffed-up pastries. They glanced at him sitting there alone several times, but he made it a point to look away in the other direction.

As the café got crowded, people constantly coming in waves, he seemingly focused his attention on the newspaper until it emptied out again. Then, by chance, the paper flipped to the local-news section, he saw an article with his photo. It was taken with a local politician and the caption read *Senator Randolph Kingsley and Ombudsman Clark Jefferson Chat at a Local Fund-raiser.* He vaguely remembered the photo. He didn't read the article, but for some reason, it made him uneasy. He made a mental note to read it later.

"Hi, remember me?"

Randolph looked up, expecting to see Alyssa. He didn't. "No, I'm afraid I don't," he said.

"That's okay," she said, sitting down across from him. "I was at the fund-raiser last Thursday with my girlfriend. She and I…"

Randolph smiled and nodded. "Yes, I do remember you now, Ms. Hall. Nina, right?"

Nina's eyes brightened as she nodded. She had no idea that he would remember her name. "Yes. That's me."

"How are you this morning?"

"Great. I can't believe you actually remembered my name," she said in wonder as she slid down in the seat across from him.

"It was only a few days ago," he assured her.

"Yeah, but still, you meet, like, millions of people every day. I could never remember them all."

"I have a very good memory and believe it or not, I don't really meet that many people."

"Well, anyway, I need to confess, it was me who asked you to come here this morning."

"Really?" Randolph said, hoping he didn't sound as disappointed as he felt. "And why is that?"

"I know it was kind of a lousy ruse and all and I know your time is precious and it was terrible of me to do. But I really wanted to talk to you." Nina talked fast because from her seat she saw Alyssa approach by way of the hotel entrance.

"It was indeed. With you having said that, what can I do for you, Ms. Hall?"

"Nina, please."

"What can I do for you, Nina?"

"Actually, I can't stay, but I see my girlfriend coming and she's so much better at doing this than I am."

"Doing what exactly?" Randolph asked, hoping that this wasn't some kind of scam to embarrass him or his office.

"Hey, sorry I'm late," Alyssa said, breathless. "I had to almost park in Virginia. I swear, parking around here is impossible." She sat, looked at Nina and then finally at the man seated across from her. Her jaw dropped. "What are you doing here?" she asked, stunned to see him.

"That would be me," Nina said, raising her hand slightly to confess.

"Nina?" Alyssa said.

"Good morning, Ms. Nomalanga, nice of you to join us."

"Ms. Nomalanga—oh, right, about that…"

Nina stood up quickly. "You know, I really have to be someplace else now. I'm sorry about all this but Alyssa can fill you in."

"Nina, you better not…" Alyssa said in warning.

"See you later. Nice to see you again, sir," Nina said quickly as she turned, shuffled through the ever-growing crowd in the café, then dashed outside and disappeared down the street.

Alyssa closed her eyes and moaned inwardly. If she could disappear, this was the perfect time to do it.

"Ms. Nomalanga, or should I call you Ms. Wingate? Which is it today?"

"Alyssa, Alyssa Wingate." She peeked over at him. His smiling eyes beamed at her intensely. She felt her heart thunder and her stomach flutter as she wondered, at what point did making a total fool of yourself constitute jail time?

"Are you sure, Ms. Wingate?"

"Yes, I'm sure, my name is Alyssa Wingate." She stuck out her hand to shake. He grasped her hand gently and they both knew that they were way past this part. "Sorry about that. Sorry about this. I didn't know Nina was going to do this, I mean, invite you here like this. She did invite you, didn't she?" Randolph nodded and half smiled again. "You don't have to stay."

"Actually I'd like to stay, if that's okay with you, that is."

"But why? You were obviously tricked into coming here. I don't know how, but I assure you, it won't go unpunished."

"I'll stay. Call it curiosity."

"Okay, umm, why don't I send flowers or write a check to your campaign, or donate to your favorite charity or something so you can forget about this whole thing? Or you can even call it a speaking engagement and I'll just pay you for your time."

"I usually get well over ten thousand dollars to speak, more if the occasion calls for it."

"You get what? That's ridiculous. Who would pay…" she began, raising her voice slightly, then looked around and continued in a whisper. "Who would pay that much to listen to you speak?"

"That's the going rate. Of course, that's the initial fee. The price goes up considerably."

"Figures, how much?" She sighed regretfully while reaching into her purse for her checkbook, knowing she didn't have that kind of money but figuring she could get the rest from her father or her grandmother if necessary.

"Tell you what, why don't I buy us a coffee and we'll discuss it?"

"I don't drink coffee," she said.

"Tea. Even better, decaffeinated, I presume," he said, and walked away before she had a chance to respond.

Alyssa sat there, still surprised by the turn of events. She and Nina met for bagels and tea from time to time, so when she got her message to meet her this morning she thought nothing of it. But to her surprise…

"Hey, isn't that that senator from California?"

"What senator, who, where?"

"Over there standing in line, see?"

"Senator or not, he is gorgeous."

"It looks like him but that doesn't mean anything. What would a senator be doing here?"

"I don't know, hanging out. He's single, isn't he?"

"Faye, you should give him your phone number. You'd be a great senator's wife. You even look the part."

"You think so. Hmm, well, then maybe I will."

The conversations that once piqued her interest now irritated her. The four women at the next table began giggling and whispering like teenagers. Why would they think that just because he was a senator he wanted a woman like that? So what if she had long flowing hair, perfect skin and was a size four? Beauty was supposed to be in the eye of the beholder, right?

Alyssa glanced around, seeing the couple seated at the next table also looking toward the counter. They obviously overheard and recognized Randolph, as well. Thankfully the line at the counter was short and he was back in just a few minutes.

"Here you go," Randolph said, placing a paper cup with two dangling tea bags in front of her, then sat down beside her.

"Umm, Senator, do you mind if we go someplace else?"

"No, of course not, if you'd like. Is there a problem?"

"Actually I think your popularity is becoming evident," Alyssa said, nodding her head slightly.

Randolph glanced around for the first time. He hadn't realized it because, since Alyssa walked in, he hadn't taken his eyes from her. But now he noticed that there were several people smiling and staring at him. He returned their smile, nodded and even shook hands with the man seated at the next table. "Perhaps you're right, shall we?" he said softly.

"Why don't you leave first? I'll follow in a few."

"Why don't we leave together?" he countered.

"But, the people—" she began.

"Will be just as curious of you sitting here alone," he returned easily.

She nodded, seeing his point. He got up and reached over to help her with her chair. She stood and they walked out together with her taking one last glance at the six women at the table. They looked completely insulted. That was the first good thing that had happened all morning long.

Once outside, they started walking down the street, blending in with the early morning crowd. Alyssa kept looking around anxiously. "Maybe this wasn't such a good idea, either," she said, suddenly feeling as if everyone were staring at them when they really weren't.

"On the contrary, it was a great idea," Randolph answered. "It's a beautiful day. I have a lovely woman by my side. I can't think of anything better to do this morning. And you went to a lot of trouble to get me here, so—"

"Actually I didn't, Nina did."

"True, fair enough. But you went to a lot of trouble to get my attention Thursday evening. I believe you mentioned at some point that you snuck in to meet me."

"Yes, I guess I did," she said, sipping the hot tea.

"So, tell me, Alyssa, what's all this about?"

The idea of lobbying for the elderly on a beautiful Sunday morning while walking down the streets of Georgetown seemed almost inconsequential. But the importance of the cause made her press on. "I work for a lobbying firm called the Foundation for Senior Citizen Reform."

"Yes, I remember very well. Nice office, very private."

She knew immediately he was referring to their kiss, but she chose to ignore his reference. "And I wanted to talk to you about legislative reform for medical-insurance subsidies for specific mental-health conditions."

"That's already on the books."

"For mental health, yes, but not specifically for seniors and not for patients suffering from Alzheimer's disease and other debilitating mental illnesses. I don't know if you already know this, but Alzheimer's is a devastating condition marked by a progressive loss of mental capability resulting from degenerating brain cells," she said, and then continued speaking rapidly, telling him just about everything she'd learned about the disease in the past two years.

She elaborated on the probable cause, genetic testing, stem-cell research, medical statistics, treatment and experimental drugs. By the time she finished, her voice had risen excitedly and animated.

"Yes, I'm well aware of the disease."

"Good, then you must also be aware that it's tearing families apart," she said with unusually high passion.

"Yes, it is," he responded calmly.

"Yes, of course you are, I'm sorry," she said, trying to calm her excitement. "I tend to get a bit overzealous at times."

He smiled and nodded. "Your passion is commendable. But the current law states that all mental diseases, including degenerative conditions, are covered."

"Again, not specifically for seniors."

"Question, how personal is this to you?" he asked.

"I don't understand. What do you mean?" she said.

"I'm asking who is it, your mother, father, grandmother, grandfather?"

She paused, then swallowed hard. "My grandmother," she said. He nodded. "Look, yes, this is a personal issue for me, but it's a personal issue for a lot of people. This isn't going away with some magic wand."

"No, it's not, on that we agree."

"So we have to do something," she said.

"We are doing something."

"No, that's not good enough," she said firmly. He didn't respond. "I'm sorry. As I mentioned earlier, I tend to get passionate at times."

"That's good to know," he said, looking at her again.

She looked over at him. His eyes were piercing into her hers, and behind them, she felt something stronger, something she couldn't put her finger on. But her body reacted, her stomach began fluttering and her heart pounded in her chest. "Okay, let's just get this out in the open. We kissed, our bodies pressed together and we touched each other in very intimate places. The opportunity presented itself and we went for it. Okay, yes, it happened, but it doesn't mean it's gonna happen again. That was a fluke for me. I don't normally just throw myself at men I don't even know."

"Again, that's good to know."

"I'm serious, Senator, I mean business."

"As do I."

"The question is, what kind of business?" she asked.

"Are you questioning my integrity?" he asked.

"On the contrary, everyone knows that you're a highly respected man."

"Apparently not everyone," he said, gazing at her.

"Senator—"

"Call me Randolph."

"Senator—"

"Randolph, please, I insist."

"Fine, Randolph," she said, then looked away. "You see, this is why you should never meet someone you admire."

He smiled smugly. "So, you admire me?"

"Crap," she muttered, realizing that she said that too loudly and he heard her. "Look, that's not the point."

"You admire me. That's nice, I think I like that."

"Fine, back to what I was saying. You were right, this is very dear to me, very personal. I was a geriatric nurse for years. Now I work for the foundation. But the fight is the same. This country's seniors are suffering and no one is stepping up for them."

"I understand your concern," he said calmly.

"Oh, please, don't patronize me."

"I don't think I am."

"If you're not interested in this, just say so. A pat on the head and a brush-off will do just fine."

"You are spirited," he said, obviously impressed. She glared at him, then looked away. He took her hand and they stopped walking. "Look, I'm not patronizing you. I just can't give you the answer you want right now."

"This is so simple," she said, shaking her head, exasperated.

"Yes, it appears that way. But there's so much more."

"There's that pat on the head again."

"What can I tell you that won't sound demeaning?"

"You can tell me the truth, how about that?"

"You're not hearing the truth. You want to hear what you want to hear. And I can't do that. That would be patronizing."

She backed up to walk away, but he still held on to her hand. "Alyssa, please, I assure you, I understand everything you're saying. But laws take time, too much time, yes. What you want and what I want won't happen overnight. I know there are people suffering and I feel their pain, I feel your pain. You love your grandmother, that much is very obvious."

She looked into his eyes, seeing that he really did understand. She nodded.

"Send me a proposal, give me some time to read up on this and I promise I'll see what I can do. Fair enough?" he asked.

She nodded. "Yes, okay, fair enough. Thank you."

"See, that wasn't too hard, was it?"

"Yes, as a matter of fact, it was."

He started laughing and shaking his head. "You are a persistent woman."

"Was that a compliment?"

"Yes, I believe it was," he said.

She looked at him skeptically. "Well, I think I'll decide later if you don't mind."

"And you're not like most lobbyists, are you?"

"What are most lobbyists like?" she asked.

"Let's just say that they've got a lot less passion and more ulterior motives."

"Not all of them," she corrected.

"No, you're right. Not all of them."

"Don't you have this same passion when it comes to your job?" she asked.

"Yes, of course," he said without hesitation.

"Then why shouldn't I?"

"You're absolutely right. But as with most jobs it's the bad ones that make it hard for those who really care and want to make a difference."

She nodded, then conceded, "Fair enough." She stuck her hand out again for him to shake.

He took it and pulled her close to his body, then leaned in close to her ear. "I think we're a bit past the handshake part, don't you?"

"What do you suggest, Senator?" she said, looking up at him, not at all shocked by the remark.

He smiled. "I have a few ideas."

"Really? Does it have anything to do with going someplace less public? Because I think you've been recognized again."

He looked around. There were several people smiling and taking photos with their cell-phone cameras. "Where are you parked?" he asked.

"On a side street in the other direction about five blocks away," she said, turning and looking back in that direction.

"Fine, I'm right over here, we'll take my car."

After a few handshakes and brief conversations with pedestrians, they got into his car and quickly drove off.

Chapter 8

"Where are we going?" she asked, recognizing familiar landmarks as they drove the circle around Union Station and headed into southeast Washington.

"I thought you'd feel more comfortable at the office."

"My office?" she said, almost in a panic.

"Yes," he said.

"No, no, we can't go there. My boss is there."

"So, I'd like to meet him."

"No, not a good idea."

"Okay," he said, hearing the anxiousness in her voice. "How about breakfast?"

"Yeah, okay, that's sounds great. Where?"

"I know a nice out-of-the-way restaurant, very exclusive, very private. We can relax and talk comfortably away from prying eyes." He drove around the block, turning in the opposite direction. Then he drove down a side street and headed for the Capitol Building.

"Whoa, you mean, the Capitol Hill Restaurant in the Capitol Building?"

"Yes, it's private. We won't be interrupted."

"No, not a good idea. I don't think I'm ready to go there yet."

"Okay," he said, again not asking her why.

They continued around the Capitol Building on Independence, heading back toward the northwest section of the city. They eventually turned onto Fourteenth Street and drove across the bridge and out of the city.

"You want to tell me what all that was about?"

"All what?" she asked innocently. He looked over at her. "Oh, that, you mean. Nothing," she said.

"You can do better than that, I'm sure."

"All right, my boss works in the office on Sunday mornings. It's quiet and he goes there to get away from his kids. He's got, like, ten or twelve or twenty or—"

"Yeah, I get it. Something with the letter *T.* What about him?"

"I don't want to disturb him."

"Okay," he said, obviously not completely buying the explanation. "And the Capitol Hill Restaurant?"

"One of my coworkers, Ursula Rogers, goes there all the time. One of the senators is a good friend of hers and they go there for Sunday brunch a lot."

"And the reason you don't want either of them to see us together is…" he asked.

"Okay," she sighed heavily, "I need to confess something."

"Go ahead."

"The truth is, I'm not a lobbyist. I'm actually a staffer at the foundation. I make no decisions and I have no power. And as such I'm not supposed to actually approach members of Congress directly. I don't have enough experience."

"Is that right?" he said.

"Yes. No. I mean I have experience in the trenches so to speak. I was a geriatric nurse. But no experience when it comes to fighting on the political front line."

"You make it sound like this is war."

"It is. The foundation has no money, so we can't influence the people we need to like those larger firms that represent tobacco, oil and big businesses. We're just a small group of people trying to do the right thing. So when it comes to lobbying I don't have any direct experience."

"But you approached me."

"Yes, I know I did. And that was different and if my boss finds out, he'll wring my neck."

"I certainly hope not. I kind of like your neck the way it is," Randolph said, smiling at her as the light turned red and he stopped the car.

"You know, you do that a lot."

"I do what a lot?" he asked.

"Flirt with me."

"Do men flirt?" he asked, looking at her.

"You know what I mean. You say things, innuendos that are innocent enough but then not really. Not when you look at me like that."

"Like what?" he asked as he glanced at her again.

Alyssa met his eyes and her stomach soared, then tumbled as a warm burn slivered through her body. "Like that."

He smiled and looked away. "Does that bother you?"

"Yes. No. I don't know, I guess not. I just didn't expect…"

"What that a senator is a man, too?"

"No, it's not that. Umm, I guess I expected you to be different."

"Different how?"

"Never mind, this really isn't an appropriate conversation.

I'm supposed to be soliciting your support," she said, deciding to end the conversation while she was ahead.

"No, tell me. Really, I'm interested. Different how?" he continued.

"This is going to sound strange…"

"That's okay," he prompted.

"Umm, I've seen you on television morning shows and doing interviews and you seem very staunch and, I don't know, rigid."

"Rigid?"

"Well, maybe *rigid* isn't the right word. Maybe, umm, conservative."

He instantly burst out laughing. "Me, conservative, that's a first."

"No, I'm not talking about politics. I'm talking about you personally. You seem rigid and almost unapproachable."

"And yet you approached me."

"Yeah, ain't that a kick in the head?"

He laughed again. "I like you, Alyssa Adia Wingate."

"Adia is really my middle name. I didn't tell you that, but I didn't have to, did I?"

"No, you didn't."

"Background check, huh?" He nodded at the inadvertent slip. She shrugged. "I expected as much."

"In my position, Alyssa—"

"Of course, you don't have to explain, I understand. I mean, you are a U.S. senator. I guess I forget that sometimes."

The car fell silent. They drove into Alexandria, heading farther south to Virginia. The early morning drive was serene and the surrounding view was breathtaking. "So, tell me more about Alyssa," he finally said.

"There's not much to tell and I'm sure my little file has some interesting highlights in it already."

"Not so little," he joked.

"Really, am I that interesting?"

"Let's just say that you quite unexpectedly kept me up the other night."

"That's not a good thing."

"On the contrary, it's a very good thing," he said, sparing a side glance.

"There, you did it again."

"Did I?" he asked innocently.

"Cards on the table?" she offered out of the blue.

"Of course," he said, smiling openly.

"I'm attracted to you. I guess that's obvious and I'm doing my best to ignore it. But you're not making it easy."

"Why try to ignore it?" he asked simply.

"Why? You're a U.S. senator."

"I realize that, so…"

"So I need to at least keep some sense of decorum, some semblance of respectability," she said.

"Why?" he asked again.

"Because whatever is going between us can't be going on," she said.

"Why not?"

"Because it can't and don't keep asking me why."

"I hate to state the obvious, but why not?"

"Because I said so," she finally said, making her point. He laughed. She tried not to as she looked away. "So just ignore it, okay?"

"What if I can't or don't want to?"

"Try," she said. He turned to her. "You're looking at me that way again."

"Was I?" he said coyly. "Cards on the table?" he offered.

"Of course," she said.

"A few days ago, I looked down and saw a stunning woman wiping a martini from my tie and I stopped breathing. In a room filled to capacity, you were the only one I saw. Ignore it? I don't think so."

Alyssa smiled, blushed and looked away, not sure how to take that remark. This man was too charming. He had the perfect answer to every question and the ability to make her heartbeat stop and skip a beat. "So, Senator, where are you taking me now?"

"Home."

Alyssa didn't bother asking him to clarify. She knew exactly what he meant. He was taking her to his house. Mount Vernon in northern Virginia, down the winding parkway traversing along the Potomac River. On one side was the river, on the other, stately homes that had been there for nearly two centuries. They drove a few miles longer, and then he pulled into a short circular driveway off a nice residential street directly across from the water.

The house was spectacular. It was located on the corner, right across from the Potomac River. It was Georgian style, two-stories high with columned porticos, a peekaboo attic and a long, precisely trimmed front lawn, littered with colorful seasonal blooms.

"Wow, this is you," Alyssa said, looking up at the large stone house surrounded by massive hedges and centuries-old trees. "It's beautiful. It reminds me of Wayne Manor."

"Wayne Manor?" he asked, pushing a button on the dash and opening one of the garage doors.

"Yeah, the stately home of Batman."

"Wasn't that the bat cave?" he asked, turning the engine off and looking over at her.

"Same thing, this is your Wayne Manor."

"I don't know about all that," Randolph said, opening his car door.

Alyssa opened her door and stepped out, looking around. "Your secret identity is revealed here."

"You think I have a secret identity?" he asked, leaning on the top of the car, staring at her.

"Sure, we all do. Don't you think? One side we show to the public and the other we keep to ourselves," she said, looking away from the intensity of his stare and walking around to the back of the car.

"Which identity are you showing me now, Alyssa?" he asked, meeting her at the rear bumper. Their eyes locked again and she instantly felt the intensity behind his. Was she crazy? Was he actually attracted to her?

She turned quickly to look out across the street. "Nice view."

He smiled, knowing that she changed the subject on purpose. Following her line of vision, he turned and nodded. "Yes, it's very serene and peaceful after a long hard day."

"I can imagine."

She walked to the garage opening and watched a jogger run by, then continue onto the jogging path across the street. She needed a few minutes to relax. Randolph came to stand right beside her.

Nervous and excited, she wasn't sure if this was a huge mistake or just plain reckless. But either way, she was walking into this with her eyes wide-open. So now what? Here she was, standing there face-to-face in an open garage with a U.S. senator. Suddenly the situation seemed surreal. "So, what's for breakfast?" she asked, turning to him.

"Come on," he said, holding his hand out to her. She looked at it for what seemed like forever, then finally touched him. His hand wrapped securely around hers and guided her through the garage as the door closed behind them.

"How about a quick tour?" he said as soon as they passed through the large mudroom into the great room.

"Oh, okay. Sure, sounds good," she said nervously, hoping that they wouldn't end up in his bedroom, then again hoping they would.

The foyer, the living room, the dining room, the downstairs office, the restroom, the conservatory, the small parlor, all exactly as she expected, old and stately, fitting for the centuries-old manor.

The house was lavishly adorned in bold, deep, rich colors with architectural moldings everywhere. The hardwood floor shone, interrupted only by very expensive oriental carpets.

"How old is this house?" she asked as they stood at the conservatory window, looking out across the street to the boats cruising by on the Potomac.

He stood right behind her. "Very old. Some parts are from an old plantation, and the cornerstone is dated to around 1820, but some say the house was here as a wooden structure much earlier."

"Wow, that is old," she said.

"It's been remodeled, refurbished, restored, partially overhauled, additions added and removed over two-dozen times, but the main stone structure still remains."

"It's remarkable, all that history, right here."

"Yeah," he said, gently placing his hands on her shoulders. She leaned back into him, feeling the strength of his body behind her. They stood silent a moment, breathing in the comfort of their bodies pressed together. Standing there with Randolph was beginning to feel too good and too comfortable. She stepped away, sensing his hands casually drift down her shoulders, then away.

"Your home is beautiful, Randolph," she said, walking to the other side of the room to examine more closely a painting over the fireplace.

"Thanks," Randolph said, watching her move away, "but I had very little to do with it."

"Really?" she said, turning back to him. "But it suits you so well. It seems to fit your personality perfectly."

He nodded. "It's comfortable, I like it. My sister and some very dear friends did it for me while I was away in Africa last year. Before that, this place was a joke. I basically had a sofa, a TV and a bed."

"It sounds like a typical bachelor pad."

"Maybe not that bad," he said.

"Is your sister a professional decorator?"

"No, Juliet is, was a professional ballerina. She's married and retired now but owns and operates a dance studio and is expecting her first child. Then there is Madison, who's an art historian and college professor, and Kennedy, who's a museum curator, and their mother, Taylor Evans, an incredible professional artist."

"Are they all related to you?"

"Just Juliet. The others have adopted me, so to speak. I don't have much family left. My mother died young and my father marries every other weekend so I don't see him much. As a matter of fact, he recently married again. I believe this will make number six."

"Interesting."

"And then there's Hope and Faith, two sisters from New York. They did this room with the flowers and plants with, of course, help from Mamma Lou."

"Mamma Lou?" she questioned.

"Yeah, Louise Gates—" he began, then was interrupted.

"Louise Gates… Wait, I know her."

"You know Mamma Lou?" he asked, suddenly skeptical of their meeting after everything he'd heard over the last few months about Louise's cunning.

"Well, not personally. Actually I don't know her at all personally, but my grandmother knows her. They were good friends at one time. I remember my dad telling me when we saw her photo in the newspaper."

"Oh, really? This is the same grandmother with Alzheimer's?"

"Yes, my maternal grandmother. She raised me when my mother died. I was four and my dad was completely devastated." She went silent a few seconds and took a deep breath to calm herself down. Talking about that time in her life was still very emotional for her.

"Hey, how about some breakfast?" he offered.

"Yeah, that's sounds good."

She followed him back through the foyer, down the hall and into the kitchen. "Wow," she said as they entered the kitchen, "this is really nice. Not exactly from old George Washington's time, is it, my brotha?"

"I think not," he said as he opened the refrigerator and looked inside. "I don't get called the brotha tag a lot anymore."

She slid onto a stool at the center island counter. "You're right. I guess Senator is more appropriate."

"I thought we were past that. It's Randolph, remember?" he said, turned to her, then turned back, bending over to see what might be on the lower shelves.

Alyssa watched his long legs column to his tight butt when he bent over and she unconsciously licked her lips. She suddenly remembered touching and squeezing him there, and a flash of heat instantly shot through her. "Why not Randy or Dolph or something?" she asked, hoping to distract herself.

He grimaced. "Dolph! Oh, I hated that name as a kid. Mostly everybody called me Randy when I was growing up. My sister called me Dolph for a time, especially when she wanted to make a point, but then finally everyone settled on Randolph. Most of my close friends back home still call me Randy."

Still trying to distract herself, Alyssa looked around the ultramodern kitchen. She was surrounded by every high-end gadget imaginable. Chrome, glass and black lacquer were everywhere. "This is really a nice kitchen."

"It's comfortable. But I miss my real home."

"That's right, California. Tell me about it. I've never been there before."

"You have to go there at least once. It's amazing," he said, after grabbing a half dozen sealed containers and placing them all on the counter in front of her.

"What's all this?"

"Breakfast, or brunch, whichever."

They started opening lids, finding all kinds of goodies tucked away inside. "Who made all this?" she asked.

"My housekeeper comes by every day and she loves to cook and she loves my kitchen. You wouldn't believe the food she prepares for me. She knows I usually get home late and seldom do I eat at receptions or events, so she fixes meals for me." He pulled out two place settings and two glasses. He went back to the refrigerator and held up a water bottle and a soda. She chose the water, so he placed two waters on the counter in front of them.

"This is fantastic. I wish I had someone cook my meals every day. I hate to cook."

"So you can't cook, huh?"

"I said that I hate to cook, not that I can't."

"You have to cook for me one day," he said.

She nodded. "We'll see."

They scooped out pasta salad, cut slices of roast beef and added spicy horseradish mustard with crackers and cheese.

Munching on the countertop, they continued talking about their daily schedules and the differences in their responsibilities. When they finished eating, they covered the leftovers and placed them back in the refrigerator. Helping out, she spotted summer fruits in a small basket.

"How about some fruit for dessert?" she offered.

"Sounds good," he said, placing the last of the dishes into the dishwasher.

Alyssa pulled out some strawberries, blueberries, raspberries, blackberries and different-colored grapes. "These are the biggest berries I've ever seen in my life. They look like they're right out of someone's garden."

"They are. My assistant, Kent, has this amazing garden. Actually it's really like a small farm. He grows just about everything. Fruits, vegetables, herbs. You name it, he grows it. I don't know what he uses, but the size is always amazing."

"These are from his garden?"

"Yes, I believe so."

She took the dish of raspberries and blueberries and went over to the large open sink and turned on the water. He followed with more fruit. They washed the fruit side by side.

"What are they?" she asked, seeing the dark and bright green berries he washed.

"Boysenberries, huckleberries and gooseberries," he said.

"I don't think I ever tasted them before."

"Try them."

"I don't think so."

"Come on, it's something new. Here, try this one." He picked out a plump, nearly black boysenberry and held it near her lips. She opened her mouth and he placed it on her tongue. She bit into the luscious fruit, tasting bittersweet juice. "Umm, it tastes kind of like a raspberry."

He nodded. "Okay, now try this," he said, holding a yellowish green ball out to her. She leaned in and took the fruit from him.

She grimaced and shook her head. "Yuck, I don't like that one at all. It's way too bitter."

"Not exactly a great-tasting wine, either."

"That's right, you probably know all these berries because of your vineyards."

"Not all of them, some of them," he said. "Here, taste this." He held a huckleberry out for her. She took his hand and guided the small fruit to her lips. As soon as she bit it, juice spilled. He traced his finger over her lips, then licked the juice from his finger.

"Umm, it's tart but good. What was that?" she said.

"That's huckleberry," he told her.

"I like it. Here, you try one," she said, holding a strawberry out to him. He bit the red berry while staring into her eyes. She watched intently.

"It's sweet. Here, your turn." He gave her a raspberry. She gave him a blueberry. He gave her a blackberry. She gave him a huckleberry.

"Umm, taste this," he said, holding a strawberry out for her. She bit it and sweet juice ran down the side of her mouth. She reached up to stop the juice from dribbling, but he took her hand and licked it. Her heart lurched. Then he licked her lips. She swallowed hard. He kissed her, nudging his tongue into her mouth. She opened up to him and that was all they needed to fall into each other's arms.

Chapter 9

Pressed against the sink as the water continued to run, Alyssa could think of nothing else except kissing the man in her arms. Harder and more ardently, they kissed as a power beyond them propelled their desire. The thunderous sound of her heart beating overshadowed even her thoughts. Logic and reason vanished as she surrendered to his kisses and the dizzying feeling of passion poured out of her.

The space between their bodies vanished as his hands caressed and cherished every inch of her. Breathless and hungry, his appetite for her seemed insatiable as he pressed her back against the counter. "You are so beautiful," he whispered, his voice deep and raspy.

"Maybe, umm," she whispered breathlessly, then stopped. "Maybe, umm, maybe we should, umm…" she began again, but stopped when he stepped back away from her. The sudden startling release stunned her. He lowered his head and closed his eyes, fighting to regain control of his wanton desire.

He nodded. "You're right," he said huskily. "I'm sorry, this is too soon, we shouldn't—"

"That's not what I was gonna say," she interrupted, smiling coyly.

"It's been a while for me, I mean, being with someone. I'm not exactly the tomcat the press makes me out to be."

"I didn't think so," she said, then moved close again and leaned into him. He opened his eyes and looked at her. She reached up and gently traced the soft line of his lips with her finger. The passion in his eyes was unmistakable. "I was gonna say that maybe we should turn the water off. I'm getting splashed and the back of my shirt is soaked." She smiled. He smiled. She spun around and turned the faucets off.

Randolph saw her saturated cotton shirt. He moved close and reached around the front of her and slowly unbuttoned it. As soon as all the buttons were released, he opened her shirt, removed it, then let his hands caress her soft mounds. She rolled her head back, and his hands continued touching her gently as his lips came down to nibble on her neck and shoulder.

Alyssa moaned, closing her eyes to the sensual sensations, his hardened body behind her and his soft hands in front of her. His palms rounded her breasts; then his fingers tweaked her nipples. She gasped. Then he found the front clasp on her lace bra and released her. The firm weight of her breasts filled his hands and he massaged the fullness as her pebbled nipples begged to be touched.

He obliged, then pressed closer and she felt more of his body hardened. He reached out and grabbed a strawberry from the bowl in the sink, squished it and let the sweet juice drip down onto her chest. Sweet syrup poured everywhere. He touched her shoulder to turn her to face him, then leaned down as soon as she did. His tongue lapped up the fruity essence and his mouth devoured everything else.

She tugged at his shirt, releasing it from his pants, then quickly discarding it over his head and across the room. His arms, shoulders, back and chest were magnificent. Broad and powerful, they were hard and toned obviously from working with weights. He was chiseled to perfection. Her hands drifted lazily over his shoulders and down his arms, then across his chest as he held her tight, gripping her body relentlessly.

She grabbed a berry from the sink and bit into it, and instantly his mouth was on hers. Together they tasted the tart bitterness, then began laughing. The sensual moment had changed to lighthearted humor.

"What was that?" he asked, still chuckling.

"I don't know, I just grabbed something." She grimaced. "I think it was the gooseberries," she said as a generous twinge of embarrassment gripped her. She looked down at her bare breasts, then readjusted her bra and brought it together in front and held it securely without fastening it.

After witnessing her obvious discomfort, he tipped her chin up with his finger and smiled into her eyes. "You are so lovely, Sundari Adia, my beautiful gift from God," he said, then leaned in and kissed her lips chastely. "I didn't plan this," he whispered to her, "and nothing will happen here today between us that we both don't want to happen." She didn't respond. "I can take you back to your car if you'd like."

Alyssa smiled slyly, then reached over and grabbed a strawberry. She bit into it, then touched the juicy fruit to his bare chest. A drop of red juice fell and inched its way down to the tip of his nipple. Without a second's hesitation she opened her mouth and licked it away. He moaned and grasped her arms tight, holding her still. His labored breathing stoked the already ignited fire burning inside her. She knew power when she heard it.

Everyone had a place on their body that, when stimulated, caused immediate sexual arousal. Apparently she had found his. She licked him again and he quivered, then inhaled quickly, breathlessly.

She kissed him, then suckled him, then felt his body lurch and shudder. She knew his legs weakened because she felt his weight adjust accordingly. She smiled with power as she unbuckled his belt and dipped her hand beneath to touch him there. Suddenly a strong hand clasped her wrist, halting her progress. "Adia," he groaned heavily, breathlessly, "we don't have to do this. We can still walk away if you want."

She smiled and shook her head. This newfound power felt too good to just walk away from. There was no way she was going anywhere. She touched, then rubbed down the length of him, full, hard and long. He groaned his pleasure as his mouth came down to hers in a blazing instant.

In a feverish reply, a tangle of hands touched, caressed and stroked, teasing and tempting the pleasure they both sought. Dizzy with longing, they were drunk with anticipation.

Through their sexual haze, they let the power of their desire overtake them until there was only one place to go. He pulled back and took her hand, then led her from the kitchen, down the hall, up the stairs and to his bedroom. They crossed the room and he sat her down on the side of the bed. Then he knelt down in front of her.

He removed her bra, then leaned in. Her breasts perked eagerly to him and he devoured each in turn. He tasted and teased her fullness while his tongue leisurely languished on her pebbled nipples. She arched back, offering more, and he gladly accepted as he wrapped his arms around her body, securing his treasure.

She placed her hands on the sides of his shoulders. His powerful hands held her tight and added to the sensual rhythmic pull of his mouth on her. His tongue thrust hard, then soft, tantalizing each peak. She sighed and moaned breathlessly, raking her teeth over her bottom lip as the fiery burn inside her blazed.

His fervor was unending and her rapture was soaring.

"Lie back," he whispered breathlessly. She did. His hands circled lovingly over her breasts, then eased down her stomach to the waistband of her pants. He slowly unzipped them, then loosened and pulled them free. Now lying there with just lace panties, she closed her eyes, expecting and hoping for everything. She intended to savor every last second of this moment.

She felt the bed move as he got up, and then she heard the sound of a drawer open and close. She opened her eyes, seeing him toss several condoms on the bed beside her. She smiled and leaned up on the palms of her hands. He came back over to her and gently stroked her face. "My Sundari Adia, you are so beautiful."

"I think you like that name."

"I do. It suits you perfectly, my beautiful gift from God."

She lowered her eyes, then looked away.

"What is it?"

"You don't have to say that," she said.

"Why not? You are—"

"Ten pounds overweight," she interrupted, continuing his sentence.

"In all the right places," he added, licking his lips, then looking down at her body relaxed on his bed.

"My ears are too big."

He leaned in, moved her hair to the side and kissed each earlobe. "The better to taste you, my dear," he whispered.

"My eyes are—" she started.

"Luminous," he said before she could finish.

"And I have ten freckles."

"Fourteen actually," he said, correcting her.

"Fourteen? Are you sure?"

He nodded. "Oh, yes, Adia, definitely fourteen."

She reached up to touched her face, but he took her hand and pulled her up against his body. "Not on your face, here," he said, tracing his finger down the front of her, then circling each breast. "Five here and nine here."

"You take my breath away," she said.

"Fair enough," he said, then grabbed and kissed her, holding her neck firmly with one hand while securing her to him with the other. Aggressive and powerful, he devoured her mouth.

Then, in a tangle of wanting, she tugged at his zipper, then at his briefs. Freeing him finally, she felt the hard shaft of his excitement throbbing fiercely and sighed. She stroked the length of him as his kisses intensified even more. He moaned his delight, then edged her lace barrier free. She held him and he felt her.

Then in a burst of unrestrained passion, he shifted up as she lay back on the bed. He grabbed a condom and while covering himself, she pushed up and guided him beside her. Reversing their positions, she straddled to hover above him and smiled at her pending victory. She looked down at him, expecting to see his wanton desire, but instead she saw concern. She knew he was asking her if she was sure.

As she grasped him, her answer was simple. She impaled herself in one quick steady movement. The sudden intense burn of her long-overdue passion stunned her as she held her breath, then closed her eyes until the sting of her tightness subsided. He went deep inside her and she felt every inch of him. Slightly dazed, she sat back motionless, relishing and enjoying the feel of him.

"Adia, are you okay?" he asked, sitting up quickly, obviously concerned.

She opened her eyes and smiled. "Oh, yes, I'm most definitely okay," she said as her fingers bit into his shoulders to hold on as she began grinding into him with her hips.

He smiled.

She smiled.

The rapture began.

He held on to her back while guiding her waist as she released, then plunged down, sinking him into her body and loving the feel of his fullness. She gasped as she sat up and leaned back and his mouth captured her breast. In eager ecstasy they moved to the rhythm of their hearts, quickening the pace and feeling the surging power building in them.

She shrieked and gasped as her rapturous climax neared and the swell of her breasts filled his mouth. He held tight, absorbing the stark pounding she delivered each time she slammed down onto him. Inching closer and closer, she thrust onto him until the overpowering release exploded and she screamed her orgasm and felt him pouring into her.

Then in a split second, Randolph turned her on her back and pushed deeper inside. She wrapped her legs tight around his waist as her nails bit into his arms. A second orgasm crept up and blinded her. She screamed her pleasure again, panting feverously beneath him. He released, then sank deep again. She called out his name, then climaxed so full she swore her heart stopped beating. Afterward he rolled over again, resting beneath her.

Shaking almost violently by the succession of climaxes, she held on to him. Their bodies damp, he lay there holding her tight as she sprawled on top. Her body lay limp, drained. She closed her eyes and waited for her world to stop spinning.

She was no virgin, but she had never been so completely satisfied in her life. When she finally regained her composure, she tried to move away, but he held firm. "No, don't go. Stay," he whispered huskily.

"I don't think I could go even if I wanted to. That was... I don't know, that was..." she began.

He reached up and stroked her back lovingly. "Umm, yes, that most definitely was," he muttered slowly. "I've never felt..."

"Me, either," she said. "It's like my whole body was..."

"Exploding, yeah, me, too, over and over again," he added. "I can't..."

"Believe it, I know, neither can I. How do you think we..." she said.

"I don't know." He smiled and kissed her forehead, then her cheek, then the tip of her nose until finally their lips met in a slow, long, leisurely, passionate kiss.

"So, if we ever..." she muttered.

"Give me ten more minutes..."

She did.

They did, again and again.

Chapter 10

Nina had been checking her watch every two minutes. It was almost eight o'clock and Alyssa still wasn't in yet. For anyone else it was fine, since work didn't actually begin until eight o'clock, but for Alyssa it was totally uncharacteristic. She was never on time or late for anything. She was always twenty to thirty minutes early.

A twinge of guilt struck her. What if she was wrong and Alyssa and Senator Kingsley didn't hit it off as she suspected they would? She grabbed her *I'm not a morning person, so don't bother me* coffee mug and walked over to the coffee station and poured herself a cup.

Adding sugar and cream, she stood stirring pensively a moment, then looked up when she heard the office door open and close. "Finally," she muttered, then hurried over as soon as she saw Alyssa walk in and sit down at her desk. She stood waiting impatiently as Alyssa reached down and dropped her purse into the bottom drawer, then adjusted her keyboard on the desk. "Well?" Nina asked curiously.

"Don't even think about speaking to me after that stunt you pulled yesterday. You are in so much trouble."

Nina smiled brighter and comfortably parked her hip on the side of Alyssa's desk. "But did it work?" she asked.

"Did it work? Is that all you have to say?"

"Oh, please, don't give me all that I'm-so-wounded, I'm-so-stricken crap. Did you get together or not?" she half whispered, leaning in closer. Then she saw Alyssa blush. "Oh, did you and he…"

Alyssa opened her mouth wide in exaggerated shock. "I'm not even going to dignify that with an answer."

"Damn, you didn't," she said, leaning back again.

Alyssa blushed again and looked away, trying to busy herself by turning on her computer and scanning the daily calendar she always kept on standby.

"You did," Nina squealed, "you did."

"Would you stop saying that? It's not what you think," she said, and lowered her voice even more.

"Well, something happened, it's all over your face."

Ursula walked by and smiled. "Good weekend, ladies?"

"Yes, thanks, and yours?" Alyssa said nicely.

"Oh, I worked as usual, then did a bit of gardening. I have some beautiful tomatoes and nice big strawberries coming up already. I'll bring some in for you."

"Sounds great," Nina said, not really caring, since all she wanted to hear was Alyssa's account of Sunday afternoon.

Alyssa blushed. The thought of strawberries and the memory of tasting them on Randolph's body made her stomach lurch like a mile-high roller-coaster drop. Their fruity foreplay at his kitchen sink was only the beginning. Later they had dipped strawberries in melted chocolate and whipped cream and even honey. Then a quick flash of Randolph's chest drizzled with honey and chocolate and her twirling a strawberry on it stoked the fire inside her to burn even hotter. She picked up a folder and began fanning herself.

"See," Ursula said, nodding her head, "I told you it's always hot in here, but nobody listens to me. I'll go turn up the air conditioner on my way out. Talk to you later."

"Uh-huh, now look what you did. We'll be freezing all morning thanks to you. Okay, tell me everything," Nina said as her eyes widened with anticipated interest.

"Alyssa, line four," someone called out.

"Thanks," she said, and picked up the phone on her desk as she smiled at Nina. Nina glared at her, having gotten no information.

"Good morning, this is Alyssa Wingate."

"Good morning, Adia," he said softly.

"Hi," she said cautiously, then quickly glanced around the office, seeing that Nina had already gone back to her desk and started working and everyone else in the office was busy with their own duties.

"Hi," he said, "I just wanted to hear your voice."

"Oh, isn't that nice?"

"I miss you," he whispered.

"Oh, isn't that nice?" she repeated, feeling the sweet sexy softness of his voice caress her body.

"I bet you're blushing," he whispered softly.

"You'd win that bet."

"I gather you can't exactly talk right now."

"Umm, yeah. That would be correct."

"Okay, I want to see you tonight." She didn't respond, so he clarified, "A date, dinner, a movie, dancing, bowling, roller skating, whatever you'd like."

Another flash shot through her body as very vivid memories of the day before surfaced. Whatever she'd like was too tempting an offer. But she needed to be realistic. "Umm, I'm not sure that's such a good idea."

"Don't tell me that you were just using me for my body."

This man was killing her. She picked up the folder again and started fanning, half expecting to spontaneously combust at any moment. "Umm, why don't we discuss this later? Where are you exactly?"

"In my car on my private cell phone on the way to work. I had a meeting out of the office earlier."

"Really? How'd it go?"

"Good, very productive. So how about dinner tonight?" he asked again.

"I can't. I already have plans."

"Should I be jealous?"

"No."

"Good, then how about meeting me after your plans? We can have dessert and tea someplace."

"Umm, that might not be such a good idea."

"Are you trying to let me down easy?"

"Um…"

"Don't answer. I'm not sure I want to know," he joked.

Alyssa didn't respond again. Then out of the corner of her eye she saw her boss approach. He waved and pointed to his office. She nodded. "Umm, I have to get back to work now."

"Okay, I'll call you later tonight," he said.

"'Bye."

Randolph pushed the end-call button on his steering wheel and disconnected the call. He pulled to a stop at the traffic light, then just stared across the street at nothing in particular. The phone call troubled him. Alyssa was detached and distant. He understood that she couldn't exactly talk comfortably at the office, but all he wanted was a firm commitment for dinner that night, and she seemed somewhat withdrawn.

The light changed. He made a mental note to call her again around noon. Hopefully she'd be at lunch and more available to talk.

He turned into a small private entrance, then followed the path down several levels until he came to his parking space. He turned off the engine, got out and headed to the elevator. As soon as he got there, the doors eased open. The elevator operator stood smiling.

"Good morning, sir," he said happily.

"Good morning."

"Going to your office?"

"Yes, thank you."

Moments later, the doors opened again and he strolled down the hall toward his office. As soon as he walked in, a bustling commotion began as assistants and aides tried to get his attention.

As soon as he went into his office and closed the door, the noise stopped. Kent was sitting at the conference table surrounded by several books, folders and laptops. "Morning," Kent said, looking up as Randolph entered.

"Good morning, Kent," Randolph said, dropping his briefcase on his desk and removing his suit jacket. "Okay, let's get started. What's first?" He picked up a government report in a blue folder, read the title, flipped through the pages, then opened to the first page. His day had begun.

Louise and Otis signed in at the security desk, then took a seat and waited to be escorted on their Capitol Hill tour. There were several other people sitting around waiting, including what looked like a number of student groups on class trips and a delegation from Japan.

"I hope he won't be too busy to give us the full tour. I'm really looking forward to it," Louise said as Otis sat beside her, admiring the intricate stonework surrounding the huge atrium.

"Oh, I don't think the senator will actually be giving us the tour. He's far too busy for that. He'll probably have an assistant or an aide give us a nice walk around a bit. He's a very busy man."

"Well, of course he is but that won't do, now, will it? How am I supposed to help him if he doesn't tell me what he wants?"

"Help him?" Otis questioned. "Help him with what?"

Louise smiled. Otis shook his head. "No, Louise, now, this is too far. Messing around in your grandsons' lives is one thing and even delving into the lives of their friends and relatives is marginally acceptable, but you can't start disrupting the life of a United States senator. That's just going too far."

"Too far! Of course not. He invited me here."

"To take a tour, yes. But he never asked you to play matchmaker, did he?"

"No, not in so many words, but the spark in his eyes was there. Believe me, I recognized it instantly."

"Maybe he was just tired."

"No, he's interested and he needs my assistance."

Otis shook his head, knowing that there was no reasoning with her when she got this way. He only hoped that Randolph would have the good sense to stay as far away from them today as possible. He was wrong.

"Mamma Lou, Colonel Wheeler, welcome."

Louise turned and smiled happily. Given her reputation, few men were happy to see her. In fact, most ran for their lives, Trey Evans being the one who immediately came to mind. "Hello, dear. We were just talking about you. We're fine and we're very excited to take this tour."

Otis's jaw dropped. Louise never ceased to amaze him.

"Colonel Wheeler, how are you, sir?" Randolph asked, shaking his hand.

"Just fine, Senator, and thank you for the invitation. It's always exciting to be here. We know you're a busy man, so we don't want to take up too much of your time. As a matter of fact, if you have an aide or an assistant we'll be just as delighted to take the tour with them."

"Not at all. I wouldn't dream if it. I've been looking forward to this, as well. I've cleared a nice break in my schedule for us. We'll start off with lunch in the Senate Building and go from there."

"Excuse me, Senator Kingsley, can I get your autograph?" A student walked over to him with pencil and paper.

"Sure," Randolph said, signing his name. Then suddenly a mass of kids began surrounding him as teachers and chaperones tried to control their sudden excitement.

Louise and Otis looked on as security stepped in and Randolph continued talking to the students. "You never cease to amaze me, my dear," Otis said into Louise's ear.

Louise smiled. "That's the whole idea."

"We better get out of here before I start another riot," Randolph said, escorting Louise and Otis down the hall toward the elevators. "Hungry?"

"Starved," Louise said happily.

Ten minutes later, they were seated in the main dining hall of the Congressional Building. Large and ostentatious, the room was crowded with members of Congress, staff and guests. They sat at a table off to the side near the center courtyard. They each ordered the special of the day, then talked and enjoy a nice leisurely meal filled with laugher, good conversation and welcome friendship.

As usual Colonel Wheeler was spotted by someone he

knew. The two men chatted a few moments, and then Colonel Wheeler was extended an invitation to sit in on a security meeting that his friend was facilitating, leaving Louise and Randolph to sit sipping tea after lunch.

"Have you spoken to Trey Evans lately?" Louise asked. Randolph's blood pressure spiked as Louise chuckled, enjoying his flabbergasted expression. "Don't answer, I wouldn't dream of asking you to betray his confidence."

"Confidence?" Randolph asked, recovering his coolness.

She chuckled again. "I know he's been hiding from me. You can assure him that I am quite busy using my talents elsewhere."

"I'll make sure to pass that along if I see him."

"That will more than likely be at the poker game this weekend."

"Is there anything you don't already know?"

"Not much," she said. It was Randolph's time to chuckle. "Okay, now, why don't you tell me about her?"

"Tell you about whom?" Randolph asked, refusing to be taken off guard again. Louise looked at him steadily and smiled. He nodded, knowing that his coy restraint was more than likely futile given her talents.

"The reason I'm sitting here," she said.

Randolph surrendered. "Her name is Alyssa Adia Wingate."

"That name sounds familiar," she said.

"As a matter of fact, she said that she knew you, or rather, her grandmother knew you and she remembered her father talking about you a while back."

"Who's her grandmother?"

Randolph opened his phone and quickly scanned the message Kent had sent him earlier with all of Alyssa's information listed. "Alyssa Granger."

"Alyssa Granger, now, there's a name I haven't heard in years. Yes, I know Allie. She and I were very close at one time. How is she?"

"I'm afraid she's apparently in the early stages of Alzheimer's disease."

"Oh, no, how heartbreaking," she said, obviously affected by the sad news. "The last time I saw Allie was at her husband's funeral and before that, it was at her daughter's funeral. Seems we meet at the worst possible times."

For the first time, Randolph really considered the woman sitting across from him. As others were far more frail and delicate, Louise Gates, at over eighty years old, was as spry as a jackrabbit and just as spirited. She was part of the group his senate committee was trying to help.

Passing legislation for financial, medical and home-care assistance, he felt obligated to make their lives as trouble-free as possible. But there were so many issues that his job was made even more difficult just by doing it. There were insurance and pharmaceutical lobbyists, medical and fair-housing agencies and senior social-services agencies all vying for his attention, not to mention Social Security, Medicare and discrimination issues.

Louise Gates, of course, was the exception. But there were the others, like Alyssa's grandmother, who were depending on him to make their retirement years as comfortable as possible, and he intended to do just that.

"You said you were close, and now?" he asked her.

"Yes, we were, but we drifted apart," she said, still shaken by his news.

"If you'll excuse my directness, Mamma Lou, you don't seem like the type to allow a friendship to just drift apart."

"Very astute, Senator. No wonder your numbers are through the roof. Yes, it's true we allowed our friendship to lapse. It was best. There were personal issues on which we didn't agree."

"I see."

"And now, her granddaughter is all grown up. The last time I saw her she was barely a teenager. So, tell me about your Alyssa."

"She's not exactly my Alyssa."

"But you'd like her to be."

"What makes you say that?"

"I'm sitting here, aren't I?"

"Very astute, Mamma Lou."

Alyssa stifled a yawn, covering her mouth casually so as not to draw attention to herself. She was still tired. She'd gotten to bed late the night before after spending the afternoon and then all evening at Randolph's house. They ate, made love, laughed and talked and then ate and made love again. It was the most passionate day she'd ever had. By the time he dropped her off at her car and followed her home, it was after eight and she was exhausted.

He called her and they talked again the whole time he was driving home. The whole day was like something out of a fantasy or one of those romance novels. Things that never happen to real people, but it did—it happened to her. Then morning came too early and she needed to come down to earth.

It was sex. It was fantastic. And it was over. She'd seen the women on his arm in the past and she was nothing like them. They were all tall, wildly successful in their professions and drop-dead gorgeous and that definitely wasn't her. She was average by any standard. Nowhere near what he was used to, so the only logical reason for her being with him was opportunity. She was his little secret and the tryst was all too familiar.

She yawned again, but this time she didn't cover too well,

and Nina, sitting directly across from her at the conference-room table, looked at her, questioning. Earlier, she'd managed to avoid all of her questions and leave her with the idea that nothing actually happened between them. That they had left shortly after Nina did, and that she did go home and start packing. Alyssa just didn't elaborate on what she did in between.

Now it was almost five and she couldn't wait to get home. She'd worked through lunch and tried really hard to focus on the job, but it was difficult. Everything reminded her of Randolph, and then when Ursula returned to the office unexpectedly and mentioned that she'd seen him having lunch with a woman in the Congressional restaurant, she knew that everything was back as it should be.

She'd gotten his message, of course. He called twice. But returning his call was the last thing she intended to do. She intended to just put him out of her mind and consider last Sunday a sweet memory just as her grandmother once did.

By the time the meeting was over, she'd managed to refocus on what was going on and offered some good suggestions and answered a few questions. Later, she turned off her computer for the day, gathered her things and left.

Chapter 11

"Hello."

Louise and Otis looked around, hearing the greeting.

"Over here," the voice called out again. "Yoo-hoo."

They looked next door and saw a woman standing on her front porch, holding a broom and waving. "Are you lost?"

"Good afternoon," Louise said. "No, I don't think so. Actually we're looking for someone, Allie Granger. Do you know if she still lives here?"

"Yes, she does and she should be at home. You might want to try knocking a bit louder. The doorbell sticks and she might be in the back of the house. Sometimes it's hard to hear the doorbell in the kitchen, especially when the television is up too loud."

"Thank you," Louise said as Colonel Wheeler knocked firmly on the side panel. A few moments later, they heard a small voice calling out from the other side of the door, and then the lace curtain pulled back and an older woman peeked out. Louise smiled. The door opened.

"Louise, Louise Gates, is that you?" Allie asked, not sure if her memory was failing her again.

"Hello, Allie," Louise said, smiling happily.

"What on earth?" Allie said, opening the door wider.

"It's been a long time," Louise said.

"Yes, it has. You look great."

"Liar," Louise joked, then smiled and laughed.

"Well, don't just stand there in the doorway, come in, come in, please." She stepped back and allowed them to enter.

"Allie, this is a dear friend of mine, Otis Wheeler."

Colonel Wheeler nodded and smiled as he always did. "Good to meet you, Allie."

Allie took his large hand and barely shook it. "Come on into the parlor, we can talk there."

"Actually, Allie, I'm gonna let you two young ladies sit and chat for a while. You don't need an old rooster like me in the way. I saw a nice little shopping center a few blocks away. I'll pop over there and make myself useful." He nodded and smiled wide. "It was good meeting you, Allie." Then with a quick peck on Louise's cheek he stepped back outside and down the front steps to the car.

Allie closed the door and turned. "Well, isn't this a blast from the past?"

"It certainly is, Allie."

"It's been a long time, Louise. What on earth brings you here today?" she asked, leading the way to the parlor.

"That's just it, it's been a long time, too long a time. Someone mentioned your name to me recently and knew I needed to stop by and see you. We're getting too old to drag hard feelings around."

Allie smiled and opened her arms wide. She and Louise

hugged long and hard and tears started to fall. "Oh, look at us, a couple of old broads crying like babies. Enough of this parlor stuff, let's go in the kitchen and get us some tea and cookies."

"Sounds like a perfect idea."

The two women spent the rest of the afternoon in the kitchen, talking and catching up. Louise was heartbroken to hear several old friends had passed, and Allie was amazed that both Matthew's and Raymond's sons were married.

"Time is passing us by, Allie."

"Lord knows that's the truth. So, what have you been up to? Are you still living on the island?"

"Crescent Island will always be home. I've been traveling a bit, visiting. My grandson Tony and his wife, Madison, had twins recently and I just needed to see them, although I'm still waiting for my other grandson, Raymond, and his wife, Hope, to slow down enough to start having children. I tell you, there's nothing like welcoming babies into the family."

"I know, my Katherine was a beautiful baby. She's a little over two years old now. I don't know where she is, probably outside playing with the next-door neighbor or upstairs taking a nap," Allie said.

"Excuse me?" Louise said, suddenly confused.

"Why don't I call her in or wake her up? You have to meet her. She's so precious, has these big brown eyes just like her father."

"Allie, are you okay?" Louise asked, reaching over and holding her hand tight.

"Of course I'm okay, Louise, I'm just glad we put all this behind us. It was silly, really, and yes, you were right, but I love him and I always will. But if my Henry ever found out that Katherine wasn't his—" she smiled and giggled "—he'd divorce me and take her away."

"I'm sure everything will be fine, Allie. He will never find out from me."

"I know. You're a true friend, Louise. But that damn press is starting to mess around and now Vincent's wife won't let him an inch out of her sight. He promised me that we'd be together and he'd marry me, but being a United States senator is so demanding. But we love each other and our child needs a father. Henry's here, of course, and he's wonderful, bless his soul, but I don't love him. Vincent and I need to be together."

Louise sat heartbroken. Her friend was obviously drifting back. She knew that her friend had had an affair with Senator Vincent Dupree years ago, but she didn't know that their union had produced a daughter. A child she obviously passed off as her husband's. "More tea?" Louise asked.

"Yes, please," Allie said, then continued to tell Louise about Katherine and Vincent.

"Grandma, hi, it's me. I just stopped by to…"

Allie stopped talking and both she and Louise turned to the kitchen doorway. A woman entered and smiled. "Hi, I didn't know you were gonna have company today. Hi, I'm—"

"Who are you?" Allie asked, her eyes glazed in shock.

"Grandma," she said quietly.

"Louise, who is this woman? Is it Vincent's wife? Does she know about us?" Allie stood and backed up. "If you came for him, he's not here and you're not taking our daughter. Katherine, Katherine…" she called out.

"Vincent, Senator Dupree?" Alyssa muttered.

"You know exactly who Vincent is. Now, what are you doing in my house?" Allie shouted.

"No, Allie, this is a friend of mine, remember?" Louise said, trying to calm the now very agitated Allie. She stood and smiled at her. "I'll tell you what, why don't I tell my friend to wait in the parlor while we talk, okay?" Louise said. Allie nodded her head quickly, but still glared at Alyssa.

Louise walked over and asked Alyssa to wait in the parlor. Alyssa nodded slowly, turned and walked out sadly.

"There, that's done. Now, come on, sit down and we'll have another cup of tea." Allie agreed, then sat as Louise re-filled their cups.

"I'm sorry about that, Louise. It's just that that woman has me all wound up. She can't have children of her own and I know she wants my baby. Do you know that Vincent actually wanted me to put Katherine up for adoption so that he and his wife could take her? Now, how was I supposed to do that with Henry right here?"

"That's terrible, unthinkable."

"Yes, I know. I told him no, of course. I haven't seen him since. He says he's busy and now he won't take any of my calls. But I know it's his wife. She did all this. She wants to take Katherine and break us apart."

"Allie," Louise said assuringly, "ease your mind. No one is going to take Katherine from you and Henry, trust me."

"Oh, Lord, we need more cookies," Allie said. She stood, grabbed the doily-covered plate and walked over to the counter. She added more cookies to the plate, then replaced the lid. "You know, I thought about making lemon squares today and I'm so sorry I didn't now. Alyssa loves lemon squares. Did I tell you she's moving in again?" Allie said.

"No, you didn't," Louise said evenly, but now slightly thrown off by the new conversation.

"Lord, I don't know what I'd do without her. She's a real treasure. I can't wait until you meet her."

"Allie, I'm gonna get my handkerchief out of my purse. I think I left it in the parlor, I'll be right back." She walked down the hall and returned moments later with Alyssa behind her.

"Alyssa," Allie said, seeing her walk in just after Louise sat down. "We were just talking about you. How was work?"

"Good, Grandma, how was your day?" Alyssa said, glancing at Louise for added confirmation.

"Not bad, not bad at all. Lord, where are my manners? Louise, this is my granddaughter, Alyssa Wingate. Alyssa, this is Louise Gates, a very dear old friend." As Louise greeted her with a polite handshake, Alyssa opened her arms and hugged her. "Thank you, Mrs. Gates," she whispered.

"Call me Mamma Lou, darling, everyone else does."

Alyssa nodded happily.

"So, what are you ladies up to?" Alyssa asked.

"Louise stopped by and surprised me," Allie said, and she reached across and took her hand. "We've been sitting here laughing and talking and catching up."

"And having a wonderful time," Louise added.

"Sorry I missed it."

"Did I mention that Alyssa was moving back in, although I have no idea why? She needs to find a nice guy and settle down and start having babies of her own. No need looking away like that. You need to have your own life."

"I have my own life, Grandma. I'm happy."

"But you could be happier. Louise, do you still match people up like you used to do back in the day?"

Louise smiled. "How do you think I got my great-grandkids? If I left it up to my two grandsons, I'd still be waiting."

"Perfect, why don't you find someone nice for Alyssa?"

"Grandma, I'm standing right here. You can't just do that right in front of me like this."

"Of course I can," Allie said. "I want someone kind and generous with a sweet, even disposition, maybe a good job and an excellent work ethic. But no one who'll break her heart. And keep in mind, I want lots and lots of grandchildren before my ticket is punched."

"Grandma, please," Alyssa said.

Louise smiled and winked. "I'll see what I can do."

"Did I mention a sense of humor? Yes, he must have a good sense of humor. But absolutely, positively, without question, no politicians, that's nonnegotiable."

Both Alyssa and Louise looked at her. Allie smiled happily, having said her piece and placed her order.

"Well, as I said I'll keep my eyes open and see what I can do. Oh, gracious, look at the time. It's getting late and I just know Otis must have bought out the entire sporting-goods and fishing departments by now. I'd better give him a call, so he can pick me up."

"Do you need a ride, Mamma Lou?"

"No, that's okay, you stay here with your grandmother. It was a real treat meeting you, Alyssa."

"You, too, Mamma Lou. I heard so many wonderful stories about you and Grandma from years ago and I'm so happy to finally meet you. You're like a legend."

"I don't know if that's a good thing or a bad thing," Louise joked.

"It's a very good thing and thank you for keeping Grandma company today."

"My pleasure, dear, we'll talk again soon."

Louise called and Otis arrived a few minutes later with the back of the car filled with new fishing gear. After introductions were made, Louise and Otis said their goodbyes and promised Allie that they'd stop by again to visit before they left town.

Allie closed the door and smiled, seeing Alyssa standing in the parlor doorway behind her, holding the big white box with the red ribbon. "Grandma, you brought your silk dress downstairs?"

"Yes," Allie said.

"Any particular reason?" Alyssa asked, fearing that her grandmother might have had another episode earlier, prompting her to bring the dress down.

"Yes, I'm giving it to you and you're taking it home tonight."

"Grandma, we talked about this."

"Don't *Grandma* me. Take the dress home, Alyssa Adia Wingate, or I'll turn you over my knee right this minute."

"I don't go any place to wear it."

"You will. With a dress like that, something will most certainly come up."

"Yes, Grandma," Alyssa said, deciding not to argue.

"Now that that's settled, are you hungry?" she asked.

"Maybe a little."

"Good, I made a couple of nice big Cobb salads earlier. They're in the refrigerator. Why don't you pull them out for dinner while I go upstairs and wash my hands?"

"Sure, Grandma," Alyssa said, and watched her grandmother head up the stairs. Then Alyssa walked over to the sofa and sat down slowly. The long tiring day had turned into an even more stressful evening. And the fact that her grandmother was talking about Senator Vincent Dupree and had another episode wasn't good.

She knew about the affair, of course. Everybody knew at some point. It was the affair that brought down the senator and led his wife to shoot him. The newspapers covered it for weeks. She'd seen and read them all. Not from her grandmother, of course, but from the library archives. At the time, the story dominated nearly every newspaper in the county.

"Senator Dupree Questioned by Ethics Committee."

"Dupree Quits the Senate, Embroiled in Sex Scandal."

"Possible Dupree Mistress Questioned on the Hill."

"Dupree Shot by Wife Over Speculated Affair."

Although there was never any physical proof and the senator never revealed her grandmother's name, it was widely assumed that Alyssa Granger was his mistress. She never denied it even as her husband stood by her side and adamantly did.

Now hearing his name mentioned tonight sent a chill through her. Her grandmother's past had been rifled through dozens of times. She even had several authors request interviews for books they were writing on the scandal. Unlike today, in the sixties a senate sex scandal was major news. And the fact that her grandmother was black and the senator was Creole and his in-laws were old-school Southern only added to the controversy.

"Alyssa, why don't you make some iced tea? We can have that with our salads," Allie called down.

"Sure, Grandma," she said, then stood, but just as she was about to go into the kitchen, she heard her cell phone ring. She answered.

"Are we on for this evening?" Randolph asked.

"I can't," she said.

"You're still busy?" he asked skeptically.

"Yes, something like that." She looked behind her into the hall at the steps leading to the second floor. Thankfully her grandmother was still upstairs.

"Are you okay?" he asked.

"Yes, just a bit tired." He didn't respond for a short while. "Are you still there?" she asked.

"Do you want me to be?" he asked. She didn't answer.

"Yes, I'm still here, although I'm not sure if I should be. If you're not interested, Alyssa, tell me and I'll back off."

She took a deep breath and lied boldly. "I'm not interested.

We've run our course, Randolph, and I think we both know that we don't have a future together. Where can this really go from here?"

"I presumed we were going to try and get to know each other."

"We did that yesterday."

"I'm not talking about making love, Alyssa. I think you know that. You're pushing me away, I get that. I just hoped you'd tell me why." Again she didn't respond. "I guess not."

"It would never work. You know it and I know it. So why don't we just cut to the chase before hearts and reputations get broken. I'm not saying that you're not a great guy. You are. You are. You're incredible and I had the best time of my life yesterday. It was like a fantasy. But that's just it, really, a dream, and that's all it can and will ever be."

"I'm very sorry to hear that."

"Goodbye, Senator." She hung up and took a deep breath, then went into the kitchen, crying silently, and made iced tea.

Randolph closed his cell phone and laid it down. He hated losing a battle, but more than, that he hated not even getting the opportunity to prove himself.

He was scheduled to make a personal appearance at a fund-raiser tonight, but being gracious and charming was going to be almost impossible now. Spending one day with Alyssa was all it took for him to know that he wanted her. Not sexually, although their time together was beyond incredible, but completely; he wanted all of her.

So what now? he wondered, considering his alternatives. Forget her? No, he didn't see that happening anytime soon. Make her change her mind? No, he already knew that she was too stubborn for that. Bribe her with an unbelievable future?

No, she was way too smart for that and would see right through him. Then a slow, easy smile crept across his face. Of course! He picked up his cell and dialed.

"Mamma Lou, it's Randolph Kingsley."

"I was just thinking about you, dear. Otis and I had a wonderful time. We're here at the auction house. If you haven't had dinner, why don't you stop by and join us? We're going to Dennis's restaurant in a few minutes."

"I'd love to, but unfortunately I have a previous engagement this evening."

"Oh, what a pity. So, what can I do for you, dear?"

He paused. "I'm not sure how to ask this…" he said.

"Consider it asked."

He smiled. Of course, he'd obviously forgotten to whom he was speaking. "She decided that we weren't a good idea."

"I suspected as much."

"How do you mean?"

"Otis and I stopped by to visit Allie this afternoon."

"Her grandmother, but I thought that the two of you…"

"Gray hair has a way of opening doors and easing soured feelings. The past is the past. You learn to leave it there with age. Allie and I talked, but unfortunately she isn't as well as I'd hoped."

"I'm sorry to hear that. Is there anything I can do?"

"To help her, I'm afraid not. We are how we are. Our bodies fail us. There's nothing anyone can do about the ravages of time and disease. But seeing her granddaughter happy would ease Allie's mind considerably."

"Unfortunately that's out of my hands at the moment."

"Let me see what I can do."

"Thanks, Mamma Lou."

"In the meantime, give my regards to Trey."

"Trey?" he questioned.

"Yes, tomorrow evening at the American Alzheimer's fund-raiser gala."

"How do you know he's gonna be there?"

"You'd be surprised what I know," she said.

Randolph smiled. Mamma Lou was too much.

Chapter 12

"Good news, people," Pete Lambert said, walking into the office, clapping his hands to get everyone's attention. "We've all been invited to attend a fund-raiser at the American Grand Hotel this evening." Everyone moaned and groaned. There was nothing more boring than attending a fund-raiser at a posh hotel in Washington, D.C.

"That's not a request, it's a mandatory. Someone has generously offered us two tables and I want us to be there in full force. No excuses. This is for our foundation and our partner in the fight, so we must show our support."

"But what if we already have plans?" someone asked.

"Now, listen up, folks. One of the board members has very generously given us these tables and we're going to represent, understand? Cancel, postpone, reschedule, do whatever you have to do. We need to fill up two tables. That's twenty seats. That means we all need to be there."

"What's the fund-raiser for?"

"It's the American Alzheimer's gala," he said.

Suddenly interest perked up. Last year, this same event had raised close to two million dollars and it was crawling with celebrities.

"Can we bring a guest?"

"If you want to bring a guest and someone else seriously can't make it, then set it up between yourselves."

"Who's gonna be there?" someone shouted out.

"The usual. Senators, congressmen, judges, maybe a retired secretary of state or ambassador. And no, before anyone else asks, I don't have an advance list of who will be attending. So if you want to see and hang out with celebrities, you're going to have to show up and see for yourself. Are there any more questions?"

"Yes," Ursula said, raising her hand. "I'm gonna need at least three hours to look presentable. Are you closing the office early today?" Several other staff members began nodding in agreement.

Pete stood there shaking his head. Ursula was a partner in the foundation and, at times, worse than his two-year-old. Pete was in charge of the support staff, and Ursula was the director of outside staff. If Pete, as the founder, was its backbone, she was the ribs that held everything together. For him to say no to her was nearly unheard of.

He looked at his watch. It was two o'clock, three more hours left in the workday. After a heavy sigh, he nodded his head. "All right, go on, get out of here, everybody." There was instant cheering. "Just remember to be there on time, seven o'clock. Dress is semiformal to formal."

"Boo," several of the younger staff shouted.

"If you've got a tuxedo, pull it out. If not, a nice business suit will do. Ladies, dress gowns or dinner suits, nothing too flashy or too sexy and remember, no sneaks. Thanks. See you tonight."

"Oh, great," Nina moaned, "I had a date tonight."

"With who?"

"None of your business. See, I can be just as restrained with my personal life as you," Nina said firmly, glaring at Alyssa. "All right, who am I kidding? It's with Oliver Watts."

"Good for you, or rather, good for both of you. Tell you what, just make the date for later. We'll go to the fund-raiser at seven, hang out for an hour, then I'll tell Pete that you got sick and had to leave."

"Seriously?" Nina said happily.

"Of course. No need for both of us to wind up alone and miserable with an apartment filled with cats."

"Oh, that's a pretty picture. But I thought you and a certain person might be hitting it off."

Alyssa looked around, seeing no one paying any attention to them. "Nah, it didn't happen."

"I can't believe he ended it. That stinks," Nina said, immediately assuming Randolph had broken it off.

"Actually it would be me that stinks. I ended it."

"Alyssa, but why?"

"It was best. No sense starting something that neither one of us could finish."

"Are you all right?"

"As right as rain," she assured her friend. "Come on, let's get out of here. Pete closes this office early once in a blue moon and I don't want to be here if he suddenly changes his mind."

"Good point," Nina said, then rushed back to her desk and gathered her things. By the time she finished, Alyssa was waiting at her desk. "I'm ready, let's go."

Once outside they quickly discussed what they might be

wearing, then said their goodbyes and headed in two different directions

Alyssa drove to her apartment.

Going straight to her closet, she pulled out the box and untied the red ribbon. She gently took the dress out and laid it on the bed. There was no doubt about it, it was still stunning.

She quickly removed her clothes and very carefully unzipped the side of the dress and stepped in. She pulled it up over her hips, then secured it with the small clasp and zipped it up. It fit as if it had been made for her. She pulled out the shoes and slipped them on. Perfect fit. She added the matching shawl and looked at herself in the full-length mirror behind her bedroom door.

"Oh, my goodness, it's gorgeous," she muttered.

She turned to the side, then to the back and then removed the shawl. Everything looked perfect. Then she tried to sit down and to her surprise the dress gave with her every move. She took it off and hung it up on a padded hanger, then stood back and looked at it.

Her grandmother said that it was a gift, so she wondered who gave it to her. It was far too expensive for her grandfather to give. Then a sneaking suspicion told her that it was her grandmother's lover, Senator Vincent Dupree. She looked closer at the dress. It had never been worn and the idea of wearing it now seemed strange.

Then out of the blue, she wondered if Randolph would attend and what he would think seeing her in this dress. She smiled and hoped he would be there.

After a short nap and a quick cup of yogurt, Alyssa took a shower, curled her hair and added a touch of makeup. She lotioned, perfumed and styled her hair, pulling wispy ringlets down to accent her face. She checked the clock, took a deep breath and removed the dress from the hanger. Forty minutes later she walked into the hotel ballroom, turning heads in her wake.

"Check you out, hot mama," Nina said, smiling. "Look at you, you look fantastic. Girl, when you said you might wear one of your grandmother's old dresses, I was seriously beginning to wonder. But you pulled it off and then some."

"Thanks, I still can't believe it fits so well."

"It looks like it was made for you."

"Actually it was made for my grandmother. Now, look at you. You look incredible."

"Thank you," Nina said as she spun around slowly, and struck an alluring pose.

"Go ahead, girl, work it," Alyssa said as Nina twirled again, and they both started laughing. "So, are we the first ones from our crew here?"

Before Nina could reply the sound of a wolf whistle got both women to turn, seeing Oliver walking up smiling. "Wow, am I a lucky stiff or am I a lucky stiff?" he said, carrying three glasses of champagne. "You two look ravishing. And speaking of ravishing, this is just like a dream I once had. Let's see, Nina, you were reclined on a sofa waiting for me and, Alyssa, you were—"

"Stop right there. I don't want to hear it."

"Suit yourself but, ladies, you two look absolutely mouth-watering. One in black and one in white. Man, what I could do with that image. Shall we?" He stepped between them and gave each his arm. They tucked their arms through and he escorted them into the main ballroom.

"Whoa. Stop. Back up. What do you mean, Mamma Lou sends her regards?"

"Just what I said," Randolph said. "She asked me to send you her regards."

"You told her I was coming here tonight?" Trey asked.

"How could I? I didn't know you were coming until she told me. You know Mamma Lou has a way of predicting things."

"I don't know how you can get away with it."

"Get away with what?" Randolph asked.

"With not getting matched up. She's got everyone else hooked up. Why not you? What's your secret? Did you threaten her with an IRS audit or something?"

"What makes you think she doesn't have me targeted?"

"Because you're too calm," Trey said. "Tony and Raymond sweated bullets. J.T. was double-crossing her and still she got him. Juwan, well, brother didn't have a prayer. But you, you just ease through this like it's no big deal. You even have the nerve to contact her. Are you nuts?"

"She's a sweet lady."

"Hey, you think I don't know that? Mamma Lou is the best, only I'd feel much better if she were back on Crescent Island. So, just in case she's thinking of showing up here tonight, I think I'll call it an early night."

"You're not gonna let an eighty-year-old woman chase you away, are you?" Randolph challenged.

"Watch me," Trey said without flinching. He turned, but stopped short and smiled. "But on the other hand…"

"Changed your mind already?" Randolph asked.

"Momentarily," he said, staring across the room.

Randolph turned and glanced at the open ballroom door. A vision entered and he could hardly contain himself. "Adia," he whispered.

"You know her?" Trey asked.

"Yes, as a matter of fact, I do."

"She's gorgeous, man."

"Yeah, she is."

"Where have you been hiding her?"

"Good question."

"Still, I'm out of here, just in case," Trey said, shaking Randolph's hand. Then he pulled a check from his pocket. "For the cause."

"Thanks, I'll pass it on."

"Don't forget the poker game this weekend."

"I'll be there. Take care," Randolph said. And as soon as Trey walked away, several guests walked up to Randolph and introduced themselves as his staunchest supporters. He greeted them with his usual charm.

Heads turned and eyes stared. The dress was obviously a sensation and Alyssa felt like a million dollars wearing it. Her coworkers remarked how great she looked, but the one person she wanted to notice never said a word. He never even acknowledged that she was there. She spared a glance across the room several times, but was never able to catch his eye. He was either surrounded by other guests, quietly speaking with someone one-on-one or at the main podium.

Then there were the women. Like her, they couldn't keep their eyes off of him, particularly one woman who made it her business to stand by his side at every opportunity. Small, slender and beautiful, she was constantly at his side.

But who could blame her? He was Senator Randolph Kingsley and he looked fantastic in his tuxedo. Of course it fit him perfectly. She expected no less. But in an unspoken truce, their paths never crossed. She stayed on her side of the ballroom and he stayed on his.

When the fund-raiser was over Alyssa said her goodbyes and drove home alone. Regret tortured her the whole way— what she should have done, what she should have said, how she should have acted. But it was too late now. She'd heard that Randolph would be out of town the rest of the week. She had

had her opportunity, and being too afraid of taking a chance and too proud to admit how she felt, she missed it. The evening was over. He was back in his world and she was back in hers.

A few minutes after she closed her front door, her phone rang. She picked up. "I'm downstairs."

She answered by pushing the button on the wall by the door and buzzing him in. Her heart raced a mile a minute. Standing there waiting for him, she started to panic. What was she doing? She must have been insane to buzz him up. But it was too late to change her mind. He was coming and every part of her soul wanted him to.

Moments later, she turned the knob and opened the door. He was standing there motionless, staring at her. Still wearing his tuxedo, he'd loosened his bow tie and let the ends hang down on either side of his collar. He didn't knock or call out her name, he just stood there. She opened the door wider, then reached out and took his hand. He didn't move.

"I'm asking you to come in."

"Are you sure?"

"Yes," she said.

As soon as he stepped inside, he grabbed her up and kissed her fiercely and powerfully. He slammed the door and crushed her against the wall, holding her secure with his hardened body. She yielded to him completely. He took her hands and pinned them above her head, then ravaged her bare neck and shoulders until she was weak with desire.

She pulled her hands free and grabbed at his tuxedo jacket, removing and tossing it down, then tore at his shirt, sending small black button covers scattering across the hardwood floor. She felt for his pants, but he grabbed her hands again and held them tight.

Then, breathless, he stood panting and dipped his head to her shoulder, while still holding her neck and head with one hand and her wrists with the other. "Whatever you're doing to me, Adia, keep doing it," he said.

The tickle of his hot breath on her neck made Alyssa shudder. Her body melted and her heart soared as she realized that what she was doing was simple, she was loving him. "If you insist," she whispered huskily.

They kissed again, this time tenderly, long, languishing with tongues intertwined, feeling the sweet pleasure of connecting. Alyssa felt her whole body burn as it came to life for him. Then without warning, he stopped and pulled away from her.

He stepped back and let his eyes roam down the length of her body. His smile was slow and telling as his eyes burned hot with desire. The dress, still flawlessly formfitting, clung to every perfect voluptuous curve. He reached out and touched the delicate embroidery just below the sweet swell of her breast, then traced it all the way down her body. His gentle touch burned like fire as she watched his descent.

When he finished, he walked around behind her and touched the bodice of the dress, down her back and over the curve of her buttocks. She gasped and arched straight as his hand continued down her thigh, then slowly drifted back up.

He stepped in close behind her and captured her arms at her sides, then whispered into her ear, "Do you have any idea how hard it was for me not to grab you into the cloakroom and make love to you tonight?"

She leaned back against him. He was already ready for her. "No, tell me." She smiled seductively.

"I'd rather show you."

He raised her one arm, taking her hand up around his neck, then he felt the zipper along the side of the dress. He pulled it down slowly, loosening the dress on her body. It fell loose, threatening to fall to the floor. He grabbed it tenderly, lowered it and she slowly, carefully stepped out, barely seeing him rest the dress on the chair beside them.

Now, with her standing there with just her lace panties and high heels, he moved her other hand up to his neck and cupped her breasts. She moaned and closed her eyes as his thumbs tweaked her nipples, causing them to harden. Then as one hand softly massaged her breasts, the other drifted down her stomach and traced the line of lace at her waist.

"You're driving me crazy, I'm gonna explode," she warned, then tried to turn to him, but he stopped her.

"No, Adia, not yet," he muttered. "I want to touch you."

She swallowed hard and opened her eyes as the blur of the living room became a dream. "Randolph, over there…now… bed," she muttered incoherently, and pointed to her small bedroom. His mouth came to her neck and shoulders and he kissed and nibbled freely. "Over there," she repeated, barely audible through the haze of desire.

His fingers dipped below the lace and her legs weakened and nearly gave way. He quickly held her secure to the front of his body. Her breathing was erratic as his fingers touched the soft hairs, then traveled lower. His other hand left her breasts and slid between their bodies. She gasped when both his hands connected in front and slowly traced the lace, inching it down.

"Randolph…" she muttered again. "Randolph…"

"I'm right here, Adia," he said sweetly. "Let me touch you."

"I…I…I…" She started to speak, but never finished. Between the hardness she felt behind her and the probing hands in front of her, her mind dizzily fantasized in the throes of rapturous pleasure. The torture was nearly unbearable, but she savored every second.

He slowed, then stopped, then gently turned her around to face him. His shirt was still on and his loosened tie still hung around his neck. She reached up and eagerly grabbed his tie and flung it across the room, then busied her hands removing his unbuttoned shirt. She unzipped his pants and freed him.

With them standing there face-to-face, she took his hand and led him toward her bedroom, then stopped. "I don't have any…" she began. He smiled and nodded, then picked up his jacket and pulled a single condom from the pocket. "Only one?" she questioned, remembering that they had used several the last time they were together.

"I guess we have to make this one last," he said, smiling at the possibilities.

She took the small square, opened it, then led him into her bedroom. She crawled onto the large bed, and he followed. She protected them as he removed the lace barrier, and then two seconds later, he was on top and inside her.

She gasped at the explosion of power throbbing and pulsating within her. The fullness, thick and deep, stroked and stimulated the tiny nip of her pleasure. He thrust into her, and she took all of him over and over again in a quickening pace that ravaged each other nonstop.

Thrusting with unimaginable intensity and unrestrained aggression, they delved into their primal hunger. Never missing a beat, she rolled on top of him and leaned over. He captured her breast and suckled. Her body nearly burst as they surged ever closer to the prize. He held her waist securely as she held on to his shoulders, biting her nails deep.

The pleasure crept up quickly as, seconds later, they both reached the pinnacle. He groaned long and forcefully as his body stiffened rigid and he poured into her. She gasped, trembling as the climactic tremors undulated through her body. She came again, screamed with the second unexpected orgasm. Seconds later, she twitched and jerked again. In spite of his stillness she experienced his presence.

The pleasure, immense beyond anything she'd ever experienced, continued as he began to move, his hips first, then his mouth captured her breast again and she started shaking, trembling, wanting more of him. He gave all he had, then reaching down between their bodies, touching her, he gave more.

Whimpering gasps escaped from her as his fingers gave and she took, her whole body ablaze with pleasure. She tried to rise, but Randolph held her firm to his body while tenderly massaging her rear. Using his hips, he rocked into her quicker, grinding into her again and again while holding her in place. She screamed loud this time as her climax came in a shocking release.

He started to repeat the action.

"No, no, please, I can't...can't breathe," she muttered, completely breathless, knowing that she was well past the level of tolerance.

He stopped immediately and just wrapped his arms around her and held her close. They lay still in perfect serenity. His strong arms were wrapped securely around her as she snuggled back against his hard body. Their lovemaking had reached yet another milestone.

"So what was that *we've run our course* thing all about?"

"I have no idea." She smiled wickedly, knowing that her evening was complete.

Chapter 13

The next few days passed with Randolph out of town. Alyssa took the opportunity to continue packing for the move. Every evening, she loaded the trunk and backseat of her car with boxes and drove to her grandmother's house in preparation. By the end of the week, she was covered with bruises and ached from muscle strains, not to mention being completely exhausted.

The one thing that always soothed her bumps and bruises was the nightly conversations with Randolph. After a hot shower, she climbed into bed and waited for the phone to ring. When it did, they talked for the next couple of hours, usually early into the morning. She'd be exhausted the following day, but it was more than worth it.

"I need a massive dose of caffeine injected directly into my veins," Nina said, yawning sleepily as she plopped into her chair and grabbed her coffee cup.

"Sounds as if you had another great time with Oliver last night," Alyssa said jokingly, looking up from her desk, knowing that Nina and Oliver had seen each other every night that week.

"The man's insane, I swear. He's like a wind-up puppy without an off button. I thought I had energy…but nothing like his… Do you know he actually had me running around the Washington Monument at eleven o'clock last night? I thought the Mall police were gonna arrest us."

"And you loved every minute of it, didn't you?"

"Yep, every single minute," she said, smiling happily. "You know, Alyssa, you could have come with us last night. We were only going to hang out."

"I know, and thanks again, but I'm glad I went home. I needed to take care of some things."

"Well, anytime you want to hang out, let me know."

"I will. But since I'm moving this weekend, I doubt I'll have much time to hang out."

"Okay, what time do you want me over to help? I can bring Oliver, too."

"Actually I don't have that much to do and my dad is gonna help me out, so don't worry about it. I got it covered."

"Are you sure? 'Cause I can—"

"I'm positive."

Nina's phone rang and she walked back to her desk to answer it. As she talked Alyssa thought about the freedom Nina had to tell everyone about her relationship with Oliver. It was something she knew she could never do. The understanding between her and Randolph was of her doing.

She insisted they keep this relationship secret, much to Randolph's vociferous objections. It's not that she had any other sort of shady past, but she knew that once word got out about them, life would never be the same.

So she came to an uneasy decision to keep a low profile.

Like having an affair with a married man, she decided to hide in the shadows of Randolph's life.

"Okay, so what's up?" Nina asked, standing at Alyssa's desk.

"What do you mean?"

"Oh, I don't know… Check it out. Look familiar?" Nina said, holding a copy of the *Post* out to her.

Alyssa took the paper, expecting to read another one of Nina's comics, but instead, she was shown clear photos, Senator Randolph Kingsley with an unidentified woman walking down the streets of Georgetown in one and them driving away in another.

Alyssa stared at the photo. Although her head was turned quite by accident in both pictures, it was definitely her and she was sure that Nina knew it. She looked up at her friend and winced.

"Yeah, I'd cringe, too, if I were you. Are you nuts?" she said, then began whispering, "If Pete sees this, he's gonna annihilate you and me both."

"It's not what you think, Nina. We were—" Alyssa began.

"Oh, please, it's exactly what I think and you know it, so don't even try to deny it. I can't believe you were going behind my back with this," Nina said, seemingly furious. "And even worse, you didn't tell me any of the juicy parts. Some friend you are." She smiled and placed her hip on the side of the desk and leaned in.

Alyssa leaned in, too, and smiled, nearly busting. "He is unbelievable," she whispered.

Several coworkers walked by and glanced at them with their heads together. Nina nodded and leaned back. "All right, that's what I'm talking about. I'm so happy for you."

"Alyssa, line three for you," a coworker called out.

Alyssa's phone rang, but she looked up at Nina still at her desk. "Maybe we should talk later."

"Most definitely," Nina said, going back to her desk.

"Good morning, this is Alyssa Wingate."

"Alyssa, this is Mamma Lou. How are you, dear?"

"Mrs. Gates, Mamma Lou, hi. Fine, how are you?"

"Can't complain, dear. I'm calling because I'm in town and I'd love to have lunch with you today if possible."

"Oh, I'm not sure I can. We're swamped over here and I was just going to send out and eat at my desk."

"Oh, that will never do. I'll have something brought in. What's the address there?"

Alyssa was still stumped at Mamma Lou saying that she'd have something brought in. What exactly did that mean?

"Alyssa, are you there?"

"Yes, I'm sorry," she said, then gave her the address.

"Good, that's settled. I'll see you at twelve-thirty. Good-bye, dear."

Louise hung up before Alyssa could question her. She had no idea what had just happened.

Pete came over to her desk. "Alyssa, I understand you have a lunch with Louise Gates this afternoon."

"No, I mean, yes. Wait, how do you know that?"

"Never mind about that," he said, waving. "I need you to see if she might consider taking a more active role with the foundation, particularly with us."

"With us?" she asked.

"Yes, I realize that she's already involved nationally. I just want to know if we can rely on her support locally. I realize she lives in Virginia, but if we can get her on board on some of these issues, we'd be able to make some real headway."

"Wait a minute, are we talking about the same woman?"

"Yes, of course."

"I don't think so. The Mrs. Louise Gates I know is my

grandmother's friend and I'm sure she doesn't have the kind of power and influence you think she does."

"Actually she does." Alyssa looked at him, still questioning. "See what you can do," he said, then turned to walk away, but stopped and turned back. "And don't forget to thank her again for the two tables."

"Two tables, right." She nodded and watched as he hurried back to his office at his usual top speed. The conversation made absolutely no sense. There was no way they were talking about the same woman. She shook her head and went back to work.

At a quarter after twelve the office received a massive delivery. It looked as if someone had raided an Italian restaurant. Foil-covered trays topped with fresh meats, breads, salads and pastas started filling the conference-room table. The staff, totally awestruck, piled in and began opening and filling plates. It was unbelievable.

A few minutes later, Louise Gates arrived.

"Hello, anyone here?" she called out to the now seemingly empty office. Ursula, sitting at her desk, eating pasta and salad, greeted her.

"Mrs. Gates, it's an honor to finally meet you," Pete said, obviously impressed.

"You must be Pete Lambert. How are you? I've heard some wonderful things about your organization here. I'm very impressed."

"Thank you, and thank you for this wonderful buffet."

"My pleasure. Now, is Alyssa here?"

"Hi, Mamma Lou," Alyssa said, walking over.

"Hello, dear, are you ready for lunch?"

"Sure," she said, pushing her purse onto her shoulder. "Do you have any particular place in mind, Mamma Lou?"

"As a matter of fact, I do. There's a quaint little family-owned restaurant not too far from here. I hear the food is wonderful and the owners are quite interesting. I believe the family just won the lotto a few months back. Isn't that a wonderful story?"

"The American dream," Alyssa mused. "Unfortunately most dreams don't actually come true."

"Ah, but some do. You just have to have a bit of faith."

Alyssa drove and moments later, they were seated in the small restaurant, eating lunch. They mainly talked about Alyssa's work at the foundation and Louise's many philanthropic ventures. The conversation finally got around to a more personal subject.

"I presume that was you in the photo with Senator Randolph Kingsley in this morning's newspaper," Louise said, smiling.

"How did you know it was me?" she asked, obviously caught off guard by the statement.

"You'd be surprised at the things that come my way."

"Yes, it was me."

Louise smiled happily. "I'm delighted. Randolph is a wonderful man and you, my dear, are as sweet as can be."

"Yes, he is, and I really like being with him. But I don't think my grandmother would quite agree with the relationship."

"Because he's a politician?" Louise asked.

"Yes, exactly. Plus the obvious similarities between Randolph and her friend from years ago are too apparent."

"Randolph is single and unattached. Unlike Vincent Dupree, who was a very married man."

"You remember everything that happened, right?" Louise nodded. "Could you tell me? I mean, I've read all about it in the newspaper archives, but you were actually there. I tried asking my dad or grandma, but they never wanted to talk about it. All I can gather from her is that she was accused of having an affair and publicly humiliated."

"First of all, there was never any proof, know that. As far as the newspapers and public opinion go, they could only speculate."

"Mamma Lou, you don't have to sugarcoat it for me. I'm a big girl, I know it happened. When Grandma is having an episode, she talks about the senator as if he's right there with her. I remember Grandpa and she never talks about him like that. She really loved this senator, didn't she?"

"In her way, yes. I believe she did."

"But he didn't love her back, did he?"

"It was complicated. His family and his career were very important to him. It was a different time. The sixties were extremely turbulent—the war, civil rights, the deaths of King, Kennedy and Malcolm X—there were so many things happening all at once. We were no longer the innocent kids on the block. We had to open our eyes and take responsibility for our actions. Vincent and Allie got caught up in all that."

"And all that was to say that there was no way they were gonna be together, right? And he knew it. So why did he use her like that?"

"I can't answer that."

Alyssa nodded her understanding.

"When did Allie start showing signs of Alzheimer's disease?" Louise asked after a few minutes.

"A few years ago, I think. I can't really pinpoint when exactly. She started forgetting things, easy things, like turning appliances off and losing stuff. I was still a registered nurse at the hospital at the time."

"And you stopped to work at the foundation?"

"Yes, I loved being a nurse, but working to help change public policy is very exciting. Unfortunately it's not as simple and straightforward as I thought it would be. There are so many twists and turns. I sometimes wonder how anything ever gets done in this city."

"But things do happen and laws are made that really help people. Washington is a remarkable city, vibrant and exciting. I enjoy the energy here."

"But you don't live here, right?"

"No, I live on Crescent Island in Virginia."

"Crescent Island. Where is that exactly?"

"It's a picturesque paradise about twenty-five miles off the Virginia coast, and it's absolutely beautiful this time of year. It's not called *God's Garden* for nothing. It's paradise with a rich history and beautiful scenery."

"Wow, it sounds absolutely incredible."

"It is, and I'd like you to consider coming to visit me. I have more than enough room and it might do Allie good to get out of the city awhile, and I'm sure you could use vacation from work."

"Thank you, I'll definitely see about arranging that, even if it's just for a long weekend. But speaking of vacations from work—" she glanced at her watch "—I'd better get back there or I won't have a job to go back to."

"I wouldn't worry about that, dear."

The check was paid and they walked outside into the warm sunshine. "Where can I drop you, Mamma Lou?"

"Oh, don't worry about me, my ride will be here in a minute."

"Are you sure?"

"Yes. As a matter of fact, here he comes now," she said as a large dark town car parked across the street at the traffic light.

"One more thing, Mamma Lou. You paid for the tables at the foundation fund-raiser Monday night, right?" Alyssa asked. Louise nodded. "Then you knew Randolph was going to attend, right?" She nodded again. "Is that why you invited my office, so that he and I would meet there?"

"But the two of you had already met," Louise said.

"Are you playing matchmaker like Grandma said?"

The car pulled up and a driver got out and opened the door for her. "Goodbye, dear. I had a wonderful time. We must do this again."

"'Bye, Mamma Lou," Alyssa said, realizing that she wasn't going to get an answer one way or the other. She waved as the town car drove off, then got in her car and went back to work.

With the weeklong conference finally over, Kent walked back into the meeting room just as the last presentation was over. He took a seat in the last row as the final acknowledgments were being given. Nodding agreeably as some passed and glanced at him, he watched as large groups of attendees began filing out, all eagerly discussing the two-day program, excited to put their newfound knowledge to good use.

Kent looked around, quickly spotting Randolph standing in front surrounded and talking to several attendees. As usual, he waited patiently in the back for the last few people to file out. Several men walked over and joined the small group, all listening intently to what Randolph was saying.

Kent smiled and shook his head. His friend and employer was the most promising political figure in years. When he spoke, others listened. His record was impeccable and he was known for his honesty and openness. When he made a promise, he stuck to it, and one way or the other, he would find a way to enrich someone else's life.

Kent knew that recently Randolph had been distracted. His solitary lifestyle was beginning to take a toll. He unintentionally cut himself off from exactly what he needed.

Kent opened his leather binder and looked at the news clipping one more time. He smiled. The clipping was news to him and he prided himself on knowing everything there was to know. He knew his boss well, but apparently not well enough. The photo was clear and the woman by his side was definitely with him. He held her hand securely, but unfortunately her identity in both photos was obscured.

He looked up, seeing that small group beginning to disband, then called for the driver to have the car waiting out front. He'd already made arrangements to go directly to the airport, then back to Washington that evening. The only concern was the weather.

The forecast called for heavy rains, high winds and the possibility of scattered hail. There was also a tornado warning in effect. With all that, he knew that there was a real possibility that the flight might be canceled. He only hoped that it wouldn't be.

Kent glanced over at Randolph again, then nodded, indicating that all had been arranged. He discreetly held up his open palm, signifying that they had about five minutes. He refocused on the folder in front of him. After one last look at the clipping, he flipped it over and started reading a report he'd been working on all week.

The last four days were completely exhausting for Randolph. He and Kent had left early Wednesday morning and hadn't stopped since. The first two days were both physically and mentally torturous in and of themselves. In a burst of political energy, Randolph had crisscrossed two states, five cities and a countless number of counties and townships campaigning and supporting fellow politicians. He shook hands, talked, joked and attended rallies. He made speeches, introduced candidates and generally lent his face and name to candidates he believed in.

It was an election year and a lot of very important seats were up for grabs. Two were of congressmen whom he respected and admired a great deal. Three others held great promise and he wanted to add his voice to their campaigns.

Afterward, Randolph had attended a two-day conference on health-care reform for senior citizens. There were presentations, speakers from all over the globe and a number of very prominent health-care-reform advocates.

Inundated with medical research and scientific studies, the proposal offered interesting possibilities that he considered developing for a broader audience.

When the conference was over, he had the opportunity to speak at length with several medical experts about the latest developments in the treatment of Alzheimer's disease. They offered little hope, but were extremely helpful in directing him to other specialists in the field of degenerate mental conditions.

While he was busy to the point of exhaustion, the one thing that kept him going was his nightly conversations with Alyssa. Even now, he smiled just thinking about them. He usually called her late when she was already in bed and they talked about everything under the sun until early the next morning.

When they hung up each time, he realized that he missed her all over again. Now the knowledge that he would see her in a few hours was all he needed to prompt his hasty exit.

"Hey, we all set?" Randolph asked standing over Kent.

"Yeah, just finalizing transportation," he said, as he received a text message that the driver was already out front and waiting. Already checked out of the hotel and their bags stored with the bellmen, they headed straight to the lobby.

Randolph stopped several times to shake hands and talk briefly, adding a few minutes to their departure. Kent got their luggage and the driver put it in the trunk. By then, Randolph had gotten into the car and they were on their way to the airport.

The weather was horrible and traffic was disastrous.

Kent opened his folder and handed him the clipping.

Randolph looked at it and smiled, half chuckling. "I'm surprised it took so long to get into the papers. This was more than a week ago. My popularity must be slipping."

"I doubt that. Looks like it was a telephoto-lens photo, nicely detailed. I'm surprised it looks so good." Kent smiled. "Did you need a report done?"

Randolph smiled at him. "You already did."

"Ms. Alyssa Wingate, I presume," Kent said quietly, well aware of the driver in front. Randolph nodded. "Good, I like her."

"So do I," Randolph said.

"I gathered that," he said. "Okay, next order of business…"

They talked briefly about several reports and decided to forgo the next medical conference, since it would most probably interfere with an important vote on the Hill. Both men took important phone calls, then concluded by discussing last-minute travel plans.

"What's this weekend look like?" Randolph asked.

Kent opened his small PDA and scanned through. "Just family and friend obligations. You have dinner with the Evanses Sunday evening and brunch with Senator Andre Hart Sunday morning after church. A card game switched to Trey Evans's house tomorrow evening and a two o'clock lunch with your sister. I've already confirmed them. This evening and tomorrow morning, you're free. Our flight leaves at seven o'clock tonight. James will pick us up at National."

Randolph looked at his watch. It was already five-thirty. When they arrived in D.C. with the hour time difference, it would still be relatively early. If he planned it right, he might get to see Alyssa this evening.

The car arrived at the airport and Kent glanced at his watch. "We'd better hurry."

The two men walked purposefully through the airport, breezed through security checkpoints and arrived just in time to see that their flight had been canceled because of severe weather, high winds and tornado warnings.

So much for his evening plans. He opened his cell phone and made two calls, one to Alyssa and one to his sister. While Randolph was talking to his sister, Kent walked up to him looking very stoic.

"Excuse me, Senator, you need to take this call," Kent said, handing him the phone.

Randolph took the phone.

Chapter 14

"I hate moving," Alyssa moaned as her father looked around at the last few boxes in the living room.

"Eighty percent of it is already done," he said.

"I've been taking boxes over to Grandma's house all week long. I didn't want to keep you all day moving me. I know you have to get back to work this afternoon."

"Don't worry about that. What we need to figure out is how you and I are gonna move this sofa into the freight elevator and load it onto the truck. It looks like it weighs about eight hundred pounds."

"I don't need it, but I can't leave it here, so I have to donate it. I tried to get them to pick it up, but apparently they don't do that anymore. We have to take it to them."

"Yeah, yeah, that still doesn't get this thing out of here." He walked over and picked up one end to test the weight. "Yep, it's eight hundred pounds, all right," he said, exaggerating.

"Hello, anybody here call for room service?" Nina said, standing in the open doorway, smiling with Oliver right behind her, also smiling while looking over her shoulder.

Benjamin and Alyssa turned. "Just in time," Benjamin said, turning his cap around backward.

"Good morning, all," Oliver said in his usual jolly tone. "Need a hand with that, Mr. Wingate?" He scooted past Nina and headed over to the sofa.

"We drove Oliver's flatbed pickup truck just in case you need more room," Nina said. "The thing is massive, I swear. We could get a ton of boxes on it."

"Dad, this is Nina, my girlfriend from work, and you remember Oliver, Mrs. Watts's son."

"Good to meet you, Nina," he said, nodding and smiling, then turned to Oliver. "This is Oliver? Skinny little Oliver from next door to your grandmother's house? The one you used to babysit?" Benjamin asked.

"One and the same, although not so little and skinny anymore, Mr. Wingate," Oliver said happily, raising his arms and flexing his muscles, then continued to turn and pose while flexing again. Alyssa and Nina laughed. Benjamin shook his head.

"Yep, that's the same Oliver, all right," Benjamin said.

"What do you mean?" Nina asked curiously.

"Never mind that," Oliver said quickly before Benjamin could respond. "Let's get this show on the road. Where do you need me?"

Benjamin laughed. "Good point. Why don't we put all the donated furniture on the moving truck and the rest of the boxes on the flatbed. That way we can make one stop at the drop-off on the way to Allie's place."

"Sounds good," Alyssa said, picking up a box. Nina picked one up, too. "We'll take these boxes down to the truck."

"Is this the only thing to get donated?" Oliver asked.

"No, come on, I'll show you the rest," Benjamin said, taking Oliver through to the rest of the apartment.

Alyssa and Nina went downstairs and put the boxes on the back of Oliver's flatbed. They stood awhile and talked. "You and Oliver are great together," Alyssa said.

"Yeah, I really like him, he's so different, a total nutcase. He always has me in stitches laughing my head off, I swear."

"He is funny, always was."

"So, what's going on with you?" Nina asked.

"I'm moving, duh," Alyssa joked, knowing exactly what Nina meant.

"Yeah, I got that part. You know what I mean."

She smiled. "Everything's good. Randolph was supposed to get back last night, but his flight was grounded by weather so he's coming back this morning. He wants to get together for lunch later this afternoon. He has a surprise for me."

"A surprise, nice," Nina said, smiling from ear to ear.

"Why are you smiling like that? You don't even know what it is."

"Who cares, you know how I love surprises. But wait a minute, back up. You're meeting him later this afternoon?"

"Yes, around two o'clock at the restaurant, why?" she said.

"Because it's almost eight o'clock already. We'd better hurry up. We still have to pack the rest of the truck, get the donated furniture to the drop-off, then take the rest of the boxes to your grandmother's place."

"We have plenty of time. The apartment is just about empty. The only things left are my clothes, shoes and computer."

"That's it?" Nina asked.

"Yep, I've been packing and moving all week long."

"So that's why you were so tired all week. Why didn't you tell me? I would have come over and helped."

"Girl, you were having too much fun with Oliver. Besides, I had everything under control."

"So, what does Randolph think about your moving back into your grandmother's house?"

Alyssa grimaced. "Actually I haven't told him yet."

"You haven't told him. Why not?"

"Because," she answered slowly, "I'm not exactly ready for the two of them to meet just yet."

"Are you kidding me? Your grandmother is gonna be ecstatic that you're seeing a U.S. senator. Hell, who wouldn't be impressed?"

"She wouldn't be, believe me. She'll be furious for starters. After that, she'll really get angry."

"What? Why?"

"Uh-huh, see, I told you they were down here talking and lollygagging, while we were upstairs doing all the work. Sorry, Mr. Wingate, you owe me a beer."

"Yep, you were right," Benjamin said, "I sure do."

"We were not just down here talking and lollygagging. And who says *lollygagging* anymore, anyway?"

"I do," Oliver said, readjusting the sofa they carried down and easing it into the moving van.

Nina shook her head as the two of them began a comedic routine that sounded as if it should have been onstage at the Apollo in New York.

Alyssa and Benjamin laughed and enjoyed their antics as the four of them continued loading the truck. An hour later, the apartment was empty and everything was loaded and ready to go. Oliver followed the moving van to the drop-off. They emptied the donated furniture, then continued to Allie's house. By eleven-thirty, the truck and moving van were unloaded and everything was in the house.

Allie fixed sandwiches, cookies and lemonade while doing

her best to tolerate Benjamin. The tension was there, but since Benjamin ignored her, she didn't have a lot to complain about. Oliver was on his best behavior, since his mother had specifically called over and asked him to bring Nina over to meet her.

After everything was done, Nina and Oliver stopped next door and Benjamin helped Alyssa rearrange her bedroom. He helped her hang up her clothes and put away her shoes, then took care of removing the empty boxes. They carried out the flattened boxes and paused to stand by the truck a minute.

"Thanks, Dad, I really appreciate everything. You were wonderful today," Alyssa said.

"You're very welcome, sweetheart. Now, are you sure you want to do this?" he asked, looking up at the front of the house as if it were haunted or something.

"Dad, we just moved everything in."

"And I can just as easily move everything out again."

"Dad, I gave up my apartment."

"You can come stay with me."

"I'll be fine here with Grandma. Really, I promise."

"Are you sure?" he asked, still not completely sure.

"Positive. This'll be good for both of us."

He nodded. "Okay, now you can tell me. What's all this about you being in the newspaper with a U.S. senator?"

"Huh?" she said, stunned that he knew it was her.

"*Huh* isn't an answer," he said sternly. "Did you think I wouldn't know my own daughter when I saw her? Just because your face was turned, I still know you. So what's all that about?"

"It was just someone with a camera phone. They took the picture that day I went to Georgetown."

"To meet your girlfriend?" he questioned.

"Actually she had to leave early."

"So then it was just the two of you." She nodded. "And you're dating now or what?"

"More like the latter, the *or what* part," she said.

"Do I need to ask his intentions?"

"No, of course not," she said quickly. "It's nothing, really. We just see each other from time to time."

"Time to time. Last I heard, that's called dating."

"We're acquaintances."

"What does that mean? Is he using you?"

"No, no, of course not. Nothing like that, Dad, I promise. We're just good friends hanging out and having a good time. No big deal, really. It's nothing superserious. We talk a lot," she said, knowing she was lying when she said it.

"You look pretty serious in that photograph to me," he said, seeing it in her eyes even now.

"Dad, I have no intention of getting hurt."

"Sweetheart, no one has any intention of getting hurt or of hurting someone else, but it still happens."

"I'm a big girl, Dad, I know when to back off."

He nodded and looked back up at the house. "Does Allie know yet?"

"No, I think it's best if she doesn't know right now."

"Probably not a good idea. You might want to tell her just in case the next picture is a lot clearer."

"I don't want to upset her, and there's really nothing to tell. We're just friends."

"Friendship between a man and a woman has a way of developing into something entirely different. Sometimes you don't even see it coming," he said.

"Friends," she reiterated.

"Just be careful, he's not exactly the guy next door. He's a senator. That means power and publicity. Don't go diving in the deep end before you've tested the water. I don't want to have to go to Capitol Hill and call him out."

She smiled at his occasional parental advice. "Yes, Dad. I'll be careful, I promise."

"See that you are," he said as she nodded, agreeing with him. "Now, one last time, are you sure—"

"Dad, stop it. Yes, I'm sure. Go, goodbye. Thanks again. I'll stop by in a few days," she said, then kissed his cheek. She stepped back on the curb and watched as her father pulled off. Turning to go up the front steps, she wondered exactly what her grandmother would say about Randolph. After all, what had happened to Allie was totally different. Her senator was married, and Randolph wasn't. The two situations were totally different. But Alyssa knew that it didn't matter. Her grandmother would still have a fit.

After her father turned the corner, out of sight, Alyssa walked back into the house and excitedly headed up to her bedroom to get ready. This was going to be her first actual date with Randolph and she wanted to look fantastic. Midway up, she stopped.

"So, what are we going to do this afternoon?" Allie asked as soon as she walked out of the kitchen.

Alyssa came back downstairs. "Umm, Grandma, I have this lunch thing to do this afternoon, but after that, we can do whatever you want."

"Sure, that sounds fine. Is this lunch thing a date?"

"Yes, kind of," she said cryptically.

"Is he good enough for you?"

"Yes, Grandma, he's incredible and he makes me very happy. I love being with him."

"Oh, my, looks like you didn't need Louise's help after all. But knowing her, she would have brought you a politician anyway just to spite me. I love her dearly, but she can be so difficult at times, always wanting her own way. So, when am I going to meet this Prince Charming of yours?"

"Soon, he's really busy at work right now."

"What does he do?"

"He owns a wine business out West."

"Ooh, that sounds lovely. I'll look forward to meeting him real soon, I hope," she said pointedly. "In the meantime, I'll make us a nice supper for your first night here."

"I have a better idea, why don't I take you out to dinner tonight? You know, to kind of celebrate my being here."

"You know what, that sounds like a bet. Let's do it."

"Great. I'll go to my lunch thing, then come back and we'll have dinner at your favorite restaurant." She looked at her watch. "And I'd better get ready or I'll be late."

"Okay, better hurry up. I don't want you to be late. I have a feeling this might be my future grandson-in-law."

Getting dressed took longer than Alyssa had expected. The shower was too cold. She couldn't find the outfit she wanted to wear and she never did find her curling iron. But even after all that, she decided that she looked great. Maybe it was that she was back home or maybe it was the fact that she was meeting Randolph; whatever it was, she felt great and was on her way.

After a short drive, she walked up to the restaurant and a feeling of wonder flowed through her. The marquee was subtle, but everyone knew exactly what it was. This was *the* restaurant in Washington, D.C., The Capital Grille. Popular with the power elite in Washington, it catered to the influential, the affluent and the politically connected. The address was impressive, located right on Pennsylvania Avenue, just steps away from the Capitol Building.

Greeted by the lions guarding the entrance, Alyssa walked inside and looked around. There was already a small gathering in front of her, so she stood beside the miniature encasements of private stock and waited her turn.

Peeking into the dining room, she saw it was nothing like she had expected. Rich mahogany wood, white linen tableclothes, starched and pressed, candles, stately pictures and, of all things, buck's and ram's heads mounted on the wall.

Waiters and busboys and wine stewards all hustled at top speed, performing an intricate ballet of precision service. Dashing from kitchen to wine cellar to table, then back again, they looked perfectly choreographed.

Not seeing Randolph, she moved to the side just beyond the bar and paused, sitting in one of the comfortable cushioned chairs looking out onto Pennsylvania Avenue. A steady flow of pedestrians kept her attention for a while, but still, her heart thundered at the thought of seeing Randolph again.

She looked at her watch, noting that she was now exactly on time, but Randolph was nowhere in sight. She stood and walked back to the lobby area and waited a few more minutes, then returned and sat down again. Time passed and suddenly the fear of being stood up seemed very real.

"Excuse me." Alyssa turned to see a nicely dressed woman standing over her. "Are you waiting for someone?"

"Yes," Alyssa said, then turned away and continued looking out the large front window.

"Have you been here before?"

Alyssa turned again. "No."

"Have you been waiting long?"

"No, not long," she answered, looking at her strangely, then at her watch.

"I'm Juliet Bridges, uh, sorry, Juliet Evans," the woman said, putting her hand out to shake.

"Hi," Alyssa said, not understanding why a perfect stranger would come up and introduce herself to her. When the woman continued to stand there smiling, Alyssa looked at her even more strangely. "May I help you?"

"Yes, I hope so. Are you Alyssa Wingate?"

"Yes, I am."

"I'm Juliet Evans, Randolph's sister."

Alyssa's heart jumped. Having lunch with Randolph out in public was one thing, but meeting the family was too real. "Oh, I'm sorry, I didn't know he was meeting you, I thought—"

"He's meeting us both, but unfortunately something came up and he's running late, so why don't we grab a table and wait for him there?"

"Sure, sounds great," Alyssa said, smiling happily. She had no idea why. She didn't usually act so scatterbrained and giddy, but then again she'd had no idea that she was going to meet Randolph's sister.

They walked toward the maître d's, then were escorted to a table in the dining room. "This is really nice," Alyssa said. "I've never been here before."

"That's right. You're gonna love it. The food is wonderful and they wait on you as if you're royalty. This is one of our favorite restaurants. Randolph and I used to come here all the time when I was still dancing."

"Oh, right, Randolph told me that you were a prima ballerina. I'm sorry I never got a chance to see you perform. Do you miss it?"

"Yes, every now and then, but being an instructor is an amazing job. Seeing the faces of the students makes everything worthwhile. It feels like I've come full circle."

"It must be amazing."

"It is. Now, tell me about you. What little I could get out

of my brother was that you two recently met at a fund-raiser and really hit it off."

Alyssa nodded. "Yeah, something like that. He's an incredible man."

"I have to agree with you there."

"I think he told me that you just got married and that you're having a baby."

"I am," she said, glancing down at her small bump. "I'm in my second trimester, so I'm still getting used to all this."

"Do you know what you're having?"

She nodded. "I had an ultrasound last week. My husband didn't want to know, but I couldn't wait to find out. But I promised I wouldn't tell."

"As long as the baby is healthy, that's all that matters, right?" Alyssa said.

"Exactly," Juliet agreed, then glanced around. "Okay, I think we've given him plenty of time to get here. I'm starved, so let's say we order and let him catch up."

"Sounds great."

They ordered, talked, ate, talked and then talked some more. It wasn't until they were sitting at the table laughing about the strange coincidence of both of them knowing Mamma Lou that Randolph finally showed up. He kissed Juliet on the cheek, then kissed Alyssa on the mouth. Juliet smiled, humored by her brother's public display.

Completely out of character for him, she knew when he first told her about Alyssa that she was someone special to him. He'd never gone out of his way to introduce any of the other women in his life to her before.

"We've already eaten," Juliet said.

"Like I didn't know you'd start without me," Randolph joked. "How's mother and baby?"

"We're both just fine."

"Excellent, any hints you want to share?" he asked.

"No, and you're not supposed to ask, remember? You'll have to wait and see just like everyone else."

"Hints?" Alyssa asked curiously.

"It's a long, crazy story, but the gist is that the family's betting on the date of arrival."

"Betting, really?"

"Oh, yes, when my sister-in-law, Madison, had her twins my husband won the pot."

"That's funny," Alyssa said.

"Oh, but that's only the beginning. You'll see."

Randolph looked at Alyssa and smiled.

Since he'd already grabbed something to eat, he walked Juliet to her car and said goodbye, then walked Alyssa to her car. They stood there awhile talking, both glad that he was back in town.

"What are your plans for this evening?" he asked.

"I'm taking my grandmother out to dinner."

"Your grandmother, Allie Granger, I can't wait to meet her. She sounds like a great lady."

"She is," Alyssa said, hoping to postpone or possibly avoid their meeting as long as possible. "So, what about you, any plans tonight?"

"I have a poker game with the fellows tonight."

"The fellows?"

"My brother-in-law and the rest of the family."

"Sounds like fun."

"I'll let you know."

"So I guess this is it. I'll see you later," she said.

"When later exactly?"

"I don't know."

"How about joining me at a small dinner party tomorrow?"

"Family, friends or colleagues?" she asked.

"Family and friends. Juliet will be there."

"She's wonderful. We had a great time."

"I figured you would. She likes you, too."

"Really? And how do you know that?"

"It's a brother thing. So, tomorrow night, dinner?"

"I'll let you know, okay?" she said evasively.

He nodded, knowing that was all he would get at the moment. And since they were still standing on the street, he didn't press her for a definite answer.

They said goodbye, and he headed back to his office.

He caught up on some work for the next two hours, then went home, changed and drove back into the city.

The poker game was at Trey's house in Woodley Park.

He heard the rowdy group before he even rang the doorbell. When the door opened, J. T. Evans, his brother-in-law, shook his head sadly. "My brotha, you might want to turn around and leave while you still can. Trey has been philosophizing all night."

"Excellent, I could use a bit of comic relief."

They chuckled and hugged as he walked in and greeted the rest of the players. Tony Gates and his cousin Raymond Gates, Dennis Hayes and Juwan Mason were already there. J.T. handed him a drink as they all took seats at the poker table already set up in the center of the huge living room.

The entire house was designed for a bachelor—rich dark paneled wood, large-cushioned sofas, sleek electronics and of course, a fully stocked bar. A massive flat-screen television hung on the main wall and was turned to a sports channel with the picture-in-picture split screen tuned to two other sports channels. A humidor filled with cigars sat on the coffee table. An enormous buffet of spicy Buffalo wings, smoked meats, fruit and sandwiches was laid out on the side table and a tub filled with bottled beers, sodas and spring water covered with ice sat on either end.

Several brand-new decks of cards were already unpacked and being electronically shuffled and color-coded chips were already stacked at each setting. And of course, Trey started the whole thing as usual.

"So, where is our host?" Randolph asked after greeting everyone.

"An important phone call," J.T. said. "Business, of course."

"As usual," the rest chimed in unison.

"There he is," Trey said as soon as he entered the room and saw Randolph. "Finally a little backup from a true believer."

Randolph shook his head, already seeing where this was going.

"Told you to leave while you had a chance," J.T. said.

"No, no, no, don't go influencing him with that. J.T., Randolph and I are the only ones here with common sense enough to avoid the plague."

"The plague?" Randolph asked, looking at Raymond. Raymond just chuckled and shook his head.

"Yes, the plague," Trey reiterated as a round of moans and boos interrupted his tirade. "Okay, now, if you'd just listen to what I was saying, it's very simple, but only a few of you will really understand 'cause the rest of you are already a lost cause." There was another loud uproar as everyone started booing Trey.

"And what exactly is this evening's topic?" Randolph asked.

"What else?" Dennis said.

"Mamma Lou," they said in unison again.

"Same as it always is, women—" Juwan started.

"Romance, love—" Dennis added.

"Marriage—" Raymond continued.

"And of course, Mamma Lou," Tony ended.

"Okay, okay, now wait a minute, keep an open mind and hear me out. Here's my latest theory." There was another round of groans and moans. But Trey, forever calm and collected, cleared his throat and continued. "The plague is upon us, my brothers. Spread by tender bodies, sexy lips, long, luscious legs and seductively innocent smiles. Now, a number of you are already lost. Consider yourselves extremely blessed to have found the good women you have. But not everyone will find what you have. The rest of us, specifically Randolph and myself, will hold up the honor of bachelorhood because we all know that only lunatics get committed to marriage and this is why."

The groans and moans got even louder.

Chapter 15

"Hi, perfect, you're right on time," Alyssa said, hurrying down the front steps just as Randolph got out of the car.

"Hi," Randolph said, looking at her, slightly puzzled as he walked around to open the door for her. "Is this your grandmother's house?"

"Yes."

"I was curious about the different address you gave me when I called. Are you visiting for the day?"

"No, actually I moved in with her."

"When did all that happen?" he asked, then closed the door and went back around to the driver's side. "When did you move in?" he repeated as he sat behind the wheel and started the car.

"Umm, Saturday morning and all last week."

"I see," he said, pulling away from the curb.

"She needs me right now and I need to keep an eye on her and her Alzheimer's to make sure she's safe. The disease is so unpredictable. There's no way of telling when it's going to come on."

"Okay, speaking of which, when do I get to meet this remarkable woman? I expected to meet her this evening," he said.

"Soon. She was napping when I left," Alyssa said, happy that her secret was still safe. She wasn't entirely sure how long she could avoid the two of them meeting, but she was definitely going to do her best to make it as long as possible.

"I hope so. I'm looking forward to meeting her, and your dad, as well," he said, steering onto an access ramp leading to northern Virginia. "What's he like?"

"My dad, he's great. He knows everything there is to know about beer and wine and I'm seriously not just bragging. His name is Benjamin Wingate and he owns Wingate Lounge in D.C. It's one of the few bars that still has its own distillery on the premises. He even knows how to run it."

"A distillery, cool. And he still operates it, that's very interesting," he said.

"Yeah. Of course, he doesn't actually make his own alcohol or beer, but my grandfather did when he had it years ago."

"Your grandfather owned it first?"

"Actually, my great-grandfather owned it first, back in 1933. It was right after Prohibition was over. Apparently everybody and their brother was opening a bar or lounge or pub when the laws changed. Few of them survived, obviously, but Wingate was one of them."

"It's been in the family for over seventy-five years?"

"That's right," she said proudly, "through riots and wars and storms and everything else, it's been there."

"And what about you? You ready to be a barkeep?"

"Actually I work there on the weekends sometimes when my dad needs help. I started when I was in college. The tips helped pay for my books."

"Really? I've always thought that there was something particularly sexy about a woman behind a bar."

"Uh-huh, is that right?"

"Oh, most definitely," he assured her. She smiled and shook her head. "So that means that someday you'll be taking over for your dad, right?"

"I don't think so. As a matter of fact, my dad's talking about retiring soon and moving to a warmer climate. He said that he's tired of the business and he's ready for something new and different."

"I can see that," Randolph said.

"So, tell me about the wine business. What's it like to own a winery in San Francisco?"

"Not as glamorous as you might think."

"What's the day-to-day like?"

Randolph started talking and Alyssa listened and asked questions. The conversation continued until they pulled off the beltway, at McLean. They continued onto the main road, then turned down a few side streets and traveled a few more miles until they drove down a long private driveway.

They pulled up in front, then drove around the circular brick driveway already crowded with stylish late-model cars. "Wow, look at all these cars, it's like a private showroom or something. Dinner with just family and friends, huh?" she confirmed as the car came to a stop.

"Precisely," Randolph answered, parking between a gray Saab and a dark green Lexus.

She nodded, looking around anxiously. "Nonbusiness, nonpolitical associates, no newspapers or photographers, right?"

"Not a politician or photographer in the bunch, I promise you," he assured her, then reached over and took her hand, bringing it to his lips and kissing her. She nodded weakly.

He could feel the tension in her stiffness. "Come on, relax. It'll be fun and you'll be fine. Trust me, remember, just family and friends."

"So, what exactly did you tell them about me?"

"I said that I would be bringing a guest, a friend, a very close friend."

"And they'll be discreet?"

"They're like family to me. Believe me, they're not likely to take out a full-page ad in the newspaper. Why?"

"I just don't want this getting around."

"This?" he asked.

"This, us…hanging out, you know."

"Why not? We're not doing anything wrong. We like each other and enjoy being together. That's nobody's business but ours, and if by chance, others know, so be it."

"It's not that easy. I mean, for you. You have a reputation—" she began.

"I also have a life and I want you to be part of it."

"I'm just not ready to be publicly outed yet. Can you understand that?"

He paused, seeing the angst in her expression. "Okay, as you like. We'll be discreet."

She nodded again as Randolph got out and walked around to her side of the car. She tried to relax, but her nerves were just too jittery. Meeting Randolph's sister was one thing. Now meeting others in his life was definitely another. Suddenly she wondered how many women had been in her very same position.

The door opened. He took her hand and she followed him down the brick-lined lane to the front door. He rang once. And a few seconds later, the door opened and the evening began.

Dinner at the Evans family home in McLean, Virginia, was beyond memorable. What started off looking like complete chaos turned out to be a very elegant sit-down dinner for sixteen in a home that could only be described as utterly breath-taking. By the end of the evening, Alyssa felt like a princess at Prince Charming's ball.

First they were immediately welcomed at the front door by Jace and Taylor Evans, who were the perfect hosts. They made her feel instantly welcome. Taylor introduced Alyssa to Madison, Tony's wife, who did the honors of introducing her to everyone else. Dispersed through the first floor and out on the veranda, everyone was cordial and amiable, greeting her with open arms.

J.T., Kennedy, Juwan, Raymond and Hope were in the living room discussing art therapy. They paused to welcome her and to chat a few moments. Randolph told them how they met and the conversation turned to great first meetings as everyone talked about theirs. Then as the discussion turned again, Randolph and Madison stayed to add their two cents as J.T. got up and continued with Alyssa.

"Hi, Gorgeous, miss me?"

Just exiting the living room, Alyssa looked up at a large blue and gold bird in a huge elaborately adorned, gilded cage standing in the corner beside the floor-to-ceiling windows.

"And this is Gorgeous," J.T. said, making another introduction.

"Oh, my goodness, he's beautiful. What kind of bird is he?" The large bird flew down to the nearest wooden post and sidestepped to get closer.

"He's a South-American macaw and he's outrageously spoiled, so don't let him fool you."

"May I?" she asked, before moving closer.

"Sure," J.T. said.

"Hi, Gorgeous, miss me?" the bird repeated, nuzzling closer to the edge.

"Hello, Gorgeous," Alyssa said, smiling, then sticking her

finger in and stroking the shocking neon-blue and gold feathers. The bird dipped his head repeatedly, encouraging her to continue. She did happily.

"A word of warning, if we don't walk away now, he'll have you doing that the rest of the evening. As I said, he's really spoiled thanks to Keni and Madi."

"I heard that," both Kennedy and Madison said in unison as J.T. chuckled and continued to the dining room where Juliet and Tony were setting the huge dining-room table. J.T. made introductions. Having already met Juliet, they hugged and talked about their lunch at the Capital Grille. J.T. and Tony joined the conversation, then escorted Alyssa out onto the veranda where Jace and Colonel Wheeler stood at the grill cooking and Mamma Lou sat talking to Randolph.

"Hey, there you are," Randolph said, standing.

"Hi, you're out here now?"

"Yeah," Randolph said, walking over and kissing her briefly. "That living-room discussion was getting too deep for me. Chatting with Mamma Lou is more my style." He watched J.T. walk over to the grill and begin giving instructions. A few seconds later, he followed.

"Hi, Mrs. Gates," Alyssa said, taking the seat Randolph had. "I didn't know you were going to be here this evening. It's good to see you again."

Louise smiled. "You never know when I'm going to turn up. How's Allie doing?"

"Good. I moved back in to be with her."

"Yes, that's right. She told me you were going to."

Alyssa nodded. "I thought you were going back home."

"I am, at the end of the week. As a matter of fact, I was even thinking of inviting Allie to join me. Do you think she'd want to?"

"To tell you the truth, Mrs. Gates—" she began.

"Mamma Lou," she corrected.

"To tell you the truth, Mamma Lou, I'm not sure she's up for it."

"Has she had another problem recently?"

"No, not since the day you were there."

"Good, then maybe I'll give her a call and invite her," Louise said, then saw the worried look on Alyssa's face. "Don't worry so much, she'll be just fine."

Alyssa nodded, not feeling much better, but decided to put it off until later. Then their conversation turned to Crescent Island as Louise began describing the most beautiful scenery.

Shortly afterward, Taylor came out and got Alyssa.

A few minutes later, Alyssa found herself sitting in the kitchen at the counter, laughing and talking as if she was part of the family. Since everyone had a job, she was assigned to help Kennedy make the salad and dressing, which apparently involved rocket science, since nearly everyone had something to say about it.

Tony wanted olives but no cheese and Raymond wanted cheese without olives, obviously to be contrary. J.T. wanted arugula and Jace insisted that arugula made the salad too peppery. Taylor finally ended all discussion when she banned them from the kitchen and insisted they finish grilling dinner without burning it, which also became a bone of contention as the battle of who made the better steak, salmon and chicken kabobs began.

Starting with drinks on the veranda, Alyssa stood talking to Hope. She was amazed to find out that she and Raymond, both doctors, ran the facility called Ray of Hope, which was getting a good deal of national attention lately.

Raymond and Randolph joined them and the four of them laughed, talked and joked like old friends. A few minutes later, Trey Evans and his younger sister, Regina Evans, arrived. Taking a short break, Regina was in her last semester of college and looking forward to starting her new career at her brother's company.

Eventually dinner was served up on platters and placed in the center of the huge dining-room table. Everyone took their seats and began to eat. Midway through the meal, Kennedy excused herself, and Juwan followed.

All talk ended as everyone began staring at each other wondering what was going on. Then, moments later, the couple returned and explained that Kennedy had a stomach flu and had been feeling ill the past few days.

Later, after dessert was served, they all sipped coffee or tea, ending what was probably the most enjoyable evening Alyssa had had in a long time. At midnight, Randolph took Alyssa home. On the drive home she felt like she was on cloud nine.

The following week proved to be even better. Randolph stayed in D.C. and they were able to spend most of their free time together. She spent the next four evenings either out with Randolph or on the phone talking with him.

Thursday evening they had plans to eat dinner at his place. Randolph called to tell her that he'd be held up and for her to stop by his office after work, so that they could leave from there. At six-thirty Alyssa signed in at the security desk, then was escorted up to Senator Randolph Kingsley's office by one of his office staff.

She'd been to the Capitol Building many times but had never actually gone to a senator's office.

"Good Evening, Ms. Wingate."

"Hi," she said. "Umm, Kent. Hi, we met a few weeks ago."

"Yes, we did. If you'll follow me, I'll have you wait in the senator's office."

"Oh, that's okay. Don't go to any trouble for me. I can just sit outside here in the outer office."

"No trouble at all. Please, this way," he insisted. "You'll be more comfortable in here."

"Okay, sure," she said, finally getting that he didn't want Randolph's guest sitting out in the open for all to see. Kent showed her into the inner office and she took a seat on the side sofa.

"There are several magazines on the table. May I offer you something to drink? We have coffee, tea, sodas, wine, brandy and water."

"No, thank you," she said. He nodded and turned to leave. "Oh, Kent, may I have a glass of water please."

"Of course, chilled, bottled or sparkling?"

"Chilled bottle would be fine."

He walked over to a side panel, pulled at the molding and opened a small refrigerator. He took out a bottle of water and grabbed a crystal glass from a tray on top. He opened the bottle and filled the glass. As he placed it in front of her he smiled. "May I offer you anything else?"

"No, thank you. This is fine."

She picked up her glass and sipped. She hadn't realized how dry her throat was until she drank the water. The cool refreshing liquid eased down her throat, relieving the dryness. She sat back and took another sip while looking around the tastefully decorated office. Dark mahogany wood, refined and classy, it was exactly as she had imagined. This was definitely a senator's office.

She picked up the magazine on top of the side table beside her and began flipping through the pages. A few minutes later, Randolph came in. He looked around quickly, then spotted her sitting on the sofa glancing through a *Washingtonian* magazine. She looked up and smiled. "Hi."

"Hi, yourself," he said, walking over to her. He dropped a leather folder down on the coffee table, then reached down to take her hand. He drew her up into his arms and held her tight, just standing there a moment with her in his arms. His comfortable moan made her shiver with delight. "I missed you," he whispered close to her ear as his lips brushed the side of her cheek.

"I missed you, too. Are we ready to go?"

"Unfortunately I'm going to have to cancel our dinner plans this evening. I have to work. But I have a better idea."

"A better idea, huh? What is it?" She smirked coyly.

"I'm scheduled to go home tomorrow morning. Why don't you come with me?"

"What do you mean home? To Alexandria, right?"

"No, my home in San Francisco," he said.

"California?"

"Of course, California," he said.

She stepped aside and walked over to the window. Her mind swirled in a whirlwind of concerns as she looked out at Washington, D.C.'s evening skyline without really seeing it. He came up behind her and put his hands on her arms gently.

"Somehow I'm not getting the gleeful response I expected," he said.

"I'm sorry." She turned back around to face him. "But maybe it's not such a good idea for me to go out there just yet."

"Why not?"

"My grandmother might have a problem."

"That's the perfect part, we'll bring her along. It'll be great. I'll finally get to meet her and I'm looking forward to showing you my California. We'll start at the marina district, then on to the Presidio, then cross the Golden Gate Bridge into Marin Country through the rolling hills of Los Carneros, which straddles both Napa and Sonoma just north of San Pablo Bay. The scenery alone is worth the trip," he said excitedly.

"That sounds wonderful, Randolph, really. But I don't think we can make it this weekend. I'm pretty sure that my grandmother already had plans."

"Then you can come alone."

"I might have to work Sunday," she lied unconvincingly. The disappointment on his face was obvious and tore at her heart. "Why don't you call me when you get back in town?" she said as she leaned up and kissed his cheek quickly. She grabbed her purse from the sofa, turned once to smile, then walked out, closing the door quietly behind her.

Randolph stood staring at the door, expecting Alyssa to come back through laughing about the joke she just played on him, but she didn't. He waited there, knowing that she wasn't coming back.

A few minutes later, Kent knocked, then opened the door.

"I took the liberty and made a second reservation on tomorrow's flight to California."

"Change it. I'm going alone. And see if there's a flight later tonight," he said, then picked up the leather folder and walked out.

It wasn't exactly a graceful exit or the smoothest excuse, but it was the best she could think of given the circumstances. There was no way she was going to take her grandmother to California to meet Randolph. And as for her going, she was already too far gone emotionally with him. When this ended, and she was positive it would, she'd have a hard enough time getting over him as it was.

Overwhelmed with regret and guilt, she left the Capitol Building quickly and drove home, trying her best to focus on traffic, but her thoughts kept slipping to Randolph's expression. He knew she was lying, but he didn't know why. She hated to hurt him, but she knew it was best.

Halfway to her grandmother's house she detoured to the Wingate Lounge to see her dad. They ate dinner and hung out awhile, and then she went home. Her grandmother was already asleep when she got there. Feeling miserable, she crawled into bed early and spent all night tossing and turning and feeling guilty.

"Good morning, Grandma," Alyssa said quickly as she passed the door and headed downstairs. Then she stopped and inhaled deeply. What was that smell? She took another step, then stopped again. Chanel No. 5 perfume, her grandmother's favorite. She walked back to her grandmother's bedroom and peeked in. The door was half open and she could see that her grandmother was up, dressed and…packing?

"What are you doing, Grandma?"

"Packing," she said simply.

"Yes, I can see that, but why are you packing?" Alyssa asked, fearing that her grandmother was experiencing another memory-lapse episode. "Maybe we should pack later and take a rest now. It's still early."

Allie, hearing Alyssa's soft patronizing tone, turned to stare at her. "What on earth is wrong with you? You sound like you're talking to a two-year-old."

"Are you all right?" Alyssa asked.

"Never mind that, are you all right? You look as if your nerves are about to jump out of your skin."

"I'm fine, I'm just a little concerned about you."

"About me?"

"Grandma, look what you're doing. You're packing a suitcase at seven o'clock on a Friday morning."

"I know it's Friday, so of course I'm packing a suitcase at seven in the morning. I have to if I'm going to be ready when he gets here."

"Ready for when who gets here, Grandma? Vincent?" Alyssa asked, using her soft, calming voice again.

Allie sat down on the bed and looked at her, shaking her head. "Honestly, Alyssa, I don't know what's gotten into you lately. What on earth are you talking about?"

Alyssa sat down on the bed beside her grandmother.

"Sweetheart, my friend, Louise—you remember Louise Gates—well, she invited me to go to Crescent Island for the weekend. I told you about this earlier."

"No, Grandma, you didn't."

"I didn't? Well, I'm sure I intended to. But I'm sure I did. Your memory must be slipping, sweetheart. Anyway, Louise and I talked again last night and she told me that her grandson Raymond and his wife, Hope, are going over to the island for the weekend. I'm sure I mentioned this to you yesterday."

"Maybe," Alyssa said, knowing she hadn't.

"So since Raymond and his wife invited me along for the ride, I accepted. I thought it would be a nice change of pace. Did you want to come, too?"

"No, thank you. I might have other plans this weekend."

"Good, looks like we're both women of leisure."

"Definitely," she said, smiling brightly, having no idea how Louise knew about Randolph's trip to San Francisco and how perfect it was for her grandmother to also have plans for the weekend.

"I think that it'll be good to visit there again. It's been over thirty years since I last visited Crescent Island. If I remember correctly, the island is like paradise, simply beautiful. Will you be all right here alone for a few days?"

"Yes, Grandma, I'll be fine. When is Raymond coming to pick you up?"

"At eight-thirty this morning, so you go on to work because I need to finish packing. They'll be here before you know it."

"Grandma, what if I need to contact you?"

"Louise's phone number is in my phone book downstairs."

"Okay, Grandma, have a great weekend. When are you coming back?"

"Tuesday," she said, smiling happily.

"Okay, I'll see you Tuesday." They hugged and kissed. Then Alyssa stood up and left. But on her way out she copied Louise's phone number into her cell phone with every intention of calling her the first chance she got.

Chapter 16

Friday was supposed to be a superslow day, but as soon as Alyssa walked into the office she could tell that there was a crisis brewing because everyone seemed to be in a panic. "What's going on?" she asked Nina, who was sitting at her desk, drinking coffee.

"I guess you haven't heard the news this morning."

"No, not yet. Why? What happened?" she asked.

Nina shook her head. "There are press conferences all over the place. No one's really talking, but what I gather is that one of the senators on the Special Committee for the Aging has been reprimanded by the Ethics Committee, and indictments are pending."

"What?" Her heart dropped. The first person she thought of was Randolph. Not that she even remotely considered the possibility of wrongdoing on his part, but she knew that the ripple effect on him would be major.

"Senator Goode?" she surmised.

Nina nodded. "Apparently there was a major uproar in the Gallery during a closed session last night. The news is sketchy and none of this has been broadcast yet, but I heard Pete mention conflict of interest, misappropriation of funds, bribery and undue influence and someone said that in an unprecedented response, Goode resigned, immediately effective last night."

"Are you kidding me?" Alyssa asked rhetorically.

"That's not all. It looks like he completely falsified his federal financial disclosure documents and now, to get leniency, he's gonna bring folks down with him like clerks, chiefs of staff, pages, parliamentarians, lobbyists and even congressmen and other senators."

"That's incredible," she said, stunned by the shocking news.

"I heard that Pete might be closing up shop early today so that he and Ursula can attend a meeting at the foundation's main office and hopefully limit whatever fallout comes our way."

Alyssa nodded slowly as she sat down at her desk. She turned on her computer as she always did and checked her daily schedule. Her afternoon was already clear. She sat considering what Nina had told her.

Since Senator Goode was chairman of the Special Committee for the Aging and also a member of the Appropriations Committee, his absence on both committees this late in the session would significantly and drastically affect the foundation's standing, plus the fact that Senator Goode was Ursula's main contact in the Senate. They frequently ate brunch on the Hill and she was supposedly very close to his wife and family.

Alyssa turned to look at Pete's office door. Usually open, it was closed this morning. Apparently he and Ursula and several other high-level members of the foundation were locked in meetings all morning and the rest of the staff were basically on hold, awaiting further developments.

After taking care of a few loose ends from the day before and checking out a few news reports, Alyssa finally got a chance to call Louise, and apparently, everything had already been planned. Just as her grandmother told her, Raymond and Hope were going to the island for the weekend and Allie was invited to tag along. The fact that both Raymond and Hope were doctors added to her relief. Since Louise knew about Allie's condition, Raymond and Hope were the perfect pair to escort her.

Everything seemed to fall in place. Now all she needed to do was contact Randolph and get herself invited to San Francisco again. That was her second call.

"Good morning, Senator Randolph Kingsley's office. Kent Larson speaking. How may I assist you, Ms. Wingate?"

So much for anonymity or the ever-popular "if the wrong person answers, hang up" exit strategy. "Yes, Mr. Larson, I'd like to speak with the senator, please."

"I'm sorry, Ms. Wingate, Senator Kingsley is unavailable at the moment. May I take a message?"

"No, thank you." She paused, then changed her mind. "No, wait. Yes, please. I realize that there's a lot happening on the Hill today and that he's extremely busy, but if you can just have him return my call, I'd appreciate it."

"The senator will be unavailable for some time. If you could be more specific."

"Okay, sure. Would you please tell the senator that I've changed my mind about going to San Francisco with him this weekend? I'd very much like to go."

"I'm very sorry, Ms. Wingate, but the senator left late last night."

"Oh, I see. Thank you," she said, knowing that the disheartened sound in her voice was evident even over the cell phone.

"Ms. Wingate, will you be at this number for the next half hour?"

"Yes."

"May I call you back?"

"Sure, yes. Thank you."

After she hung up, she sat staring across the office. It was just before ten o'clock and her mind definitely wasn't on work today. Her one meeting this morning had been canceled and it looked as if the office was getting ready to close for the day.

Moments later, Pete stepped out of his office and announced that the office would be closed until Monday morning. He tried to spin the decision to ease the obvious concerns, but the truth was he was too concerned himself.

Alyssa went straight home. As soon as she walked in the door, her cell phone rang. "Hello," she answered, removing the key from the door lock.

"Good morning, Ms. Wingate, this is Kent Larson. How soon can you get packed and ready to leave?"

Her heart thundered. "How soon do you need me packed and ready to leave?"

"I have a flight leaving D.C. in two hours and eighteen minutes. I can have a car pick you up at your house in one hour."

"I'm already home, pulling out a suitcase. I can be ready in forty-five minutes."

"Excellent, your tickets are at the counter, just insert any credit card," Kent said. "Arrangements have already been made on the other side. If you'll give me your e-mail address, I'll send you all the information."

"Kent, thank you for everything."

"My pleasure, enjoy your weekend."

A six-hour flight across the country and a half-hour drive

in a comfortable sedan later put Alyssa in front of a Spanish-style whitewashed villa in the first of the bright evening sunlight. After the car drove off, she looked up at the impressive house in front of her. It was far grander than her first impression. The open courtyard had a lovely waterfall and pond as its centerpiece and ivy crawling up the front of the two-story house that looked more like a centuries-old monastery than a private home. She half expected a monk to greet her at the door.

With her bags beside her, Alyssa rang the doorbell and waited nervously. She'd been running on sheer adrenaline since she called Randolph's number and spoke to Kent earlier that morning. She still couldn't believe that this morning she was sitting at her desk and now she was actually on the other side of the country.

It wasn't until she'd already gotten on the plane that she began having second thoughts as the what-ifs were back. What if this was actually a business trip and she was intruding? What if she got it all wrong and he was trying to keep a low profile? What if he didn't actually expect her to show up at his front door? What if he was already involved with someone here in San Francisco? After all, he didn't exactly reinvite her to go, did he? What if she was the only one who was falling in love? What if…

She took a few steps back, distancing herself from the front door. Suddenly the common sense she always prided herself on had returned and all the hoping and wishing in the world wasn't going to change anything. What was she doing here? She turned to the driveway to see that the car Kent had gotten for her was now long gone.

The door opened. She turned. A small African-American woman stood there frowning sternly. The woman's expression, the exact opposite of everyone she'd met since the plane touched down, took her off guard.

"Yes, may I help you?" the woman asked firmly.

"Umm, yes, I'm looking for Senator Randolph Kingsley."

"He doesn't do unscheduled interviews and you'll have to schedule that through his chief of staff."

"Yes, I know. What I mean is, that isn't a request for an interview. I'm a friend of the senator's from Washington, D.C."

"I see," she said with enough sarcasm in her voice to choke a horse. "How nice for you. Have a good evening." She nodded curtly, then attempted to close the door.

"No, wait, really, I am. My name is Alyssa Wingate and Kent told me that he would call and let you know that I was coming."

She opened the door slightly and looked at Alyssa, still skeptical. "I've been out most of the day. Kent might have left a message. I'll check, please wait here," she said slowly, then still closed the door in Alyssa's face.

Alyssa stood there with her mouth open a few seconds before the shock of the heavy wooden door closed in her face dawned on her. After a deep breath, she stepped back and turned around to face the driveway again. Slate bricks laid out in a circular design led right to the front porch. Beyond that was a gravel-covered road that led out to the meet the main road. She stepped down from the porch and walked to the center near the fountain and peered in.

Crystal-clear sparkling water poured from a vase held jointly by two intertwined marble figures. The water splashed, then pooled in a shell-like design that had colorful faux fish painted inside. At first glance it seemed that the fish were real, since the design looked down on top of them. It was very different. She'd never seen anything so beautiful.

Getting slightly impatient, she turned back to the house. It was definitely smaller than she had expected, much smaller than the house in D.C. This house was Spanish-style with bleached cream-colored, claylike slate shingles on the roof and what looked like large white stones covered with stucco for the outside walls.

There was a covered front porch that was just one step up from ground level and was surrounded by a heavily adorned iron rail, and there were large stained-glass windows framed by antique shutters. Everything looked old and weathered, even the people, particularly the woman who had answered the door. She turned around to see if the door was still closed. It was. Then she smiled guiltily as if the woman overheard her thoughts.

The door opened again, this time wider. The older woman stepped out onto the porch. "Ms. Wingate," she said. Alyssa turned and walked back toward the front door. "My name is Mrs. Andrews. Please come in," she said. Alyssa reached down to get her bags. "You may leave them there. They'll be taken directly to your room."

"Thank you," Alyssa said, then walked inside.

"Please forgive my tartness, but we've been inundated with reporters all day long. They're crafty little buggers with the most outrageous stories you've ever heard. One came by earlier dressed like a rescue worker and said that the senator called and requested his services."

"You're right, they are cunning."

"I presumed you were a reporter trying to get a story. I spoke to Kent and he assured me that you were okay. He apparently called earlier and left a message when I was away from the house."

"I understand completely. Is the Senator in?"

"No, the senator stepped out earlier. He should be back soon. May I offer you something to eat or drink?"

"No, thank you, I'll just wait here."

"Might I suggest you sit out on the terrace? There's a cool breeze and the western view of the vineyard is quite breathtaking this time of day."

"Thank you."

"Just down the hall and to the left," Mrs. Andrews said, then turned and headed in the opposite direction.

Alyssa followed her instructions and opened the sliding glass door and stepped out into what looked like paradise. The house was built on a hill overlooking a dramatic setting below. She walked to the rail and looked down. The house was actually three stories high with a walkout just at ground level. From there she saw a small serviceable yard with a grill, a lap pool and a connecting sauna. Immediately beyond that was a narrow path that led to a road that appeared to lead toward the vineyard.

She looked across at the endless rows of neatly lined grapevines. The sun was still pretty high in the sky, giving the lush landscape a reddish golden hue, lighting the groves of vines in a dramatic fiery flare.

"I brought you something cool and refreshing to welcome you to Kingsley Vineyard," Mrs. Andrews said as she placed a wine bottle and two glasses on the side table. She pulled the cork from the bottle, then poured a rose-colored liquid into one of the glasses and handed it to her.

"Thank you, Mrs. Andrews. You were right, the view is breathtaking."

"Yes, it is," she said, sparing a quick glance around. "Now then, I'll be leaving in a few minutes. The senator should be back shortly. He asked for something light and simple for dinner this evening, but I prepared a full meal as usual. There's plenty for two. You'll find it in the warming oven. It'll keep for a good while."

"Okay, shall I go in and—"

"Oh, no, don't bother yourself. Stay out here and enjoy the evening breeze. Your bags are in the guest room. Just go upstairs, make a left, second door on the right. My phone number is on the board in the kitchen should you need me. I'm right down the road, just call."

Alyssa nodded. "I'm sure I'll be fine. Thank you, Mrs. Andrews."

"I'll close and lock the gate after I leave so you should have no trouble with reporters."

"Thanks again. Have a good night," Alyssa said.

"I certainly will," Mrs. Andrews said, then turned and left, closing the glass door behind her.

Alyssa turned back to the view, sighing restfully. She sipped the lightly tart beverage and enjoyed the view. Fifteen minutes later, she topped off her glass of wine, then went inside to look for the guest room. She went up to the second floor, turned left and opened the second door on the right. Her bags were there sitting against the wall.

With thoughts of unpacking, she grabbed the first one, feeling instantly that it was empty. She tried the second. It was empty, too. She went over to the closet and found her clothes neatly hanging and the rest already in drawers. She went into the bathroom and found her toiletry bag unopened and sitting on the counter.

Since her things had already been unpacked, she decided to freshen up and change for the evening. Half an hour later, she grabbed her glass and went back downstairs revived and refreshed. Instead of going back out onto the terrace, she found her way to the kitchen, led there by the heavenly aroma wafting through the house.

She peeked into the warming oven and found several large salmon steaks covered with a smooth lemon-and-caper sauce nestled beside brown rice and asparagus, gently warming. The meal looked fantastic as she realized that she'd actually been hungry since morning.

"Mrs. Andrews, I'm back," she heard Randolph call out

just after the front door closed. She smiled, keeping her back to the kitchen door, intending to surprise him.

"Mmm, that smells great, I'm starved," he said as he entered the kitchen.

Alyssa turned around. "Hey," she said with a low, sexy voice, "I was in the neighborhood and decided to stop by."

Randolph's expression was perfect. He dropped his suitcase, rushed over instantly and grabbed her up, holding her tightly, sweeping her off her feet. Then he kissed her hard and long. When the kiss finally ended, he held tight to her, caressing her face gently. "Where did you come from? How did you get here? When? How long have you been here?"

Alyssa was ecstatic that he was overjoyed to see her. His smile was exactly what she needed to see. "Kent handled everything. All I had to do was pack."

He kissed her quickly, smiling deliriously. "Remind me to give him a huge raise."

"I definitely will." She laughed happily.

"I missed you," he said sincerely, "a whole lot."

"What a coincidence, I missed you, too, a whole lot."

"I can't believe you're here. Did you come alone or is your grandmother with you?" he said, looking around.

"I came alone. My grandmother had unexpected plans. Apparently Mamma Lou invited her to Crescent Island and, since Raymond and Hope were going for the weekend, she decided to accompany them."

"Great planning," he said. "Remind me to thank her, too."

"You know, if I didn't know any better I'd say that you and Mamma Lou were working together this weekend."

He smiled. "Mamma Lou is something else."

"She definitely is. So, how about dinner? It's ready."

As she turned back to the oven, he grabbed her and pulled her back into his arms. "I have a better idea." He kissed her hard and long, savoring the sweet taste of being together. When the kiss ended, he continued to hold her, smiling.

"What?" she asked, seeing his eyes bright and luminous.

He paused a second. "I love you, Alyssa," he said. She opened her mouth to speak, but he stopped her. "No, before you say anything, listen to me. Yes, I know we haven't been together long or even known each other for long, but I feel it. It's as if we've been together a lifetime. I've been looking for you my whole life and here you are, finally. You are so special to me. I can't imagine my life without you in it." She started crying. "Don't cry. I love you, don't cry."

"I can't help it," she said, "I love you, too. For everything you just said and more."

He wiped her tears.

They kissed again, this time slow and lingering. "Come on, dinner's ready and you're gonna need your strength," she said.

"Is that right?" he said, smiling.

"Most definitely." She turned and opened the warming oven. A swell of heat burst out, carrying the delicate aroma of baked fish.

"I guess you met Mrs. Andrews."

"Yes. She's pretty nice, I like her."

"Nice? The woman's a pit bull having a real bad day. And that's a direct quote from a local newspaper reporter who tried to slip in here last year."

"I'm sure she has her temperamental side if rubbed the wrong way. She's very protective of you and that's a very good thing, especially in today's political climate."

He reached up and pulled down two china plates, then got silverware, napkins and glasses and placed them on the kitchen table. "I guess you heard."

"Yes, it's all over D.C.," she said, pulling the heated platter of food out of the warming oven and placing it on trivets in the center of the kitchen table. "It's a good thing you're here already or you would have been right in the middle of all that craziness."

"Actually being here is the same thing. This is my constituency. I was at the office here all day, meeting with local leaders and explaining the ramifications of Senator Goode's pending indictment." He pulled the cork out of a bottle of wine and filled two glasses.

"I hear that he intends to take a few people down with him."

"He probably will, and I can tell you, off the record, that there are quite a few senators and congressmen who are very nervous this evening," he said, pulling her chair out for her.

She sat down, then smiled up at him. "And what about you, Senator Kingsley? How are you this evening?"

Randolph kissed her sweetly. "Very, very excited to see you."

"Really? I think I like the sound of that."

"Just wait, it only gets better."

They ate and drank and talked more about California, her trip there and the vineyard. Together they cleaned up the kitchen then sat out on the terrace, sipping his vineyard wine. The sun hovered low and was just about to set in the west beyond the vineyard.

"It's so beautiful here. How do you ever manage to leave?"

"Oh, it can get crazy around here. During harvest it's insane. There are dozens and dozens of workers and only a small window to get everything done."

"Well, my compliments. This is delicious," she said, raising her wineglass to toast him.

He stood and reached his hand out to her. "Come on, let's go for a walk."

They started out down by the lap pool, then walked through a series of sheltered arbors and trellises. Small thin vines were woven through the trellises along with sweet-smelling floral plants. They passed a large seating area with picnic tables and benches. Beside that was a nice-size playground with swings and slides and rope pulls.

She veered toward the playground, then looked back at him. "All work and no play?" she joked.

He smiled. "We have grade-school students come up here all the time. The kids sometimes get bored, so instead of letting them swing on the vines and trellises and throwing grapes at each other, we installed this small play area for them. It worked. Believe me, Mrs. Andrews was the only one who could calm them down before we installed this."

Alyssa smiled, imagining Randolph and his workers trying to control fifty or sixty excited children, then calling out to Mrs. Andrews for help.

They continued farther out into the field. With rolling hills as their backdrop, they slowly strolled through the neatly lined rows of grapevines beneath them, a soft mixture of sand, soil and knoll grass.

Between rows of posts hung thick wire that supported hundreds and hundreds of grapevines. Big, fat canopy leaves, wide and veined, floating gently in the warm breeze seemed to protect the tiny fruit, packed tightly in a triangular outline. The thick treelike vines, some slightly over ten feet, were more stable than she imagined.

"There are no grapes yet. Why?" she asked, amazed.

"No, not yet, it's still a bit early in the season. A winery has a seasonal cycle. From November through February, the vines are pretty much dormant. Then they're trimmed and cut in preparation. March and April are our spring months, but we're still concerned with the frost. By May and June, the leaves form, tiny buds develop and by mid-July, we have fat, ripe grapes at full growth."

"What happens after that?"

"The best part, in August, the grapes are ripe and ready, but disease and overwatering or underwatering can still occur. September is the harvest. October, the grapes go into fermentation tanks to bubble for a while and the first stage of winemaking begins. After that, it starts all over again."

"Wow. Okay, you said that at times—I guess, in September—dozens and dozens of people are here to harvest. How many people usually work here day-to-day?"

"That depends. We have a general manager who maintains a small staff. Then at certain times of the year, staff are added when needed."

"So every month, something's going on here?"

"Yes, all year round."

"Do you have a processing plant of some kind?"

"Yes, beyond that hill over there," he said, pointing in the direction of the sunset. "We have massive tanks, hundreds of oak barrels, a bottling system, presses, sanitizers and drainage systems."

"Why are these grapevines so small?"

"They were planted two years ago. We purchased the shoots from a small vineyard in France. They're young, but their rapid growth has exceeded our wildest expectations."

"What is it?"

"It's a cabernet sauvignon. The previous vines in this part had to be destroyed."

"How?"

"A controlled burn."

"So, how do you actually make wine? Are there a bunch of women in back stomping on grapes?"

"No. Machinery replaced bare feet some time ago. Do you want the short version or the detailed scientific version?" he asked.

"Short version, please."

"Okay, you very carefully handpick grapes from the vine, making sure not to bruise them. Wash and press, then add yeast for fermentation, which takes place in very old French oak barrels. Afterward, the liquid matures in the barrels for no less than eighteen months. Then the product is bottled for at least another four to five years, called bottle-aging. Then voilà, you have wine."

"That's it?"

He chuckled. "Yeah, that's it. Sounds easy, right?"

"Definitely. What's that building over there?" she asked, pointing through to the other side of the path.

"That's the house winery."

"The house winery," she repeated.

"It's a small storage exclusively for private use."

"Your private wine cellar. May I see it?"

"It's dark and dirty and usually very chilly and damp."

"Come on, you don't mind getting a little wet and dirty, do you?" she teased, backing up toward the small building. He followed slowly. Then as they got halfway there, she heard the sound of clicking echoing through the vineyard. The first thing she thought was that there was a wild animal, then discounted the thought instantly. Seconds later, Randolph grabbed her hand and her heart jumped. "What's that?" she asked as the sound got louder.

"Come on, run," he instructed as he pulled.

Having no idea what was happening, Alyssa did exactly as he said; she ran. Then, a few seconds later, it all made sense. The clicking stopped and a sudden spray of water shot out through sprinklers positioned around the vines. She'd never even noticed them. In no time, they were completely drenched.

Chapter 17

Laughing uncontrollably, Alyssa was near bursting with tears by the time they got to the entrance of the small building. They came through the door in a burst of laughter and quickly shut it behind them. Randolph flipped a switch and turned on soft, muted overhead lights. "Wait here," Randolph said as he walked farther into the dimly lit room, footfalls echoing on the sandy wooden floor.

Randolph was right, it was dark inside. Even with the muted lights on, she could barely see any details as her eyes tried to adjust to the dimness. The room seemed to be a huge, open space almost barnlike in appearance. There was a narrow walkway and an upper level running all the way around the building with what looked like stairs leading to a loft in the rear.

Neatly lined rows of huge wooden barrels mounted on top of each other covered one entire wall just at the entrance. Each was labeled and stamped with a date. Alyssa walked over and touched the nearest barrel. It was rough and seemed old.

Suddenly, fluorescent lights hanging from the ceiling flickered and blinked on, becoming brighter and brighter. Soon Alyssa could see all around her. She was right, it was a huge barn with barrels everywhere, but there was also a lower level.

Standing there, soaking wet, she shivered in the chilly dampness. She wrapped her hands across her and rubbed her bare arms just as Randolph approached with a towel and a thick blanket. He handed her the towel and draped the blanket around her, then rubbed her arms as she had moments earlier to ward off the chill.

Her teeth chattered. "That was fun," she said.

He laughed. "You think so, huh?" She nodded, still shaking.

"This is really nice. It's a lot bigger than it looks from the outside," she said.

"Believe it or not, it seems extremely small to me at times. During harvest we store extra barrels and cases of extra bottles in here. You can barely move."

"So there's wine in these barrels?"

"No, most of them are empty, actually. The ones over there," he began, pointing across the open area to the far side of the wall, "are being held for vintage."

She nodded, then continued to look around, noticing a sectioned-off area leading to a lower level. "What's down there?"

"My private wine cellar. Come on, I'll show you." She followed as he led her down the narrow stairs. The temperature seemed to get cooler and cooler as they descended. "Careful, watch your step."

She grasped the iron rail at the last few steps but was so

intent in looking around and taking everything in at once that she missed a step and nearly fell. "Careful," he repeated as she regained her balance. He switched on a button and light instantly illuminated the area.

"Wow, look at all these bottles," she said as her eyes twinkled excitedly each time she turned her head in a different direction. "This is amazing," she added as he moved aside and allowed her to go ahead. She stepped to the side and gently touched one of the bottles.

Some were covered an inch-and-a-half thick with dust, while others looked as though they were brand-new. She looked up, then down the narrow aisles. From the corked flooring to the wood-vaulted ceiling, the tiny compartments each held a single bottle that rested on its side at a slight downward tilt.

"How do you know which one to get?" she asked.

Randolph flipped another switch and a soft amber glow washed the bottles and backlit them, making the labels easy to read. Alyssa peeked into a compartment, tilted her head to read a label, seeing the date. "What's the oldest bottle you have?"

"That would be 1861."

"Eighteen sixty-one," she repeated. He nodded. "Do you realize this country still permitted slavery in 1861?" He nodded again. She turned down another narrow aisle and walked through, examining rows of bottles on either side. "Which is your favorite?"

He moved ahead and turned down a side aisle and walked to the end. There was a small lattice-door cabinet there. He unlatched the handle and carefully pulled out a bottle and handed it to her. She took it and, handling it carefully, gently turned it to read the label. "This is a Kingsley?"

He nodded. "A very special Kingsley, my first one."

"This is your first bottle of wine from the first year's harvest?" He nodded. "Are there others?"

"No."

"You mean, a whole year's work and all you got was one bottle of wine?"

"It was a lousy year," he said, chuckling.

She gave the precious bottle back to him carefully. "Must have been."

Afterward, she continued touring the cellar until they arrived back at the steps. "That was incredible. I've never actually been in a wine cellar before. It was certainly memorable. I don't think I'll ever forget this evening."

"I certainly hope not. But it's not over yet. Come on, let's go upstairs and get you out of those wet clothes and warmed up."

He led her through the large barrels toward the back of the room upstairs into a small office. A potbellied stove had been turned on and the room was already warming up. The room was half office, half apartment, with a desk and sink and file cabinets and refrigerator and, of course, a large, comfortable-looking daybed.

"All the comforts of home, I see," she said.

"Not quite," he answered, turning the heater up higher, then going over to the small refrigerator. "What would you like, water, juice, hot tea…"

"Wine, something dark and rich, I think," she said, standing by the heater now.

"Okay, I'll be right back," he said, then left the small room and went downstairs.

Alyssa looked around, smiling. The idea of being here was still so amazing to her. The room was getting warm, so she removed the blanket and used the towel to dry her damp hair. Her nice cotton dress was completely saturated, so she peeled it off and stood in just her lace panties and high-heeled sandals. A wicked smile spread across her face as she licked her lips and grabbed the blanket. Hearing Randolph coming up the steps, she got ready.

As soon as the door opened, he stopped and stood there. "I see you made yourself comfortable," he finally said while pulling the cork from the bottle and setting the two glasses he brought with him on the desk. He poured the wine, then walked over to the sofa and handed her a glass. She took it, swirled the dark liquid around several times, then put it up to her nose and inhaled deeply. The aroma itself was intoxicating. She sipped, letting the deep, rich, robust flavor ease down her throat.

"How is it?" he asked, sipping from his glass, then setting it down along with the bottle.

"It's missing something," she said, standing up and opening the blanket.

He looked down the length of her and smiled. "You're right, I believe it is." He took her glass and slowly drizzled burgundy down the front of her naked body. He instantly licked the wine, tasting the tart and sweet mixture as it quickly dripped down her body.

The room started to get even hotter and it had nothing to do with the heat from the potbellied stove blazing in the far corner. Alyssa took the glass, dipped her finger in and offered it to him. He opened his mouth and sucked the liquid from the tip of her finger. She repeated the action, then let the drop of wine touch the side of his neck. It started to run down but she captured it quickly, licking and kissing it away.

She unbuttoned his damp shirt and removed it. Then she unfastened his belt buckle and unzipped his pants, letting them fall to the floor. As he stepped out of them she looked down his body, seeing his readiness. She took the glass from him, smiled wryly, then poured the wine down her body. His mouth was on her instantly and they eased back down onto the daybed. He covered her, and she wrapped her arms tightly around him.

Kissing and stroking, licking and suckling, they intertwined their bodies in a twisted shape like the grapevines all around them. "We don't have any…" he muttered, breathless.

"Yeah, we do," she answered, reaching into her dress pocket and grabbing one condom as two others fell to the floor. He smiled at her preparedness.

Their clothes were removed and he protected them. Then in an instant of sensual hunger, he thrust into her and she gasped, joyously feeling the deep penetrating sensation of his hard body inside her. The intensity matched her desire as their bodies surged and thrust in unrestrained passion. Stroking hands probed willingly, as the heat burned inside them. The rapture of the moment swelled, building stronger until an explosion of passion took them over the edge.

They had loved fast and furious with passion and power. Now as they lay resting together side by side in each other's arms, he gently stroked her back as sleep tempted them.

"I love you," he said.

She moaned happily, "I love you, too."

"You know that we have to get ready to leave here," he said.

"Yeah, I know. Just a while longer, okay?" she said.

He sighed dreamily, then closed his eyes, relaxed by the simple request. Moments later, his deep restful breathing softened and she knew that he had fallen asleep. The comfort of him sleeping beside her was sheer heaven. She held on tight, vowing never to forget this moment, ever.

Later that night, after a little time had passed, they went back into the house and soon after, they made love again, this time savoring the slow, easy rhythm of each other's bodies.

The next day Alyssa put aside her worries as Randolph

showed her his San Francisco with all its natural beauty and splendor. In just one day, they devoured the magnificent city by the bay. From aquarium and Alcatraz to zinfandels and zoos, they savored the various sights downtown San Francisco and wine country had to offer.

By late afternoon, Randolph told her that they would be meeting with a doctor he had met at a gerontology and geriatrics conference recently. After lunch, they drove to a small research clinic just outside the city and spoke at great length with a doctor and his team of researchers making remarkable strides in controlling and, in a very few cases, reversing the symptoms of dementia, Alzheimer's and other degenerative mental illnesses.

The tour of his facility was amazing and frightening. An estimated forty percent of the elderly had some type of dementia, and in the next few years, millions of baby boomers would likely join them. With all Alyssa knew about Alzheimer's and mental health, she realized that it was nothing compared to the research going on at the clinic. Their research on aging was remarkable and their on-site treatment clinic was extremely impressive. But it was the patient housing that really impressed her.

After the tour, they drove back to Napa. Randolph glanced over at Alyssa and was concerned by her demeanor. She'd been exceptionally quiet since they got back in the car. "Are you okay?" he asked, noticing her pensive mood and seeing the sadness in her eyes. "Going to the clinic wasn't supposed to upset you."

"It didn't."

"But you look so sad."

"Sad, no. I'm not, really. I guess I'm just a bit introspective about all this. It's so much to comprehend and I had no idea that there were clinics like that making so much progress. But even so, there's still so much to learn, and research is still in its infancy when it comes to mental health and brain function."

"Every day, we learn more and more."

"Yes, you're right, and the clinic's phase-one studies were incredible." He nodded his agreement. "Thank you," she added softly, and reached over to hold his hand briefly.

"For what?" he asked.

"For inviting me here, for taking me to the clinic, for not forgetting about me and for not making this just another political promise," she said.

"Alyssa, the downside is that there's nothing I can really do. I can't offer you a cure to make everything all right. I can't develop a pill to cure your grandmother."

"I know."

"My part in this is small. I am sponsoring a bill to include mental-health insurance coverage. I can even get additional funding for medical research specifically for seniors, which I've already done, by the way. But for you personally, for your grandmother, I'm just as helpless as you are."

She nodded. "I'm grateful for what you've already done and I appreciate all your time."

"It's my job, remember?"

"Not all of it."

"Yes, all of it. Sometimes my fellow politicians seem to forget that, but there are quite a few of us in Washington that do just that."

"Well, in case you haven't heard lately, we, the people of the United States of America, appreciate everything you do."

They smiled, enjoying the moment.

"So, when do I get to meet the great lady?" Randolph asked, changing the subject completely.

"I guess we should probably talk about that. My grandmother isn't exactly fond of meeting new people, particularly political people."

"Oh? Define *isn't exactly fond of meeting new people, particularly political people.*"

"It's just her way. It's not exactly that she hates politicians, it's more like she doesn't trust them."

"I see."

"It's nothing personal and it's not you, it's all political people."

"Any particular reason for such contempt?" he asked.

"It's just old drama that doesn't mean anything anymore," she said, trying to avoid the particulars.

"Apparently not if she's still holding on to it," he responded.

"She's old and set in her ways, but she usually comes around eventually. Don't worry," she said, then changed the subject to talk about the breathtaking view of the valley.

Randolph nodded. He wasn't worried. Given a chance, he was sure he'd win her grandmother over. But also he had no intention of letting the conversation rest as Alyssa seemed to want. He sensed that there was a lot more to Allie Granger's dislike of politicians and he wanted to know what that was. He made a mental note to have Kent run a detailed check just in case.

"So, since I'm flying out tomorrow afternoon, what are we going to do for my last evening here in San Francisco?" Alyssa asked, looking at him.

"First I have a very private megacash fund-raiser to attend hosted by Matthew Gates at his home."

"Matthew Gates," she repeated, "as in the Matthew Gates?"

"You've heard of him, then?"

"I think everyone in the nonprofit community has. His reputation is legendary. He's an incredible businessman and an astute philanthropist. Every charitable organization on the planet would love to have him on their board. He need only mention a charitable cause and money begins to flow in like water."

"He's a really good man, a good friend and he's the son of a really great woman, Louise Gates."

"He's her son, really? I never made the connection."

"Anyway, I just happen to need a date for this evening."

"Wow, where are you gonna find a date this late?" she asked jokingly. He smiled as they both knew that she would be accompanying him. "Is it formal?"

"No, actually it's a grill-out at his home, very casual."

"Photographers?" she asked.

"No, very, very private," he said.

"In that case, I'd love to accompany you." He nodded and smiled. "Okay, so that's business. What about later? Any ideas about tonight?"

"I have a few ideas in mind," he assured her easily, then stopped at a traffic light and looked at her. "That is, of course, if you're up for it."

The obvious challenge was too tempting. "I'm up for whatever you have in mind," she replied seductively.

He turned back to the front and nodded with what looked like a mischievously wicked smile. A chill of added excitement snaked through her. She wasn't sure what he had in mind or what she would be getting into this evening, but she was sure that there was no other place on earth she wanted to be and no other person she wanted to be with.

Chapter 18

After the most incredibly romantic weekend of her life, the reality of Monday morning hit her like a sledgehammer on fragile glass, shattering her fantasy into a million pieces. She knew that as with most things in life, all good things must end eventually. But for Alyssa and Randolph, their scant perfect weekend was too sparse and their time together was far too meager.

So, now back in D.C. time, as with tides and drama, life continued even as Alyssa and Randolph cocooned themselves in their newfound love. Here, in the real world, the senatorial scandal was all anyone was talking about and it wasn't even near peaking yet. Unfortunately for them, and particularly her, she returned to be in the center of a brand-new maelstrom.

Monday morning, Alyssa yawned sleepily, feeling the remnants of jet lag since getting into town just a few hours earlier.

She'd just gotten dressed and was about to microwave water for tea when the phone rang. It was Nina.

"Hey, there," she said groggily, but still giddy from her weekend on the West Coast. "I had the most incredible weekend in the world. I can't wait to tell you about it."

"Yes, I know," Nina said.

"What do you mean, yes, you know? You couldn't possibly know. How could you?" she asked.

"Guess again, everybody knows, girl."

"What do you mean, everybody knows? Knows what?"

"Please tell me you have a plan," Nina said anxiously.

"A plan for what? Why would I need a plan?"

"Oh, I don't know, how about a plan to explain the fact that your photo is on the cover of the *Washington Daily* style section along with Senator Randolph Kingsley?"

"You mean, that photo from last week is back again?" she surmised.

"No, this is a brand-new one, taken yesterday. You and the senator are sitting in an outdoor café."

"What? No, that's impossible. I wasn't even in town on Saturday and neither was he, so there's no way I could be in this morning's newspaper."

"Oh, yes, and not just that, there's a really interesting headline that reads, and I quote, 'While D.C. Burns in Scandal, Senator Kingsley Enjoys a San Francisco Break with his New Love, Lobbyist Alyssa Wingate.'"

"What?"

"Oh, and not just that, there's more, there's another article today in the political section, questioning the senator's waning resolve and your pull on him. They think you might be influencing his votes."

"Me, what? That's ridiculous."

"Oh, yeah, but wait, that's not the worst part. Get this, they also allude to the fact that you could be using him for the foundation, since he's on the Special Committee for the Aging."

"Okay, stop doling out these tiny pieces of information a little bit at the time. Just tell me everything," Alyssa said, slowly sitting down at the kitchen table.

"Okay, here's the real kicker. There was a newspaper reporter hanging around, wanting to talk to you or your grandmother last weekend. Oliver's mom saw her before."

"Crap, not her again."

"You know her? Who is she?"

"I think her name is Gayle Henderson. She said she was a grad student at Georgetown doing a paper on senatorial scandals. But she could be anyone. I understand reporters will do anything to get a story."

"Oliver's mom said that she was parked outside all day yesterday waiting around outside the house. She finally called the police and said that woman was casing her house."

"What happened then?"

"After about forty-five minutes, the police finally came. She pointed out the car and the woman sitting there. They went over and talked to her. Two minutes later, they drove off and she stayed right there. They didn't even try to make her move on."

"Figures," Alyssa said, not at all surprised.

"Not to worry, Oliver stopped by your dad's place and they took care of it."

"Oh, no, what happened?" she asked.

"Your dad apparently asked a few of his younger, rowdier bar patrons to take a ride over to the house in exchange for free beers the rest of the evening. Just about the whole place volunteered, but only ten or twelve guys could fit on the back of Oliver's truck. They pulled up in front of her car and girlfriend was so scared to see all those brothers hopping off the back of Oliver's truck that she pulled out of there like the devil was on her tail. Mrs. Watts said she never came back, and probably won't."

Alyssa smiled, feeling no sympathy.

"So, anyway, what are you gonna do?"

"There's nothing I can do. It's already out there."

Nina sighed. "Well, I just wanted to prepare you for this morning. You know Pete and Ursula are going to know about this and there's no telling what they're gonna say. After the Senator Goode thing last week…"

"Yeah, I know, I'll just go in and see what happens."

"Okay, I'm coming in from northern Virginia and traffic is crazy, so I'll probably be late. I'll see you later."

"I'll see you in a few." She hung up the phone and sat down. Thankfully her grandmother was still away, so the chance of her seeing the article was pretty remote. She picked up the phone and called her father, knowing that he must have seen the morning papers.

"Hi, Dad," she began, "have you seen this morning's paper?"

"Yes, I have, and you and I definitely need to have a conversation."

"Yes, I know."

"You joked one time about dating a senator. Is that when all this started?"

"Yes and no. But actually, it never really started as opposed to just happened. We just started seeing each other."

"How did you meet him?"

"By accident. I spilled a drink on his tie at a fund-raiser a few weeks ago and then we kind of got arrested, but not really, we just wound up going to the police station. Then we met again by accident in Georgetown that morning I stopped by your house and then—"

"Wait a minute, back up," he said. "You got arrested?"

"Not really arrested. It was more like I was taken to the police station because I called in a burglary at the office. But it wasn't actually a burglary, it was Randolph. But I didn't know it at the time. Anyway, the police came and took us back to the station. There was no problem until I didn't have any identification. That's when Nina came in and brought my purse," Alyssa said in practically one breath.

"Alyssa, maybe you'd better stop by after work today."

"Okay."

"One more thing," he said. "What happened when you told your grandmother all this?"

"Nothing happened. Grandma doesn't know, and hopefully she won't. We both know that if she finds out…"

"Alyssa, you need to tell her," he advised.

"I can't, Dad. You know how she is. She'd be crushed."

"That's why you need to come clean and tell her."

"Dad, she's done so much for me, for us. How can I just break her heart like that? Then there's the Alzheimer's. What if this puts her over the edge?"

"That's not good enough, Alyssa. You know how easy it is for this to get out. The man's a senator, he's news and everything he does is news. I'm surprised this hasn't come out already. You need to make sure that she hears about this from you and not from a perfect stranger."

"I already know she's gonna have a fit."

"That doesn't matter. It's your life, and you live it. But you still need to tell her."

"I know. She's away for the weekend with a friend, Louise Gates. She won't be back until tomorrow. Hopefully by then all of this will have blown over. But I'll still tell her when the time is right."

"Do you love him, Alyssa?"

She didn't even need to pause a split second before answering, "Yes, I do love him with all my heart. He's a wonderful man. He reminds me of you, I think, and before you lecture me, I know it doesn't make sense and it sounds crazy, but in the short time we've been together, it feels like we've known each other a lifetime."

"I remember the feeling well," Benjamin said. "Does he love you?"

"Yes, he told me, and when he looks at me, I see it in his eyes."

"Why don't you tell me about it when you see me later?"

"Okay, I have to get to work now anyway. I'll see you this evening, Dad." She hung up, but before she could get two steps, the phone rang again. She answered. "Hello."

"I love hearing your voice in the morning, all husky and sexy. It reminds me of waking up in San Francisco, you in my arms, us making love at dawn."

Her stomach fluttered and jumped. The memory of their last morning together was still vivid. Their bodies pressed together, they'd made love in his bed beneath the darkened sky greeting a new day. They'd looked up at the large skylights above his bed and seen the glow of dawn coming. She smiled even now, in spite of herself. "Good morning, Randolph."

"Good morning, how are you?" he asked.

"I've had better days," she said quietly.

"You've seen the newspaper article, I presume."

"No, but I heard about it. How could this happen?"

"What do you mean?" he asked.

"I mean, the photograph and the article implying that I was using you. It's so wrong."

"We know the truth."

"But your career—"

"Is just fine, Alyssa," he told her before she finished her sentence. "I'm not hiding this. We have no reason to hide. I'm not married, you're not married and we're two consenting adults. If we want to pursue a relationship, so be it. It's nobody's business but ours."

"It's not that simple, Randolph, and you know it. You're a senator and I work for a lobbying firm."

"So? I also work in a vineyard and you tend bar with your dad. What we do for a living isn't who we are as people."

"I know that, but people will talk."

"Let them," he said, almost delighted by the prospect.

"My grandmother will know."

"Of course she will."

"I told you how she feels about politicians."

"She'll get over it. I would think that as long as you're happy that's all that matters, right?"

Alyssa didn't respond. She knew better. Her grandmother was far too set in her ways to yield even an inch.

"Alyssa, we have something special. Don't let prejudice and narrow-mindedness tear it apart."

"I can't talk right now, I have to get to work."

"Okay, I'll be in meetings all day, but I'll stop by this evening and we can talk on the way."

"On the way where?" she asked.

"On the way to a twenty-five-hundred-dollar-a-plate reception at the home of a very prominent political figure, followed by a quick stop at another reception for a fellow senator."

"Umm, we'll talk later, I have to go now. 'Bye." She hung up, but this time she just stood there staring. She loved him too much to let him go, but she loved her grandmother, too. She knew someone would have to be hurt and, either way, it would be her.

She grabbed her purse, locked the front door and hurried to her car. With a quick glance around, she noted the reporter's red BMW was nowhere in sight. At least that had been taken care of.

As soon as she got to the office, she noticed a very definite change in the air. Instead of the anxious drama she had left Friday morning, today everyone seemed to be quietly unnerved.

Nina hadn't gotten in yet, so Alyssa went directly to her desk, dumped her purse in the bottom drawer as usual, then turned on her computer to her schedule. Her e-mail message sounded. There were two, one from Randolph and one from Gayle Henderson. She sent one to her personal e-mail address and the other to her spam folder. She turned around to see Pete's door open. Deciding to take the bull by the horns and get it over with, she got up and walked to the opened door and knocked on the frame.

"Come in," Pete said, looking up and seeing her standing there.

Alyssa walked in and smiled weakly. "Good morning, Pete. We need to talk about what's been happening in the newspapers, why my picture was there this morning."

"Yes, Alyssa, we do. Come in, have a seat. I've asked Ursula to join us." He picked up his phone and called her cell. She was on her way and would be in directly. "First of all, I'm very disappointed with you, Alyssa. The rules clearly state that anyone working in this office is not allowed to fraternize with politicians. These aren't just my rules and regulations, they're foundation policy. And we have them for a reason."

"Yes, I know, that's what I wanted to explain to you. My relationship with—" Alyssa began, but stopped when Ursula walked in, closed the door behind her and sat down after saying good morning to them. Alyssa continued. "What I was saying is that my relationship with Senator Kinsley began outside of the office and I obviously wasn't on official foundation business. I didn't go looking for anything, for a relationship. It just happened that we became friends."

"More than friends, I believe," Ursula interjected.

"I know I'm support staff, but it was just a chance meeting, that's all," Alyssa continued, ignoring Ursula's remark. "As a matter of fact, I didn't even recognize him when I first met him."

"A chance meeting, it must have been more than that, dear. Perhaps this chance meeting, as you call it, meant more to him than you realize," Ursula said, smiling tightly.

"I don't think so. Everyone's making more of this than it really is. The newspapers just want to sell papers. We're simply passing acquaintances," Alyssa said.

"I understand that you were in San Francisco just this past weekend, staying at his vineyard, no less," Ursula said in her patronizing tone. "That sounds to me like more than a passing acquaintance. I've kept an eye on Senator Kingsley and he isn't given to flights of fancy. He keeps his personal life extremely private. I don't believe I've ever heard of him inviting a lobbyist or anyone from Washington to his California home. As a matter of fact, he goes out of his way to discourage lobbyist from getting too close to him. And you wind up at his home for the weekend…."

"Is this true?" Pete asked.

"Yes, I went to San Francisco, but we didn't actually go together," Alyssa said, hoping to clarify that point at least. "But again, I was on my time, after work, and this had nothing to do with the foundation."

"Alyssa, what you do on your time is, of course, your business, but if you're engaged in a physical relationship with the senator to further your career, the implications can be devastating to this foundation, particularly since this Goode scandal."

"My relationship, physical or not, is my private business. It has nothing to do with my work here," Alyssa said defensively as she started to get a bit annoyed.

"Be that as it may, Alyssa. We can't have everyone just

grabbing hold of senators and congressmen as they will. Keeping order here would be impossible," Pete said.

"I understand that, but as I said, our relationship has nothing to do with foundation business. We don't even talk about politics or his job or my job or the foundation and we don't—"

"Excuse me, but why don't you talk about foundation business?" Ursula asked.

"Because we just don't, we talk about other things not related to government and business and politics, we talk about personal things." Alyssa watched as Ursula glanced at Pete, then gave a slight nod and smiled.

"Well, Alyssa, if you're gonna have a senator's ear, you have to at least be able to use it, dear. That's what we do here. We use our relationships with public officials to get our cause heard and furthered," Ursula said.

"But that's not what our relationship—" she began.

"You know, maybe we can use this to our advantage," Pete said, smiling and nodding.

"I was just thinking the same thing," Ursula said, then turned directly to Alyssa. "We'll promote you from support staff to working with me directly on the outside. That means more money and more freedom, but also a lot more work. What do you think?"

Alyssa smiled happily. This was what she always wanted, to work directly with lawmakers and effect positive change in people's lives. "Yes, of course, I'd love to be a lobbyist, thank you. You won't be disappointed, I promise."

"Good. Now, Alyssa, I want you to set up a dinner meeting with the senator, Ursula and me as soon as possible. We need to get this working to our benefit fast. The Senator Goode thing hurt us a bit, but this is exactly what we need to get back on track."

"I agree," Ursula said as she leaned across the desk. She

and Pete began discussing her and Randolph as if they were commodities to be used and taken advantage of.

"This relationship with Senator Kingsley couldn't have come at a better time. It's exactly what we need to regain our standing in the community," Ursula said. "Imagine a coup like this. No one has ever been able to influence Kingsley."

"It'll definitely give us a higher leg up."

"Definitely, I totally agree," Ursula added. "Granted, Senator Goode had his issues, but Senator Kingsley's reputation is above reproach. He's our perfect in."

"Yes, yes, yes, you know we could ride this all the way," Pete said, nodding excitedly as his voice got higher and higher.

"You're right." Ursula chuckled giddily. "There's no telling where his career will take him, take us. Imagine having an ear at the White House, executive level." She smiled liberally as Pete chuckled and rubbed his hands like a greedy archvillain.

"But first things first, we need to get control of this as soon as possible," Ursula said.

"Yes, of course, we'll do the meet and start reviewing our program for next session. We can get a head start on the other lobbyists."

"Check your calendar. We need to get this started ASAP!"

They both pulled out PDAs and began scanned dates.

Alyssa sat there, looking from face to face, not believing what she was hearing. They didn't care about her or Randolph or what was going on. All they cared about was the foundation and using her to get to him. "Wait a minute," Alyssa said. "If you want to meet with Randolph, then you can just call his office. I'm sure Kent can set up an appointment for you."

"No, absolutely not. Don't be ridiculous," Ursula said assuredly. "We already have an in with you. We should take advantage of it. Besides, going through Kent Larson is like running into a brick wall. You can introduce us personally. It'll be better in the long run and far more productive."

"But I don't think that's a good idea."

Both Pete and Ursula stopped and looked at her. "Why not?"

"Because I don't want Randolph to think that I'm using my new position here to get to him or vise versa. The newspapers are already trying to make it sound like that," she said.

"Consider this a personal favor—" Pete began.

"Or, if you will, a condition of your pending promotion," Ursula added, still smiling.

"I can't, I'm sorry, it wouldn't be right," Alyssa said.

"Alyssa," Pete began again, "what we're asking isn't unethical. It happens all the time. That's what lobbyists do, we petition and influence political membership through personal contact. You know how close Ursula was to Senator Goode. That's exactly how it happens."

"Exactly, and you know Randolph's position on excessive lobbying. I can't use him like that."

"Alyssa, we know you went to the Esprit Clinic in San Francisco," Ursula said.

"How did you know that?" she asked.

"This is a very small town and an even smaller community. You show your face with Senator Kingsley and word gets out, it's inevitable," Ursula said.

"The Esprit Clinic specializes in regenerative illnesses for seniors and mental patients. We also know that your grandmother suffers from a serious malady. You've asked about us putting Alzheimer's disease on the agenda for some time," Pete said.

"Dear," Ursula began, "of course you're already using the senator, but instead of being exclusive, you can use him to help a lot more people. We're not asking you to do anything you haven't already done. Your relationship, physical or not, will help others. Think of it. There are so many people in need and he can make a huge difference. You both can. But it takes a strong commitment and a willingness to do what needs to be done to stay close," she added.

"I don't understand what you mean," Alyssa said, confused by the tone in her voice. She wasn't sure, but she could have sworn that Ursula just implied that any- and everything was acceptable as long as it furthered the greater good. "Are you telling me to sleep with him for the foundation?"

It had always been speculated that Ursula was having an affair with Senator Goode. But no one knew for sure.

"Of course not, but as you said, what you do on your time is your business. If it by chance encroaches on our agenda, so be it."

"I don't know, it doesn't feel right," she said.

"Think about it," Pete said.

"I have to say, Alyssa, hearing you now, I'm a little disappointed. Maybe I was wrong, maybe you don't have what it takes to be an outside staffer," Ursula said. "Being able to do whatever it takes to get your point across is essential. It's a frontline battle and we're understaffed and underfunded, so we have to do whatever it takes, even going that extra mile, whatever it is to get the job done for the greater good."

"Think about it," Pete repeated.

Alyssa nodded, stood and left, and as they suggested, spent the rest of the day thinking about it. She wasn't a fool. She knew what they were telling her. But in her heart she knew that it was wrong. She also knew that type of behavior went on a lot in D.C.—favors for favors, political, physical, monetary—the corruption of morals permeated the city like rotten meat on a hot August day.

But it wasn't her, so how could she possibly justify using him for her job and to further her career? It was wrong and she knew it. She loved him too much and, deep down, she knew that he loved her, too. And as promised, he had tried to help her, and succeeded before, but this was different. There had to be a better way, but she could only think of one.

Chapter 19

Home.

Finally.

Alyssa unlocked the front door, went in, then secured the door behind her. Once inside, she leaned back against the frame a few minutes, thankful to be home. The long day had worn on her, but now it was over and she was looking forward to peace and quiet. No more questions or cross-examinations. She'd had enough.

First her conversation with Peter and Ursula, then talking to Nina at lunch and telling her everything and finally talking to her father at the bar. Her head was spinning. But the day was over and all she wanted to do was sit and relax and not think about anything.

The day was long and strenuous and she couldn't imagine it getting any worse. Deciding that she was more exhausted than hungry, she chose to just head upstairs to her bedroom and lie down. Midway up, she stopped.

"You're seeing a senator, Alyssa?" Allie said accusingly as she stood in the parlor doorway, holding the now-infamous section of the newspaper.

Alyssa turned and looked back, seeing her grandmother. She must have been waiting in the parlor. "Hi, Grandma," Alyssa said, dreading yet another confrontation.

Her face contorted in pain and hurt, she turned and went back inside. "How could you do this to me?" she muttered softly.

Alyssa went back downstairs. "Grandma, I didn't know you were back. How was your weekend?"

"After everything I taught you," she said wearily, "none of that even mattered. He seduced you anyway and he ruined your life."

"No one seduced me, Grandma, and no one ruined my life. I'm fine. I was going to tell you about all this, but it was happening so fast and at first there was really nothing to tell. Then I guess we—"

"The newspaper people have been here all day, asking questions. So what is this all about?"

"It's really nothing, Grandma. We're just going out, that's all. The reporters are making more of it to sell newspapers. You know how they are."

"Imagine my surprise when as soon as I got home this afternoon, Mrs. Watts brought me the *Washington Daily* newspaper and showed me my granddaughter's photograph with a senator of all people."

"Grandma, he's a good man, not just a senator, he's—"

"You know my feelings. How could you openly defy my wishes like this?"

"I didn't defy your wishes, Grandma. I fell in love," Alyssa said respectfully, then paused a second, hearing the words leaving her mouth. It felt good to say them. "And you should be happy for me."

"Fell in love. Happy for you? Child, please, there is no love with a politician. He will use you, he will hurt you and he will leave you just like he did me."

"Grandma—"

"Don't *Grandma* me. You lied to me."

"I didn't lie, I just didn't tell you the whole truth."

"That's called lying. How could you, Katherine, after everything I went through with your father? You're not going to just throw your life away for him."

"I'm not Katherine, Grandma, I'm Alyssa."

"Are you pregnant?"

"What? No, of course not," she insisted.

"Katherine, I wanted so much for you."

"Grandma, I'm Alyssa, not Katherine."

Allie ignored her, instead staying in her own little world. "Your life was going to be everything mine never was, I was going to make sure of that. You were going to make something of yourself, something you could be proud of. Not like me." She eased down in the chair slowly. "I got married, then fell in love with the wrong man. I was the dirty little secret that everybody knew about. It was a doomed relationship, filled with pain, always hiding in secret, lying. He made promises that he knew he'd never keep."

"Grandma—"

"Everything, all his promises were lies. We made love in secret, shared clandestine meals at his place, had public lunches with a third person for appearances' sake, never just the two of us. He promised to leave his wife, to marry me. He lied. He promised to take care of me, of us. I had his child and he still left me and went back to his wife," she rambled.

"You what? What was that, you had his child?" Alyssa

repeated, in shock as she sat down beside her grandmother. "Grandma, what did you just say? You had his child? Do you mean that Senator Vincent Dupree is really Mom's biological father?"

"Don't be like me. Don't ruin your life for a man, Katherine. You're so beautiful with so much in front of you. Your father knew about you, but he never acknowledged you. And Henry," she said, smiling inwardly, "he was a good man, bless his heart. He was right there by my side the whole time and he never denounced me. He knew about me and he suspected about you, Katherine, but he never denied you."

"Grandma—"

"The heart wants what the heart wants, and my heart wanted your father. I fell in love with Vincent Dupree and gave up everything for him and watched as he walked away and turned his back on us. Our love was forbidden and it destroyed his career. That's why we have to show him what he missed out on. You can't be with that bartender. You can do so much better."

At that moment, Alyssa knew what she had to do. Her job wanted to use her to get to him, her grandmother didn't want her seeing him and his career would be destroyed once the connection with her grandmother was found out.

"I won't, Grandma. None of this matters anymore because I've decided to end it. It's over."

"Good, you're finally coming to your senses," Allie said as she saw the pain in her eyes. "It'll hurt for a little bit, but then it'll be over and you'll see that everything worked out for the best. There are thousands of bartenders out there, but you deserve so much more, Katherine."

The doorbell rang.

Alyssa got up and answered. Randolph stood there smiling, dressed in an open-collar shirt, slacks and a sport coat with sporty loafers. He reached out and grabbed her into his arms and kissed her hard. The feel of being in his arms was like coming home. She felt completely safe and secure. But she knew she needed to end it for both their sakes.

"We need to talk," she said.

"Yes, I know, I saw the pictures and articles. Don't worry about all that, it's just selling papers. I can't stop thinking about you. I missed you so much," he said, stroking her face gently, his eyes loving ever bit of her.

Alyssa backed away from him. "We need to talk, come in." He stepped inside just as Allie walked out of the parlor.

"Good evening, Mrs. Granger, I'm Randolph Kingsley."

"I know who you are." Her tone was cold and biting. "You're that senator."

"Yes, I am. It's a pleasure to finally meet you, ma'am. Alyssa has told me so many wonderful things about you."

"Really? That's funny, she hasn't told me a thing about you, particularly the fact that you're a senator."

"Grandma, please let me handle this," Alyssa said.

"No, please, Alyssa, I'd like to hear your grandmother."

Allie smiled. "Don't give me your whitewashed hypocritical manners. I know all about you politicians firsthand. You're all liars and cheaters looking out for your own interests and hurting anyone who gets in your way."

"Grandma—"

"No, please continue, Mrs. Granger," he said.

"Making promises is all you're good for, especially you senators. Sure, he says he loves you now, but just wait, he'll change his mind as soon as the heat is on and his wife finds out. You're corrupt and I'm going to expose you for what you are. You think you own the world and no one can touch you. Well, you're wrong and I'm gonna make sure everyone knows it. I'm going to tell that reporter exactly what happened."

"Grandma, please let me handle this."

Allie glared, then nodded. "Fine, you handle it. I've had my say. Now I have a phone call to make." She went upstairs as Alyssa showed Randolph into the parlor.

"When you said that your grandmother would be upset, I thought you were exaggerating. I guess I was wrong. But don't worry, I'll win her over. Give me a week and she'll adore me," he said, taking her hand and pulling her into his arms, rocking slowly to the song in his heart and humming lightly. "I missed you so much today," he whispered, then closed his eyes and kissed her neck down to her shoulder.

"Randolph," she said, pulling away, "we have to end this, now, tonight."

"What?" he said, stepping back to see her expression.

"Let's face it, this wasn't going anyplace from the beginning. We both knew that we're not exactly new to this."

"What are you talking about?" he asked.

"I'm ending this before one of us gets hurt."

"Alyssa…" he said, still holding her hand.

"Please just listen to me," she said, walking away from him. "We were good together. I'm not saying that this wasn't wonderful. It was, really. I'm going to remember our time together for the rest of my life. I loved being with you, you know that. In just a few weeks, you've made me feel like I always wanted to feel, like I was special to someone, like I mattered. You're an incredible man with so much to give."

"Then why are you doing this?"

"I can't hold you back anymore."

"Hold me back, what are you talking about?"

"I'm not the woman for you, we both know that."

"Adia," he said softly, "don't do this to me."

Alyssa turned away as tears started filling her eyes. The emotional whiplash of loving him, then letting him go was tearing her apart. She took a deep breath. "It was a physical thing and we let it go too far as it was." She quickly wiped away the tears.

"Are you kidding me? A physical thing? I'm not going to just let you walk out of my life like this. I love you and you love me. Why are you doing this?"

"Because it's best and it's the right thing to do."

"Right thing for who? You? Me? Your grandmother?"

"This isn't about my grandmother."

"I think it is. She doesn't want us together, so you're just ending it. Just like that, you're willing to end us for her."

"It's complicated," she said.

"Don't give me that."

"The longer I'm in your life, the harder it's going to be. I love you, yes. But I can't have you. I know that now."

"You already have me."

"No, the cost is too high. I'm not willing to pay it."

"Adia."

"Please, Randolph, this is hard enough already. We can't see each other. Anything more would be pointless. You're just too tempting and I love you too much."

"Then why are you doing this?"

"I'm being rational. You'll understand and thank me one day," she said.

Randolph walked over to the open door and glanced upstairs. "She wants us over and you're not even going to consider otherwise, just do exactly what she wants. If that's the case, then you're not the woman I thought you were."

"My grandmother had a hard life. She's lost so much."

"But still, she had a life, which is more than she's willing to allow you, or us."

"I can't believe you're being so difficult about this."

"If living here is the problem, then come live with me, be

with me. We love each other. Marry me, now, tonight. I know a dozen judges that would be delighted to perform the ceremony right now."

"What?" she asked.

"Come leave with me now." He crossed the room quickly and took her hand. "Tonight, right now."

"You know I can't do that."

"So you just intend to hide in the house for the rest of your life, avoid relationships, commitment and love because if might lead to something real. This isn't fair. You can't do this to yourself, to us, because your grandmother has problems with men."

"She doesn't have problems with men, only politicians, with senators." She backed up and walked from him.

"Why? Was your grandfather a politician or something?" She whipped around too quickly.

His eyes sparkled knowingly. "That's it, isn't it?"

"You don't know," she said.

"Know what? Then tell me."

"My grandmother was protecting my mother."

"Like she's protecting you now?"

"Goodbye, Randolph."

He opened his mouth to speak, but didn't. He just left.

Forty-five minutes later, Senator Bob Wellington walked up to Randolph, smiling as he always did for no apparent reason other than that he seemed to think that his boy-next-door attitude and schoolboy charm would hide the fact that he had no idea what he was doing.

"Hey, you made it," Bob said, shaking Randolph's hand as they met at the reception. Randolph nodded, still withdrawn. "You okay, buddy? You look a little shell-shocked," he said.

"Yeah, just a bad few hours, that's all."

"What happened?" Bob asked.

"You saw the newspaper this morning…."

"You mean, the beautiful woman on your arm?"

"Yeah, although, apparently she will no longer be on my arm," he said.

"Had to happen sometime, bro. I guess you found out, huh? You can't be too careful these days. I mean, it's not as bad as before. Even so, you have to be careful."

"What are you talking about?"

"The thing with her grandmother," he said.

"What about her grandmother?"

"You don't know?" Bob asked as Randolph looked at him questioningly. He stepped to the side, and Randolph followed. "Your girl is Alyssa Granger's granddaughter, *the* Allie Granger," Bob said. Randolph's expression never changed.

"Allie Granger, from the Vincent Dupree scandal about fifty-plus years ago. Father was just talking about it this morning. Apparently Senator Vincent Dupree had an affair with Allie Granger and she supposedly had a child. Then his wife found out and shot him. Of course, everything was denied, you know, hush, hush. There was no affair, there was no child, the gun was being cleaned and went off by accident five times." He chuckled. "Man, those were the days. But you know what they say, the apple doesn't fall far from the tree."

Randolph looked at Bob as he laughed. He wasn't sure if Bob was an idiot or just an insensitive fool, but either way, he needed to leave there now or he'd be front-page news having punched Bob out.

He called Kent and got a quick rundown of what had happened between Allie Granger and Senator Vincent Dupree. A few minutes later, he called Alyssa. "Meet me at the Tidal Basin."

"There's no point," she said.

"Meet me," he said, then hung up.

An hour later, Alyssa walked up, knowing exactly where to meet Randolph. They stood side by side, each staring out at the monuments as the Potomac River reflected the moonlight. The Japanese cherry trees, long since bloomed, waved gently in the warm breeze.

"Don't confuse me with Vincent Dupree, Alyssa. I'm not that man."

"I know who you are, Randolph."

"And yet you're still doing this."

"I have my reasons."

"I know your reasons. You're doing this because your grandmother wants you to."

She paused, turned and looked at him. He actually thought that she was breaking up with him because of her grandmother. Of course he was wrong, but he didn't have to know that and probably in the long run it would make things easier for him to move on. "She needs me. She protected and cared for me when I needed her. Now it's my turn."

"Fine, we can both protect and care for her, then."

"She's right, you know, it's for the best."

"Best for whom?" he asked. "I can't believe that you're letting your grandmother run your life. Her Alzheimer's—"

"What about her Alzheimer's?"

"—isn't an excuse for taking over your life and for you letting her. She needs to let go and you need to let go, too."

"Randolph, I don't want to be that woman who ended a man's life's work. You are a United States senator. Millions of voters chose you to represent them, to look out for them. How can I possibly stand in the way of that? And if we stayed together and this ruined your career, eventually you'd hate—"

"Don't even finish that sentence," he said, cutting her off before she finished. "How could you think so little of me?"

"I don't, believe me."

"Then let this pass. Scandals come and go every day in Washington, you know that. Just let it pass."

"I can't. There's too much at stake. You know, I wondered why you invited me to join you in San Francisco. Was it because it was as far away from D.C. as possible?"

"I wasn't trying to hide out with you, if that's what you're asking. California is my home and I just happened to want you there with me. I invited you to see my world outside and away from politics and D.C."

"And lunch with your sister that day at The Capital Grille. It was so public, so many people. You and me having lunch might have caused them to talk, but your sister and me having lunch, then you popping in later looked just too innocent."

He shook his head. "I invited my sister because I wanted the two of you to meet. Two of the most important women in my life needed to know each other. I got held up on the Hill because the Goode scandal was about to break and the Speaker of the House wanted me to take over his position as chairman."

"And what about—"

"Listen to yourself, Alyssa, that's your grandmother talking, suspicious and mistrusting. Remember, you wanted discretion, not me. I never wanted to hide us."

"It didn't work. Everybody found out and my grandmother was jettisoned right back in the newspapers all over again because of me."

"No, Alyssa, because of her. She needs to take responsibility for her actions. She chose to have an affair with Dupree. And now she's choosing to let that affair tear us apart. Don't let her do this to us."

"And your career, what about that?"

"What do you want from me, Alyssa? A promise? A guarantee? An assurance? You know better than that, politicians don't do promises. But there is one promise this man can make you and that's to love you for the rest of my life. I'm a politician. That's my job, not my life. This is my life, right here, right now with you. Do you think I really care what other people say about my personal life?"

"I care," she said. "You can help so many people. I can't let you just throw that away."

"I love you. We can make this work, I promise," he whispered softly.

"I know you do and I love you, too. That's why to love you I have to let you go."

"Don't give up on us, Adia," he said softly.

"I don't have a choice."

"That doesn't make any sense."

"It doesn't have to, it just has to be the right thing to do for everyone."

"I thought you were stronger than this. I guess I was wrong about you. One question, how do I stop loving you?"

"Goodbye, Randolph." She reached up and touched his face, then stepped back and walked away and went back to her car and drove off. Moments later, she stopped by her father's place and told him what had happened. Afterward she went home, closed the door, then just stood there.

"You went to him," Allie said rather than asked.

Alyssa looked up to see her grandmother standing midway on the stairs looking down at her. "Yes, I met him at the Tidal Basin."

"What happened?" she asked, already assuming the worst and glad that she'd taken steps of her own to finish this once and for all.

"We talked."

"And you weakened, didn't you?" she assumed. "You went

back to him. Of course you did. He's a man and that's what they do, they make us weak. Every man knows exactly what to say and what to do to make a woman weak. They lie, they cheat and deceive you and say anything to get what they want, especially his kind of man. He's used to getting his way and making his power work for him. But you can't believe a word they say, ever. It's all to make you weak."

"But he made me strong, Grandma."

"It's all just an illusion to get what he wants."

"But he didn't, we're not together anymore," Alyssa confirmed.

"Good, you did the right thing."

"Did I?" Alyssa asked.

"Yes, of course you did. He would have hurt you eventually, you know that."

"No, I don't. He loves me too much."

"They all say that, baby, but then they use you, then leave you with nothing but empty promises. I know, Alyssa, I went through it, too," Allie said.

"No, Grandma, not like this," Alyssa said.

"Yes, like this. Love is love, there's no differences, no degrees," Allie insisted. "It's for the best. Trust me, I'm thinking of you and your pain. I'm just trying to protect you, save you from hurt."

"Then I guess you failed because I already hurt."

"I knew this was going to happen. I knew he was going to hurt you. What did he say to you? What did he do?"

"It's not what he did, it's what I did. He loves me and I had to push him away."

"But you did the right thing, something I should have done all those years ago. None of this would ever have happened if I did."

"Grandma, this has nothing to do with you. I didn't leave

Randolph because of what you said or what you wanted. I left him because I had to in order to save his career. The papers are crucifying him and I can't let that happen because of me. He's a good man and a wonderful senator. He's done so much good in his position and can do so much more. He can help so many people. I can't just destroy his career knowing that. He told me to just wait it out, but I can't. Being with me is hurting him. I had to end it to save him. I love him too much not to." Tears steamed from her eyes as she spoke, her voice thick with emotion and pain.

Allie looked down at her, staggered by her words. The sacrifice she spoke of was something Allie knew nothing about. She'd never given anything up in order to save someone else. Yes, she was selfish just as Louise said before, spoiled and selfish. Could she have been wrong about everything all this time?

Yes, she always said that she loved Vincent, but she didn't really. Not the way her Henry loved her, without reservation, unconditionally. He sacrificed for her just as Alyssa was sacrificing for Randolph. "That kind of love fades in time, you'll see," she said, holding on to that one last thread of selfishness.

"Grandpa loved you like that and stood by you no matter what. Even when he knew you were wrong, he was there by your side defending you because he loved you that much." Allie didn't reply. "He knew, didn't he? He knew about you and Dupree."

"That was a long time ago, a different time and a different situation."

"No, you wanted me to give up Randolph because of something that happened a long time ago in a different time, so it's that same situation. Grandpa knew, didn't he?"

"Yes," she said quietly.

"And he knew about Mom, too, didn't he?"

"What about your mother?" she asked.

"That she wasn't his child."

"Who told you that?"

"You did."

"I would never—"

"No, you wouldn't, not deliberately. But it was the Alzheimer's—"

"There you go again with that. For the last time I do not have Alzheimer's disease."

"Then how else would I know about Mom?"

"Gossip, you're listening to that newspaper reporter woman and reading those rag newspapers. It's lies, all lies, it always was."

"No, it's not, Grandma. My mother, Katherine, was Vincent Dupree's daughter and Grandpa knew it."

"No," Allie said firmly.

"He loved you too much to say anything, didn't he?"

"No," Allie repeated louder.

"You had an affair with Dupree and when you got pregnant, he refused to leave his wife for you—"

"No."

"Then you passed Mom off as Grandpa's child to save face, right?"

"No, no, no, no, she wasn't his," Allie screamed, then banged her hand on the wooden railing as she broke down and cried. Alyssa rushed up to her side as she collapsed against her. She helped Allie down the steps before she fell. Together they went into the parlor and sat down on the sofa as Allie continued crying. Alyssa hurried to get water.

"Grandma, I'm sorry, I didn't mean to—" Alyssa began.

"I lied, I lied…" Allie kept saying over and over again as Alyssa put the glass of water to her lips.

"It doesn't matter now. It was a long time ago, Grandma, Grandpa is dead now and he was okay about this even then because he loved you. He never said a word about Mom not being his child."

"No, baby, that's just it. Katherine was indeed his daughter. I lied and told Vincent that she was his so that he wouldn't leave me. I thought if he knew that we had a child together, he'd leave his wife and marry me."

"But he didn't, did he?" Alyssa said. "He stayed with his wife even though she couldn't get pregnant. And even after she shot him, he still stayed."

Allie nodded slowly. "I thought I loved him, I really did. I wanted him so much, but his political career was too important, more important than me. His father-in-law's money and influence put him there, and leaving his wife meant leaving his position."

"Did Grandpa know that Mom was his daughter?"

She nodded. "Katherine looks just like his sister Claire. I have pictures upstairs of Henry and Claire together. She and Katherine could be twins."

"So Grandpa knew you lied but never said anything."

She nodded. "I thought that made him weak, but I was wrong, it made him strong." She looked into Alyssa's eyes and realized that she couldn't deny it any longer. She knew that her granddaughter truly loved her senator with a love she had never known. "He sacrificed everything for me just like you're doing for your senator."

"Grandma, Randolph isn't Vincent, he isn't like that."

"But his career will always come first. Then the affairs will come."

"Maybe, maybe not, but I needed to see that for myself. You can't protect me as if I was four years old again. I'm a woman, a woman in love with a wonderful man."

Allie looked at her sorrowfully and held her hand. "Correction, a woman who just kicked a wonderful man out of her life because of me."

Alyssa swallowed hard and the truth stabbed into her heart like a knife. Tears threatened to fall as she thought about their conversation at the Tidal Basin. It was over for good and she knew it. "No, Grandma, I did the right thing for everyone."

"It's late," Allie said. "Go to bed. Tomorrow will be a better day, I promise."

Alyssa kissed her grandmother's cheek, then went upstairs to her bedroom. Allie picked up the phone and called for help from the only person she could think of.

"Allie Granger, I never thought I'd say this to you again, but how could you do something so despicable?" Louise asked.

"I called for your help, Louise, not a lecture. I know I was wrong. I messed up. But it's not too late. Talk to him. Explain it to him."

"And how am I supposed to do that, Allie? How am I supposed to explain that you purposely tried to sabotage not only his relationship with Alyssa but also his career?"

"You know him, you know everybody. Call him, talk to him. Make him see reason."

"Allie, I may be good, but I'm no miracle worker."

"Louise, please."

Louise sighed. "Tell me exactly what you said to this reporter."

"She's not a reporter exactly. She's a grad student writing a paper on scandalized senators."

"And what did you tell her?"

"That Randolph was using Alyssa to cover up the fact that he and Senator Goode had done a number of questionable deals together."

"Oh, Allie, how could you?"

"I was trying to protect Alyssa."

"No, you were trying to manipulate the situation just like you tried years ago when you lied to Vincent about Katherine. Now you put Randolph's name out there to hurt him and you've hurt them both. You had your life, and what you did with it was your choice. Don't take that choice away from Alyssa because of your weakness."

"Louise, you haven't changed one bit. You're still the same self-righteous woman you always were."

"Neither have you, Allie, manipulative and selfish as ever. You saw me as self-righteous because I wouldn't help you hide your affair and lie to Vincent's wife so that she'd divorce him. How could I, Allie? We both knew it was wrong. I tried to tell you."

"I loved Vincent."

"No, you didn't and you know it."

Allie went still. "How can you still say that? I gave up everything for him."

"No, what you gave up was for you."

"If you won't help me, then help Alyssa. She doesn't deserve this and once that reporter writes her story and it's published, Randolph'll never have her back."

"You should have thought of that before. Randolph is a good, honest man and he and Alyssa deserve this chance to be happy."

"Then do it, make them happy."

"Allie—"

"Louise, I know I should have listened to you all those years ago. You were right then and you're right now. Maybe things would be different if I'd listened. I would still have Henry. You know I think about him a lot now. I didn't deserve him. He really loved me. It must have broken his heart, the things I did—"

"Allie, yes, Henry loved you very much and that's what love does, it forgives, and I truly believe that he forgave you."

"He really loved me," she repeated. "Why didn't I see that before?"

"We were young and foolish."

"All I saw was Vincent and everything he had and everything I wanted. I saw money and glamour. But in the end, that's all he had to give. But Henry was real. He stayed by my side the whole time, defended me to the press and everyone else. He knew the truth about me, but he never said a word, never accused me, never got angry, never even pointed a finger. I thought that made him weak, but it didn't. Why didn't I see that then? He was the strongest one of all."

"Yes, he was. And he still loved you."

"I didn't deserve him."

"Yes, you did."

"Oh, Louise, how am I going to fix this? I was so stupid, so foolish. I've made a mess of my life, but I don't want it to affect Alyssa."

"We'll think of a way. But not now, tomorrow. It's late, we need our beauty rest now."

"Yes, I guess we do." The doorbell rang. Allie looked at the clock. It was after one o'clock in the morning. "I have to go. Thank you, Louise, for everything." She hung up and went to the door, half expecting Randolph to be standing there. She was wrong.

"What are you doing here this late?"

"We need to talk, Allie," he said as he brushed past her and walked into the foyer.

"It'll have to wait until morning," Allie said, closing the door.

"No, now, right now," Benjamin said, then headed for the kitchen. Allie followed. As soon as they were both there, he turned to her and glared. "You won't be happy until you completely ruined her life. First Alyssa moved in here with you to help you and now you talk her out of seeing the man she loves. What is wrong with you?"

"Get out of my house. You ruined my daughter."

"No, I saved your daughter. There's a difference. You ruined her and now you're trying to ruin my daughter."

She turned and glared at him. "I love Alyssa. I was protecting her."

"Nobody's denying that, Allie, but your love and protection are breaking her heart. You need to butt out of her life and leave her alone."

"This is familiar."

"Yes, it is. It's the same argument we had after Katherine and I got married."

"It should never have happened."

"But it did and we loved each other fiercely and there was nothing you could do to change that. So now you're doing the same thing with Alyssa and I'm not having it."

"Well, you'll be happy to know that I changed my mind about Alyssa and her senator friend."

"What?"

"She has my blessing, but I'm afraid it's too late."

"What are you talking about too late? What did you do?"

"I'm tired, Benjamin," she said, then walked away.

For the first time in a long time he actually saw just how frail and fragile she really was. He followed her down the short hall leading back toward the foyer. "Allie, are you okay? Can I get you something?"

"I'm just tired, Benjamin. It's been a long day."

"What about Alyssa?" he asked.

"I've already asked for help."

"Help? What are you talking about, Allie?"

"See yourself out, Benjamin. Good night."

"Allie, this isn't over, not by a long shot."

"You're right, it isn't."

Chapter 20

Having just come from an early morning committee meeting on senior health benefits programs, Andre followed Randolph to his office. As they entered they continued discussing the ramifications of the new program they had committed to review. Following Randolph, Andre crossed to the desk, then glanced down at the supermarket tabloid newspaper sitting there on a stack of files. He looked down and smiled, humored by the tabloid gossip. "Nice picture," he teased.

Randolph reviewed messages left on his desk by his secretary, and chuckled. "Yeah, I really think they captured the more debonair side of my personality," he joked easily.

"Seducing two women, grandmother and granddaughter, where do you find the time?"

"I often wonder that myself."

Kent followed moments later with the extra copy of a

report Andre requested from the medical conference Randolph had recently attended.

Andre picked up the newspaper and chuckled again. "Lousy placement, though."

"I don't know," Randolph said, "sharing the front page opposite Big Foot and his bride and five alien children isn't too bad. Imagine the coverage. What do you think?" he asked Kent.

"I guess it's better than actually being Big Foot and married with five alien children," Kent pointed out.

"Good point." Andre laughed.

"Maybe next time," Randolph said as all three men chuckled at the article. Kent handed Andre the report.

"She's a lobbyist, huh?" Andre asked. His tone was disheartened as his disastrous second marriage came to mind.

"Support staff, not a lobbyist, there is a difference," Randolph corrected as he handed him a copy of the report he'd asked for.

"Semantics, same thing, this is chancy, very chancy. With the vote coming next session, this looks very messy and very indiscreet. Not exactly your style, Randolph," he said as he handed the newspaper to Randolph.

"But well worth it, I assure you."

"I hope so. Because this is exactly what Goode said and the implications are obvious. Your reputation is on the line here. And of course, you realize that this just might hinder our legislation on lobbyist reform, giving the opposition due cause and those on the fence reason to reconsider."

"I'm betting it won't."

"I hope you're right. You just might be betting your career on this woman."

"As I said, Andre, well worth it," Randolph said without flinching.

Andre looked at him, seeing the glint of love in his eyes.

Having loved and lost, he knew the look well. "My first wife, Geraldine, I called her Geri for short, did I ever tell you about her?"

"No, I don't think so," Randolph said.

"She was a hell of a woman. Spitfire, bold, idealistic, strong-willed, kind, generous, loving, the kind of woman you'd march into hell with and know that she was right there by your side every step of the way. A man searches his whole life to find that kind of woman. I was lucky enough to have her for ten years. She was killed by a drunk driver. He rammed right into her, then walked away. Why is it that you never get over women like that?"

"I don't know. I hope I never have to find out."

"Make sure you invite me to the wedding," Andre said.

"Front row."

Andre nodded his assurance. "See you in a few."

After Andre left, Randolph opened to the article page and read the headline and subhead, then smiled and shook his head.

"We're not gonna let them slide with this, are we?" Kent said as he took two bottles of water from the refrigerator and handed one to Randolph.

"I haven't decided yet," Randolph said, handing him the paper.

"It mentions that the reporter has an inside source that told of secret sexual rendezvous in the Senate rotunda and on the floor of the Senate chamber."

"Apparently I've been very busy."

"Apparently," Kent said, "but curiously enough, those are the exact same accusations that were made about fifty years ago when the Dupree-Granger scandal broke. Coincidence?" Kent asked, handing the paper back to Randolph.

He glanced at the cover again, shaking his head. "Somehow I doubt it. I think Grandma is trying to send a message and work this to her benefit."

"After what you've told me, my thoughts exactly," Kent said.

"It was a nice blow, a bit low, but I think she's going to have to do better than that if she wants to get rid of me."

"I agree," Kent added, "contacting that tabloid reporter was a pretty low blow."

"Indeed, she definitely insists on getting her way. And her way in this case means me out of the picture."

"So you're not giving up?" Kent asked. Randolph smiled at him. He knew the answer. "Still, her grandmother seems a bit cantankerous."

"She is that and more. I admire her perseverance. Don't get me wrong, I'm not at all pleased with this. Lies about me I expect, but lying about Alyssa is over the top. That part about her beating a man with a bat was extreme."

"I'll take care of it," Kent said, intending to do his usual PR spin.

"No, actually I have a better idea. I'll handle this."

"As you like," Kent said.

"Kent, do me a favor, get me transcripts of the Ethics Committee hearing meetings on Dupree."

"No problem. Your first appointment is here, Pete Lambert and Ursula Rogers from the Foundation for Senior Citizen Reform."

"Give me about ten minutes, I need to make a quick phone call," he said, picking up his cell and dialing. After a very agreeable conversation, he walked to the door and greeted his first appointment.

For the next fifteen minutes, Ursula and Pete talked to Randolph about Alyssa, thinking that he'd play along like Goode did. Randolph listened as they stated their case and informed him about their agenda for the upcoming session. Randolph asked pertinent questions as Kent sat in, listening and taking notes.

"We can't tell you how delighted we were to learn of your and Alyssa's relationship. She's like a daughter to me, to us, really. We've nurtured her career from the beginning. She's an astute and very promising lobbyist."

"Lobbyist? I was under the impression that she was support staff."

"Oh no, she's a bona fide lobbyist, has been for some time."

"Really? Some time, you say," Randolph said with interest, since both Alyssa and Kent had said otherwise.

"Yes, we're very proud of her and the fact that she's attached herself to you is very impressive."

"Attached herself," he questioned, "meaning?"

"Uh, in the most innocent and forthright way, of course," Pete said, suddenly feeling that this wasn't going exactly as they had expected.

"So you're saying that Alyssa attached herself to me to further her career?"

"No, certainly not," Pete affirmed.

"No, of course not," Ursula reiterated. "Alyssa would never use or misuse anyone. I assure you, her intentions were and are strictly aboveboard in all respects."

"Her intentions," Randolph repeated, beginning to enjoy watching Pete and Ursula squirm. "You're telling me that this was all planned? Because if it was—"

"No, of course not. Maybe *intentions* isn't exactly the right word. Let's say her objective."

"I was her objective, I see."

"I don't think we're explaining this quite well enough. What we're saying is—" Ursula began.

"No, on the contrary, you've explained it very well indeed. I have a very good picture of things and I thank you for your added insight. Now, if you'll excuse me, I have another meeting in a few minutes."

"Uh, but, Senator—" Pete began.

He stood and reached out to shake hands. "Senator," Pete began again as he shook hands, "yes, perhaps we can speak again. I don't think we adequately—"

"Yes, and perhaps we gave you the wrong impression of Alyssa and her motives and that's definitely not what we intended. They weren't as we—" Ursula added.

"It was good meeting you both," Randolph said as he nodded to Kent.

"This way please," Kent said, escorting them from the office as they each tried to explain.

By the time the door closed, Randolph was chuckling. One of his guilty pleasures was watching people like Pete and Ursula squirm, usually by letting them choke on their own words.

Kent returned to the office. "You enjoyed that, didn't you?" he said, half chuckling himself.

"Immensely. How about you?" he asked

Kent shrugged, shaking his head. "You really need to get another hobby. Making lobbyists sweat is wrong on so many levels."

"I know. It's just that they're so easy."

"So, what about what they were saying?"

"You mean, about Alyssa, that she was a lobbyist all along?" Randolph asked. Kent nodded. "Somehow I think I'll take your research and background checks over a couple of lobbyists any day."

"So you didn't believe them, then."

"No, Alyssa wants to please everyone, particularly her grandmother. That makes her endearing, but certainly not a lobbyist. She needs to step away from her sense of obligation and realize that her grandmother, although interesting in her own way, is hiding behind her."

"What are you gonna do?"

"Right now, I have to go vote, then attend a committee meeting afterward. We'll see."

Kent handed him two folders and watched him leave, shaking his head. Remembering the tidbits of conversation he'd overheard of Peter Lambert and Ursula Rogers made his day....

"We need to call Alyssa," he'd overheard Ursula say. "I think we might have messed this up for her."

"Yes, yes, definitely," Peter had responded.

Kent chuckled, then sat down and went back to work.

Alyssa didn't sleep all night. She just tossed and turned, praying that she was doing the right thing. By the time dawn came, she knew that there was only one way to make everything right. Ending her relationship with Randolph, which delighted her grandmother, wasn't enough. She knew that she needed to leave her job, as well.

There was no way she could be effective at work with a political scandal hanging over her head. It was obvious that the foundation would eventually be drawn in, and as it was, Pete and Ursula were still insisting that she use her influence with Randolph for them. If she quit, Randolph wouldn't be involved in an ethics scandal and the press would leave him alone. In the long run, he would see that what she did was for the best and that his very promising career would continue unencumbered by scandal, gossip and controversy.

By morning, the mess she found herself in had thickened. She was front-page fodder as newspapers and television newscasts ran a "like grandmother, like granddaughter" exposé, mentioning the hint of scandal referring to her relationship with Randolph and her grandmother's relationship with Vincent Dupree.

Her grandmother, having gone through this before, handled it with dispassionate cool. Her father raged, threatening every reporter in town. She, on the other hand, tried her best to find some middle ground.

As soon as she got to work and sat at her desk, she saw the latest disaster. Randolph had made front-page news in one of those cheesy supermarket rags. She briefly scanned the article, then stoically typed her resignation. She printed it and handed it to her friend.

Nina read quietly, then looked up at her. "Are you sure about this?" she asked.

Alyssa nodded. "I messed up. I ruined my career and almost ruined his. I can't let this go any further. I don't have a choice anymore."

"But are you sure you want to do this? They gave you the promotion, didn't they?"

"Yes, but I got the impression that it hinged on me bringing Randolph along. I can't do that to him."

"Wow, I can't believe that's what they said."

"They didn't actually say that. It was implied."

"Still…" Nina said.

"Yeah, still, I think it's best. That article in the newspaper is probably just the tip of the iceberg. Once they start digging, who knows what they'll come up with? This doesn't just affect me and Randolph. It affects my grandmother, my dad, even the foundation, and your jobs are at risk. I have to end this now, for everybody's sake. "

"It was a supermarket tabloid. I can't believe that woman sold this to a supermarket tabloid. I wish she would show her face around here again."

"I can't imagine where she got all this stuff."

"She made it up, you know how they do," Alyssa said.

"But about the bat, that was way over the top."

"Actually the bat part was true."

"You beat a man up with a bat?"

"No, not exactly. I was helping my dad out at his place when I was in college. Some businessman in town got drunk and tried to molest me."

"What?"

"The bar had closed and I was cleaning up. The man came back, saying that he left his wallet. I let him in to look for it and he took that as a personal invitation. He cornered me behind the bar and I grabbed the first thing I could get my hands on."

"A baseball bat," Nina surmised.

Alyssa nodded. "Yes, although the bat was plastic I still cracked his head, requiring him to get eight stitches. He told the E.R. and police that I tried to seduce, then rob him. He eventually dropped charges when his wife found out. Apparently he'd done the same thing a few times before."

"What a jerk. You should have done more than that, like grabbed a real bat," Nina said. "But still, how would this reporter know all that? It's not like all that stuff was publicized."

"No, there's only one person who could have given her this much information about me," Alyssa said, thinking out loud.

"Who?"

"Here, do me a favor and see that Pete gets this."

"Are you sure? Why don't I hold on to it until the end of the week?"

"It doesn't matter, a day, a week, I'm still quitting."

"What about Randolph?"

"After what I said and what Grandma did, I'd be happy if he didn't sue us for slander."

"Call him or write him a letter or offer him a mea culpa. Apologies are big right now. Apologize, blame childhood drama, then go to rehab. Everyone else does it, why not you?"

"Saying what exactly? I'm a fool? Sorry?"

"How about a poem?" Nina asked. Alyssa shook her head. "A dirty poem?" Nina persisted. Alyssa shook her head and smiled. "Yeah, a dirty poem like—there once was a girl named Alyssa who—"

"A dirty limerick isn't exactly gonna win his heart."

"You already have the man's heart, Alyssa, you know that. Just let him know how you feel."

"It's too late for that."

"It's never too late for love."

"It is for me. When love called, I hung up."

"So call back," Nina said.

"You're such a hopeless romantic," she said as she tossed her purse into the box she'd packed with the rest of her things.

"How else could you win the heart of the most eligible bachelor in the Senate?"

The phone rang on her desk. Nina picked up and listened, then covered the receiver. "It's for you, it's Pete and Ursula. They want to talk to you," she whispered. "They sound panicked."

Alyssa picked up the box, then shrugged, smiled and shook her head. "See ya."

By the time she got home, both Pete and Ursula had called three times along with a dozen or so reporters. Nina called once and told her that the Internet blog sites were abuzz with speculation that either she was a plant by Senator Goode to embarrass Randolph or she worked for the opposing party and seduced him in order to damage his reputation.

Add to that, the backlash against Randolph had reached a fever pitch. By afternoon, his once ramrod reputation for being opposed to special-interest groups had been seriously called into question. She was all over the news, being portrayed as either a conniving lobbyist or a scheming harlot. A scenario her grandmother knew all too well.

"You called that reporter, didn't you?"

Allie sat at the kitchen table sipping her tea. "Yes," she said softly, looking up at Alyssa.

"Why? How could you ruin him on purpose like this?"

"I did it for you."

"No, Grandma, you did it for yourself out of spite for something that happened over fifty years ago. What you did was selfish and despicable."

"I was trying to protect you."

"So you told her about me hitting a man with a bat?"

"No, of course not, at least not on purpose. I called her right after you broke it off with him. Then you went out and I knew you were meeting him someplace. She started talking about how politicians take advantage of people. Then she mentioned that she saw the two of you in the hotel lobby one day and then you went to his house. She asked if you'd ever gotten in trouble before because of a man. Then she twisted my words."

"Grandma, she was a reporter. You knew that you couldn't trust her when you called her."

"I thought she would just go after him. I didn't think she'd write those things about you, too. But that other stuff about a secret rendezvous at the Capitol…"

"I know, I read them a long time ago."

"I'm sorry, baby. I just wanted you safe. Then later, I saw how much you were hurting and I knew that you really loved him."

"Yes, I do," Alyssa said, then turned and went to her bedroom. It was a long day and she'd had enough.

The next day, the drama continued. Staying inside the house was just fine with her. She finally talked to Pete and Ursula, who urged her to reconsider her resignation and agreed to make her a lobbyist, no strings attached. But she declined. The brief taste of that world was all she needed to know that it wasn't for her.

Gradually, by midweek, the controversy subsided. Alyssa's fifteen minutes of fame had vanished like fog burned away at sunrise.

Chapter 21

Early Friday afternoon, Kent walked into Randolph's office smiling. He crossed the room to Randolph's desk as he concluded his phone conversation. Kent's broad grin was a dead giveaway. "I presume by the Cheshire-cat grin that you have good news," Randolph said dryly.

"I don't know if it would be considered good news or not, but suffice it to say it's a questionable and unexpected event."

Randolph sighed heavily. Keeping busy was his goal and, so far, he had succeeded. His desk was piled high with work and he made sure to keep as focused as possible. Thoughts of Alyssa plagued him at times, but he had managed to suppress them. He couldn't afford another lapse.

In the last three days, as the press steadily grew tired of the scandal and rumors about his ties to Senator Goode, they turned their attention to the next scandal.

Even so, he was booked solid, making the rounds of the

Sunday-morning political talk shows. He was asked about his relationship to Senator Goode, his interest in succeeding him as chairman of the Committee for the Aging and his association with the granddaughter of Allie Granger. The last of which he declined comment because of its very personal nature.

Randolph set his pen down on the desk and gave Kent his undivided attention. "Okay, let's hear it," he said, steeling himself, preparing for whatever. At this point, after the last few days, he expected anything.

The Ethics Committee had come down hard on Senator Goode, and in response he had named names and offered a list of those involved. Of course, Randolph's name wasn't on it. Neither were any of his close associates, but Senator Bob Wellington's father was.

He'd only met J. R. Wellington a few times. A braggart, his overbearing personality and boisterous demeanor annoyed Randolph. Bigger than life in all respects, he completely dwarfed his son. Senator Bob Wellington had handled the scandal as well as expected. Having his father, a former senator and now a resigned-in-disgrace secretary to the president, embroiled in this was major humiliation and had all but kicked him out of the presidential contention.

As Bob once said, "Family ties run deep. The apple doesn't fall far from the tree." Funny how what comes around goes around, he mused.

For Randolph, the latest political scandal had kicked his love life off the front pages. So he got back to work and hoped that that would ease the pain of losing Alyssa.

"You have a very impressive visitor waiting in the front lobby to see you," Kent said, standing by the desk.

"Alyssa?" he asked hopefully feeling his heart lurch.

"Close. Her grandmother is here," Kent said.

Randolph was indeed surprised. "Allie Granger is here, downstairs, waiting for me?"

Kent nodded. "Apparently so, what do you want to do?"

Randolph picked up and toyed with his pen again, threading it easily through his fingers. The idea that Allie Granger had come to him was totally unexpected. She obviously knew that he and Alyssa had broken up, so her visit was meaningless. Or was it? "Escort her up, please," he finally said.

"My pleasure," Kent said, then turned and left.

Randolph closed the folder and placed it on top of the pile of reports he intended to read that day.

Alone time was the ruse she'd come up with, but that was the only excuse she could think of in order to get Alyssa out of the house for the weekend. Surprisingly it worked. They had talked as soon as she arrived on Crescent Island and then again late last night. Then after spending the evening talking with her son-in-law, she decided to take matters into her hands and correct what she started. Benjamin agreed with her. He drove her and now they were united on one plan.

"Are you okay, Allie?" Benjamin asked as he sat, seeing the stillness of her expression. "You look a bit shell-shocked."

Allie nodded. "I guess it's just being here after all these years. This is my first time back and it looks exactly the same," she said as she shook her head. "I was such a fool all these years."

"Don't worry about it now. All that's in the past."

She nodded. He was right, but still, the ghosts haunted her.

"Mrs. Granger?"

Allie looked up. "Yes."

"Good morning, my name is Kent Larson. I'm Senator Kingsley's assistant. Welcome back to the Capitol Building. I'll be escorting you to Senator Kingsley's office."

"This is my son-in-law, Benjamin Wingate." The two men shook hands.

"Will you be joining us?"

"No, I'll wait here for you. I'm sure the senator will be visiting me shortly."

Kent nodded, understanding. "Ma'am, please follow me."

Benjamin nodded to Allie one last time for assurance.

Allie and Kent walked through the halls as memories surrounded her. It was surprisingly similar. A few new structures and a few new faces were all that separated her from all those years ago when she had worked here. It was like a time capsule unlocked.

They took the elevator up two floors, then walked down the familiar long marble hall and stopped at open double doors. They entered and, to her surprise, there were quite a few people already inside. They talked on phones or sat at desks, working on computers.

"If you'll wait right here, ma'am, I'll inform the senator that you're here."

Allie nodded silently and took a seat as Kent walked into the next office. Moments later, he returned and nodded. "The senator will see you now. Please follow me," he instructed.

Allie stood and walked into an inner office. It was empty and obviously Kent's office. Kent crossed in front of her, knocked, then opened a second set of doors. "This way, ma'am." She entered. "Senator, Mrs. Allie Granger to see you, sir."

The formal introduction was impressive. In all this time, she'd forgotten just how important U.S. Senator Randolph Kingsley really was. She looked at him impressively dressed as he stood at his desk, then walked over to her.

"Good afternoon, Mrs. Granger, please have a seat. May I offer you a beverage—water, tea, perhaps?"

"No, thank you. I won't take up too much of your time. I

realize I don't deserve to even be here after what I did and that you could just as easily have turned me away, so thank you for seeing me. I know it couldn't have been easy."

"On the contrary, it was very easy. Please have a seat." The coldness in his voice and the hard stare in his eyes assured her that this would not be easy. She glanced down at the offered seat. "Actually I'm curious as to what you feel you need to speak to me about," he said.

"Then I'll get right to the point," she said as she sat down. "Alyssa, my granddaughter—"

"If you've come here to express your disapproval again, you've wasted your time. I got your message loud and clear." He glanced at the newspaper. "And you obviously haven't spoken to your granddaughter lately. We are no longer together."

"Yes, I know. That's what I need to talk to you about. I was wrong, I shouldn't have interfered."

"Be that as it may, it doesn't change the fact that—" he began.

"Yes, I know, you're not together, but please, let me finish," she implored. He nodded, then stepped back to sit on the edge of his desk. "Alyssa loves you and she told me that you love her, too. And all this mess in between is nonsense, including me and my interfering. I'm a foolish old woman and I'm sorry. I should have stayed out of this. It was none of my business from the start, but you see, I was trying to protect her. That's not an excuse, it's an apology. So if you would call her."

"No," he said simply.

The quick answere surprised her. "No?" she repeated.

"That's right," he told her.

"I don't think you understand. It was me, I did everything I could to hurt you. I called the reporter and told her terrible things. I talked Alyssa into getting rid of you."

"Yes, I'm well aware of that."

"Then how can you profess to love her and not give her another chance?" she asked. He didn't respond. "Don't penalize Alyssa for my mistakes. She had nothing to do with the article. I called the reporter and said those things. Alyssa had no idea what I'd done until it was too late. I hurt her and I hurt you. It never should have gone this far. I was trying to protect her from my memories. Be angry with me, don't punish her for what I did. Please go to her, talk to her."

"Mrs. Granger, I'm sorry, I can't."

"Your pride—"

"My pride has nothing to do with this," he assured her.

"Please."

"I'm sorry."

Allie was heartbroken. Louise had told her that it wasn't going to be easy. She had to try anyway, but now she had no idea what to do next. "I can go to the newspapers and retract everything. Tell them the truth."

"Mrs. Granger, when lies are already out, you know as well as I that the truth doesn't really matter much anymore."

She remained still, feeling his words penetrate deep in her heart. He was right. "You're right and so was Alyssa. I ruined your chance to be together for my selfish reasons. I'm sorry. Is there nothing I can do to change your mind?" He didn't reply. She nodded, stood and turned to leave.

"How is she?" Randolph asked when she got to the door.

"Like you, heartbroken."

"I'm sorry to hear that."

"Are you?" she asked, turning back to him.

"Yes, I am."

"Then do something about it. Go to her."

"She asked me to stay away. I'm honoring her wishes."

"But don't you see why she did it?"

"I know why she did it."

"No, I don't believe you do. She didn't walk away from you because of me, she walked away because of you."

"What?" he asked.

"She wasn't doing this for me. Yes, she knew I'd be angry and hurt, but that wasn't her real reason," Allie said, walking back over to him. "I'm not proud of my behavior or what I did. I was wrong, back then, and even now. I know that. All those years ago, I was a fool and I'm right back in the same place."

"I'm sorry. There's nothing I can do."

"Of course there is. Go to her."

"She doesn't want me."

"Of course she does, she didn't push you away because of me. She was trying to protect you."

"Protect me? From what?"

"From this. The press. From yourself. From her. With her out of the picture you'd be able to go back to your nice normal political life free of distractions because of my past."

He went silent as he thought for a moment. "She was thinking of me, trying to protect me?"

"Yes, she loves you and I can see now that she was right, you love her, too. Don't be a fool like I was and ruin your chance at happiness because of meaningless lies and misunderstandings. Go to her." Allie reached into her purse and pulled out an address. She handed it to him. "She's staying with a friend of mine in Virginia on a small island off the coast, called Crescent."

"Yes, I know where it is."

Her grandmother and Mamma Lou were right, this was the perfect place to escape. Alyssa closed her eyes and relaxed back on the hammock, letting the warm, gentle breeze whisper softly in her ear. The mellow sounds of nature and the sweet aroma of the flower garden were exactly what she needed. She'd never felt so relaxed and at ease. For some reason there was always something swirling in her life that kept her on edge, but today, right now she refused to think of a single worry.

All her cares and concerns had faded as soon as she stepped off the ferry. No more drama, no more newspapers and no more reporters. The idea seemed foreign, but she had to admit she liked getting back to her less-than-glamorous life.

Alyssa never knew that Crescent Island, just hours away from D.C., was so beautiful. She only wished that her grandmother had decided to come with her. When Louise Gates invited them both to visit, she implored her, but her grandmother flatly refused, saying that she'd ridden out the storm years ago and that she had every intention of riding this one out, as well.

By Wednesday evening the boredom must have set in because the questions began to wane, restoring their lives to relative normalcy.

She spoke with Pete and Ursula and they again offered her the position, then told her of their less-than-successful meeting with Randolph. She wasn't at all surprised. She knew that Randolph was too strong and independent to fall for any of their sneaky gimmicks. He was a man of principles and purpose. Even though when it came to senior healthcare reform they'd agreed in most cases, he still had his own agenda and time frame.

By early Thursday morning it was Allie who suggested she spend a long weekend on Crescent Island. After much persistence, Alyssa reluctantly agreed, giving her grandmother the alone time she wanted. She called Louise, who extended her an invitation to visit. After packing and making travel arrangements, she called her father and asked him to look in on Allie. He agreed. Then five hours later, her ferry reached Crescent Island.

She had talked to her grandmother the night before and was surprised to hear that her father had stopped by earlier and brought Chinese food for dinner. Apparently they sat, ate and talked about her and her mother most of the night, each telling stories and sharing memories of both laughter and tears. She said, after eating, the two of them headed up to the attic and went through some of her old boxes. He helped organize a few things, then promised to return again today with wood and tools to build more shelves so that finding her memories wouldn't be so difficult.

The idea that her father and her grandmother were not only getting along but actually talking and listening to each other was a true blessing. Both stubborn and fiercely loyal to family, they had so many things in common and now it looked as though they had finally gotten past their pain and anger long enough to see that.

"So, are you enjoying yourself so far?"

Alyssa opened her eyes and smiled. "Hello, Mamma Lou, you're back," she said as she sat up and swung her legs to the side.

"Yes, thank goodness," Louise said as she sat down and relaxed. "What a long day."

"How was the flower show?"

"Good, but exhausting as usual. How was your day?"

"Quiet and peaceful," she said.

"Do anything special?" Louise asked.

"I swam this morning, then rowed a boat on the water. After that, I went into town to look around and even saw a few of the sights, including the old slave church and the cemetery this afternoon. It was wonderful."

"I'm glad you enjoyed yourself."

"I did, I'm really enjoying myself. Crescent Island is incredible. I don't see how anyone can ever leave here."

Louise sat down on a lounge chair beside the hammock. "Well, you're perfectly welcome to stay as long as you like. I have plenty of room and I love having company."

"Grandma always said that this place was magical."

"I just spoke to your grandmother."

"Is she coming down, too?"

"No, she just wanted to make sure you were doing okay."

"But I talked to her last night," Alyssa said.

"A little secret about grandmothers. We need a little extra assurance sometimes when it comes to our grandchildren and their happiness."

"I wish she came with me. She loves being here."

"Well, anytime either one of you wants to come visit, feel free. If I'm not here, just come anyway and make yourselves at home."

"Careful, Mamma Lou, I just might stay forever."

"You're welcome to do that, too. Now that Tony and Raymond are gone, it gets too quiet around here. So stay as long as you like."

Alyssa looked around wistfully. The gentle waves lapped slowly against the shoreline and a sweetened breeze caressed her lovingly. The escape was well worth it, but she knew that she needed to get back to the real world sooner or later. "I really wish I could."

"When is your next vacation from work?"

"Actually I'm going to need to find a job first."

"Why is that? You already have a job."

"Not anymore, I quit last Monday just after this mess started."

"Why, if you don't mind my asking?" Louise said. "When we talked at lunch, you seemed to love what you were doing."

"I did. But now I realize that I can't be what they want me to be."

"And what is that?"

"A lobbyist. I got promoted, but the cost was too high. It's funny, I always thought I wanted to be a lobbyist. But now all that seems so insignificant. Being a lobbyist meant that I could go out and really connect with lawmakers and politicians and make the case for the foundation. I would actually be making a difference and helping people who really need it."

"And you don't want to do that now?"

"Yes, I do, but not at that price. They wanted me to use my influence with Randolph to further the foundation's agenda. He would never do that, but he might consider it if I asked him to and I would never ask that of him."

"Of course not," Louise said softly.

"So I quit," she said. "Good thing I moved back in with Grandma," she added, lightening the mood.

"But you moved in before all this happened, right?"

"Yes, I moved back in to help care for her, but also because I needed to fill the void."

"Fill what void?" Louise questioned.

"The one my mother left," Alyssa said.

"What do you mean?"

"It broke Grandma's heart when Mom married my dad, and then when she died they were both inconsolable. I guess it was guilt maybe, because of all the time she wasted being angry with her about Dad."

"Your filling a void, as you say, doesn't make anyone happy. Your grandmother is a lot more resilient than you give her credit for."

"It sounds childish and silly, but she was there for me when I needed her, so I need to be there for her now that she needs me. I need to stand in for my mother." Alyssa looked at Louise.

"Baby, your grandmother would be heartbroken to hear this. She never wanted you to replace Katherine. Yes, she wanted so much for Katherine, but most of all, she wanted her to be happy and loved, and she was. Your dad loved her, really loved her very much."

"Yes, I know he did. He still does."

"And you deserve to be loved just like that. You and Randolph together—"

"Mamma Lou, that's over," she said. "I thought you knew, I broke it off. It's over."

"Do you still love him?"

"Yes, too much," she said.

"Then it's never over."

"It has to be. I can't be the one who destroys his career. He'd hate me eventually and I couldn't bear that."

"Trust me, he could never hate you," Louise said.

"Of course not."

Alyssa turned quickly, hearing the voice she knew so well. Randolph was standing there, looking down at her. She stood slowly, speechless at the sight of him. He smiled. She just stared at him.

"Well, you two talk. I better get back up to the house and see about dinner," Louise said as she stood and walked back to the house.

"What are you doing here?" Alyssa whispered.

"I was invited."

"Mamma Lou invited you, too…" she asked, seeing Louise walking back toward the house.

"I'm not the only one hurting here, am I? You're hurting, too. I heard it in your voice and I can see it in your eyes," he said. She looked away. "You love me, Alyssa, and I love you. This is too strong to just let go and walk away. You know that."

"I don't know what to do."

"Yes, you do, love me," he said as he walked to her.

"I do love you but—"

He reached out and took her in his arms and kissed her long and hard. Moments later, breathless, she stepped back. "This is wrong, I can't. Mamma Lou may have told you I was here but—"

"She didn't tell me."

"Then who?" she asked as the answer came to her.

"Yeah, that's right, Allie Granger told me."

"What? When? How?" Alyssa said, totally confused. "My grandmother told you I was here?"

He nodded and smiled. "Yes, she came by my office early this afternoon. We had a very interesting chat."

"She did?" she asked. He nodded. "What did she say?"

"In essence that I'd be a fool if I didn't come here."

"She said that?"

"I thought you left because you couldn't stand up to your grandmother."

"I know. It was easier to let you to believe that."

"Why?"

"Because you might have tried to talk me out of doing what I knew I needed to do. Randolph, your career is too important to too many people. They believe in you, they trust you. You do so much good. I can't be the one—"

"Adia, I have room in my life for my career and the woman I love. Never doubt that," he said softly as he gently stroked the side of her face with his thumb. "Allowing you to walk away from me was the biggest mistake I've ever made. You know we were meant to be together. I can't go another second without you in my life. Marry me, be my wife, now."

Alyssa smiled. This was like a dream come true. She'd turned him down before, but there was no way she was going to do that again. She smiled brightly. "Yes, yes. Oh yes."

Allie and Louise sat out on the terrace trying not to eavesdrop. They glanced toward the shoreline a few times but then always looked away. Their polite conversation was less heartfelt as they waited impatiently for some sign that everything would be all right.

Then hearing Alyssa's voice carry was all they needed. They looked at each other and smiled. It was done.

Epilogue

The wedding celebration of Senator Randolph Kingsley to Alyssa Adia Wingate was sheer perfection. Just after sunset, beneath the canopy of a glorious moonlit sky sprinkled with early twinkling stars and the radiance of the heavens above, Randolph and Alyssa took their vows in the vineyard surrounded by family and friends and a host of well-wishers.

It was simple and divine.

Afterward, the reception was the ultimate gathering. Beneath a canopy of green decorated and scented with fresh flowers, the large newly joined families and host of friends enjoyed the ultimate celebration. Food, wine and champagne flowed as music played and laughter echoed beneath the stars.

Everyone ate leisurely, then toasted and danced as a local band played, sending music flowing through the neatly lined rows of grapes.

Just before harvest, the vineyard was at its peak. The scent of ripened grapes wafted through the air, making their dream wedding even more sensational.

"Are you having a good time, Grandma?" Alyssa asked her grandmother as she sat down beside her in her flowing lace wedding gown.

Allie smiled happily. "I'm having a wonderful time, and you look absolutely beautiful in that dress. Henry would be so delighted to see you right now. Thank you for wearing this."

"Thank you for lending it to me. I love it."

Allie smiled. "He bought this so long ago for me but then we eloped and then when your mother, eloped I thought I'd never see anyone wear it." She reached up and gently touched her granddaughter's face. "You look absolutely lovely."

"Thank you, Grandma, for everything," Alyssa said.

"She's right, you look beautiful," Benjamin said as he leaned down to kiss his daughter on the cheek. "Your mother would have been so proud of you."

"Thanks, Dad."

"Mind if I join you?"

"Sure," Alyssa said, making room beside her.

"So, how do you like your new home?" Benjamin asked as he looked around at the beautiful Napa Valley landscape.

Alyssa looked around. "It's a different world out here, but I love it. Of course, I'll be going back and forth with Randolph at times. What about you, Dad? Selling the business after all these years must have been difficult."

Benjamin looked around, smiling. "I think I can get used to retirement. And of course, working here might not be too bad, either."

"I think you'll fit right in."

"I think so, too, and, since my new son-in-law is looking into adding a small brewery, I might just come in handy. And what about you, Allie? Can you handle living at the Esprit Clinic?"

"It's beautiful there. I'm think I'm gonna like it."

"I'm glad," Alyssa said, overjoyed.

This was her day and everything was perfect. Mrs. Watts walked over and sat on the other side of her grandmother. "I don't know what I'm gonna do with those two," she said of Oliver and Nina playing on the swings like kids.

"Wish them the best," Allie said happily.

Alyssa nodded, then turned her attention to Ursula and Pete as they chatted eagerly with Senator Andre Hart and a few other politicians. They were all in their glory, making contacts and exchanging business cards.

She glanced across at her new husband laughing and talking with his friends and family. She couldn't believe the family she married into. They were all so wonderful and were overjoyed to have her in the family.

"He's a lucky man," Benjamin said, seeing the direction she was looking.

"And I'm a lucky woman," Alyssa said.

"I have to give him credit. He did the right thing, walked in, introduced himself, then asked my permission to marry you."

"I still can't believe he did that."

"It showed respect. I appreciated that. Shall we discuss my grandchildren yet?"

"No, Dad. Not yet. Give me a few months."

They laughed happily as she stood and walked over to her husband surrounded by her new family and friends.

"Wait, wait let me get this straight," Trey said, still staggered by the preposterous idea. "You actually went willingly to Mamma Lou." Randolph smiled and nodded. "No deception, no trickery, no coercion, no one forced you?"

"That's right," Randolph said as Tony and J.T. chuckled at Trey's stunned expression.

"And you actually asked her to help you?"

"Yes, I did."

"Willingly?"

"Yes."

"Are you being blackmailed?"

"Trey," Randolph said, joining with Tony's and J.T.'s laughter, "I met Alyssa and told Mamma Lou about her. She helped me and I will forever be grateful to her. And, no, I am not being blackmailed."

"You actually went to her and asked for her help."

"That's right," Randolph said, smiling as he watched Alyssa across the terrace talking to her grandmother and father.

Trey shook his head. "I don't know what to say. I've never seen a man walk directly into a lion's den with a T-bone steak hanging around his neck, purposely get eaten, then come out looking so happy."

The guys laughed. "You'll see," Randolph said.

"What do you mean, I'll see? What have you heard, is Mamma Lou planning something? Do you know what it is, who it is, when she's gonna do it?" Trey continued as the idea of being next on the list was suddenly a very real concern. He turned and glanced at Mamma Lou across the terrace. She smiled and nodded. He panicked all over again.

Randolph walked away laughing, meeting his bride midway. They stood face-to-face smiling into each other's eyes. "So, Mrs. Kingsley, are you happy?" he asked.

"I am deliriously happy, Senator Kingsley," she said. They kissed beneath the arbor under the stars, sealing their love forever.

* * *

"So, are you ever going to take on the ultimate matchmaker challenge?" Colonel Wheeler asked, standing beside Louise as she basked in the happiness of another perfect pair.

Louise looked across the room at Trey Evans as he happily joined in the celebration, standing and talking with Randolph, Tony and J.T. She watched as he turned to her. His worried expression was exactly what she had expected. She nodded and smiled, having already begun working on him without him even knowing it. "Trey is already hooked, he just doesn't know it yet," she said slyly.

"I'm not talking about Trey," Otis said.

Louise looked at Otis questioningly, then glanced around the outdoor terrace at the other guests. It was a beautiful sight. Knowing that she'd had a hand in joining together in happiness several of the couples there filled her with joy. Having eloped a few weeks earlier, Dennis and Faith sat with Jace and Taylor talking about their impromptu elopement and their honeymoon in Africa.

Madison, with her two little ones, sat with a very pregnant Juliet and now-pregnant Kennedy and Hope by her side. Word spread quickly about Kennedy and Hope having the same due date, and bets as to who would deliver first sparked a renewed round of excitement.

Yes, the next generation was very promising. Louise was proud of her accomplishments but even prouder of the love she was able to share. Matchmaking was all about love.

She spotted both her two sons standing across the way, talking with several politicians. "Yes, I agree, you're absolutely right, both my sons have been widowers for long enough. Maybe it's time I do something to rectify that situation."

"I'm not talking about Matthew or Raymond," Otis said.

Louise looked at him oddly, having no idea who he was talking about. "Then who are you talking about?" she asked.

"I'm talking about us. Don't you think it's our turn?"

Louise's mouth opened. She was speechless.

Dear Reader,

I hope you enjoyed reading the story of Alyssa Wingate and Senator Randolph Kingsley in *When Love Calls*. In this story I wanted to show how one person's past directly affects another person's future and consider at what point we truly let go of the drama that is holding us back. With Washington, D.C., as the backdrop, Alyssa and Randolph needed to find strength in each other in order to overcome their many challenges to answer love's call.

My next much-requested and much-anticipated release is entitled, *And Then There Was You*. In this story, Mamma Lou has finally set her sights on the ultimate bachelor, the always slippery, always skillful, Trey Evans. The two meet head-to-head and all bets are off when the challenge is on.

Don't forget to read my upcoming young-adult novel, *She Said, She Said,* coauthored with an amazing new writer, my daughter, Jennifer Norfleet. Two generations, two voices and two strong-willed Norfleets in one book; it's definitely a winner for all ages.

Please feel free to write me and let me know what you think. I always enjoy hearing from readers. Please send your comments to conorfleet@aol.com or Celeste O. Norfleet, P.O. Box 7346, Woodbridge, VA 22195-7346. Don't forget to check out my Web site at http://www.celesteonorfleet.com

Best wishes,

Celeste O. Norfleet

"Ms. Craft is a master at storytelling…"
—*Romantic Times BOOKreviews* on *Star Crossed*

Author favorite

Francine Craft

Designed *for* PASSION

Second chances never looked so good…

When Melodye Carter's husband's mysterious death is linked to another shooting, Detective Jim Ryman must protect Melodye and her twin boys. Jim shut down his heart after losing his wife, but proud, vulnerable Melodye makes him remember what it means to be a man in love.

Coming the first week of March, wherever books are sold.

KIMANI™
ROMANCE

*He was the best thing
that had ever happened to her...*

The FOREIGNER'S CARESS

Favorite author

Kim Shaw

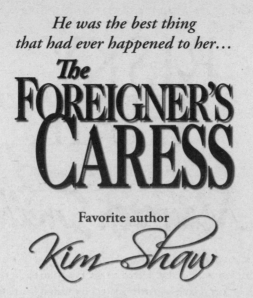

Determined to change her wild ways, Madison Daniels finds
the man of her dreams in handsome Jamaican billionaire
Stevenson Elliott. But when her past indiscretions earn the
disapproval of Stevenson's family, she must convince him that
a lifetime with her is worth more than his family's billions.

Coming the first week of March, wherever books are sold.

KIMANI ™
ROMANCE

A RISKY AFFAIR

Award-winning author

Maureen Smith

Private investigator Dane Roarke leaves Solange Washington
breathless with desire. Hired to do a routine background
check on her, Dane unearths secrets regarding her parentage
that force him to walk a thin line between his growing
suspicions and his consuming hunger for this vibrant woman.

"With Every Breath [by Maureen Smith] is engaging reading
that is sure to provide hours of pleasure."
—*Romantic Times BOOKreviews*

Coming the first week of March, wherever books are sold.

KIMANI
ROMANCE

www.kimanipress.com

Featuring the voices of eighteen of your
favorite authors…

ON THE LINE

Essence Bestselling Author

donna hill

A sexy, irresistible story starring Joy Newhouse,
who, as a radio relationship expert, is considered
the diva of the airwaves. But when she's fired,
Joy quickly discovers that if she can dish it out,
she'd better be able to take it!

Featuring contributions by such favorite authors
as Gwynne Forster, Monica Jackson, Earl Sewell,
Phillip Thomas Duck and more!

Coming the first week of January,
wherever books are sold.

sepia™

www.kimanipress.com   KPDH0211207

"King-Gamble's engaging African American romance has broad appeal."
—*Booklist* on *Change of Heart*

NATIONAL BESTSELLING AUTHOR

Marcia King-Gamble

Hook, Line and Single

For newly divorced Roxanne, the new age of speed dating, singles parties and noncommittal encounters is all a bit awkward. Between keeping her business afloat and coping with a teenage daughter, Roxanne feels like a fish out of water. But she plucks up her courage and boldly goes where only singles dare to go—the world of online dating. Because maybe, just maybe, Mr. Right is out there looking for her....

Available the first week of January, wherever books are sold.

sepia™

www.kimanipress.com   KPMKGI180108

From acclaimed author

DWIGHT FRYER

The evocative prequel to *The Legend of Quito Road*...

The Knees of Gullah Island

A beautifully rendered novel that explores the complex racial dynamics that shaped the South through one family's extraordinary journey to freedom. Born to free parents, Gillam Hale realizes he can never be truly free until he finds his lost loved ones and faces the legacy of his own rash decisions.

"Dwight Fryer's debut novel is a scintillating mixture of love, betrayal, hope and redemption disguised in the incredible human condition of a sleepy little 1930s Tennessee town."
—*Rawsistaz Reviewers* on *The Legend of Quito Road*

Coming the first week of March wherever books are sold.

These women are about to discover that every passion
has a price...and some secrets are impossible to keep.

NATIONAL BESTSELLING AUTHOR

ROCHELLE ALERS

After Hours

A deliciously scandalous novel that brings together
three very different women, united by the secret lives
they lead. Adina, Sybil and Karla all lead seemingly
charmed, luxurious lives, yet each also harbors a
surprising secret that is about to spin out of control.

"Alers paints such vivid descriptions that when Jolene
becomes the target of a murderer, you almost feel
as though someone you know is in great danger."
—*Library Journal* on *No Compromise*

**Coming the first week of March
wherever books are sold.**